Waking the Dead

by

Kerry Blaisdell

Book Two of The Dead Series

This is a work of fiction. Names, characters, places, and incidents are either the product of the author's imagination or are used fictitiously, and any resemblance to actual persons living or dead, business establishments, events, or locales, is entirely coincidental.

Waking the Dead (Book Two of The Dead Series)

COPYRIGHT © 2019 by Kerry Blaisdell

All rights reserved. No part of this book may be used or reproduced in any manner whatsoever, including for the purposes of training artificial intelligence technologies. In accordance with Article 4(3) of the Digital Single Market Directive 2019/790, the author and publisher expressly reserve this work from the text and data mining exception. Only brief quotations embodied in critical articles or reviews may be allowed.

Lello Ball Enterprises
P.O. Box 331
Beaverton, OR 97075

Publishing History: First Edition, 2019
Print ISBN 978-1-951141-06-6
Digital ISBN 978-1-951141-07-3

Published in the United States of America

Dedication

This one's for my Aunt Carol:
Your insistence that I let you read the then-unpublished,
un-contracted DEBRIEFING THE DEAD is what
finally got this crazy ball rolling. From the bottom of
my heart, thank you. You rock!

Chapter One

The only truly dead are those who have been forgotten.

~Jewish Proverb

I'm pretty sure my landlady's alive, but you never know. At least, I don't.

My name's Hyacinth Finch, and a couple of months ago, I died and was brought back to life—sort of—by Saint Michael the Archangel, who's now my boss. Also sort of. It's complicated.

Basically, if you met me on the street, you'd think I was one hundred percent alive, no strings attached. But if I met you? Thanks to the "side effects" of rebirth, I wouldn't know if you were alive, dead, or somewhere in-between, unless you told me.

Then there's this whole thing where my former neighbor, Jason Jones, turned out to be related to my nephew, Geordi Dioguardi, and they both might have demon blood in them.

Well, Jason does for sure; it's Geordi we won't know about until puberty. And *he* doesn't know I'm the Walking Undead, or that he's being babysat by a newly dead cop named Eric Guilliot. See? Complicated.

Anyway, since my landlady wanted money—cold hard cash she could spend at the market—it's a safe bet she's a breather. She blocked the stairwell leading up to the Zürich flat I share with Geordi and Eric, looking like a six-foot-tall Swiss-German metal door in her gray sweater, matching slacks, and sensible black shoes. Her hair was gray too, but her eyes were a watery blue. Not a hint of black, thank God, so at least she wasn't a demon. Probably.

I suppressed a shiver and shifted the heavy paper grocery bag in my arms, putting on my best Trustworthy Tenant smile. "Frau Blauch. So lovely to see you today."

Her frown deepened, and she pointed a finger at my nose. "Rent. You pay now."

She'd appeared from her basement apartment just in time to prevent me getting under cover of the small overhang above the stoop. The late-October drizzle that had fretted all day wasn't much more than a mist now, but it was enough to dampen my bangs and drip cool rivulets into my eyes. I blinked them away, wishing again that Jason hadn't ditched us. For one thing, he's even taller than Frau Blauch. For another, he can charm the pants off just about anyone. Me included.

I suppressed a shiver of a different sort and said to Frau Blauch, "I'm happy to pay you. But you said I could have an extra week to sort out my finances."

"*Ja*," she said agreeably. "Rent. Due now."

The bag started to slip, the weight of peanut butter, milk, and fresh veggies pulling my aching arms as I hiked it up. The thing is, she was right. The rent was past due, and deal or not, I don't flake on responsibilities. I bend the truth now and then, and my past is shadier than you might think. Okay, I'm a former graverobber and dealer in goods of, er, questionable origin. But I'm an honest thief. Think Danny-Ocean-charming, not He-Who-Shall-Not-Be-Named-evil.

To make matters worse, Michael was also past due, with my first official orders. He's a busy guy, leading all those souls to their Final Destination, while also fighting Satan's minions. Since, like the kid in the movie, I see dead people, we struck a deal. If I "pre-sort" some of the Dead for him, I get time to find Geordi a foster family. But once he's settled, I'm off to whichever afterlife is reserved for semi-reformed grave-robbing liars.

I have other ideas, like staying with Geordi permanently. But that's a whole other problem.

Frau Blauch's gaze flicked over the wet grocery bag. "You haf little boy, *ja*? He is upstairs, *allein*—alone?"

Crap. I switched gears to Conscientious Parent and nodded toward the store, one door down. "I only left him for a minute, just to get food."

Her brows lowered further, and she glanced pointedly at the streetlights now coming to life. It might be afternoon, but the heavy skies were dark. I couldn't very well say, *My dead roommate is babysitting*. But our flat faces the street, and Geordi'd leaned over the windowsill to watch me go into the store, then waved when I came back out. Both times, Eric hovered behind him like a moody, blond—and *built*—guardian angel.

If only he wasn't invisible to everyone but me.

Frau Blauch said, "Is not safe, little boy *allein* like zat. He has nightmares, *ja*? I hear him at night. You leave him again, I call *Polizei*. You pay rent—tomorrow."

She ducked through the side door that led to her basement rooms. She was right about this too. I shouldn't leave him, and he did have nightmares. What kid wouldn't, after what he'd been through? Was *still* experiencing?

I sighed and stepped into the musty stairwell, lugging

the now-soaked grocery bag up the stairs. Geordi, bless him, heard me fumble with the lock and ran to open the door, flinging himself at me.

"Tata Hyhy!"

"Oof!"

By some miracle, I didn't drop the groceries, and I managed to get one arm around his shoulder, squeezing back. He smelled of moist earth and sweet, late-blooming flowers, and I surmised he'd been digging through the angel geraniums in the window box planter, searching for bugs. I leaned back and sure enough, his fingernails were black and his face was smudged.

"Find any as-yet undiscovered species of insect, Professor Finch?"

That made him giggle, but I detected uncertainty too. I dropped the bag—who cared if a few jars broke?—and pulled him tight for a full-on, aunt-who-loves-him-more-than-life hug. Frau Blauch was right. Regardless of the market's proximity, a child shouldn't be left in what he perceived as an empty apartment.

I sought out the only adult support I had in this new life of mine. From the window seat, my gaze was met by a habitually cynical jade-green one, now oddly tense. I tightened my grip on Geordi and raised an eyebrow, but Eric shook his head and turned back to the window. The lowering sun broke through the clouds, electrifying his golden hair and limning his rigid profile, making him look like a downed wire about to arc.

Had something happened?

I tamped down my frustration. How much easier this would be if my babysitter wasn't dead. But Geordi's the only son of Nicholas Dioguardi, himself the only son and heir of a very nasty capo in the Sicilian Mob. Nick died recently, trying to kill Geordi's mother, my sister Lily. She died too, but after Nick, and now *la familigia* wants Geordi back.

I will *never* let that happen.

Geordi swiped a grubby hand under his nose, making a dirt mustache. His black hair and blue eyes were so like Jason's that a hot lump rose in my throat.

"Tata, when you were gone, I heard a man's voice."

Shit. The Dioguardis—they *had* found us. I tried to sound calm. "Outside on the street?"

He frowned. "Inside."

"Actually *in* the apartment?"

He nodded, and my first thought was, *Thank God.* Nick's family would hardly break in and speak once, then hide in the back room. They'd snatch Geordi, and he wouldn't be in my arms now. Then his words sunk in, and my pulse rocketed.

I said carefully, "You mean out in the hall, right?"

The frown became a glare. Usually I took him more seriously. "*Inside.*"

I blew out a breath. "I'm sorry, sweetie. I know you meant in here. But—" I made a show of glancing around, my gaze lingering on Eric, who studiously avoided eye contact. "—there's no one here. Is there?"

Geordi shook his head again, but less certainly. "I heard something. And when I looked, I heard it again."

A faint flush rose on the back of Eric's neck, and I forced my jaw to unclench. "Sweetie, I need to get the milk in the fridge. Can you help put stuff away?" Geordi nodded, and I gave him another squeeze. "It's okay. It was probably someone outside after all, or in the flat above or below us. These old buildings—sometimes the sound carries too well."

"Really?"

"Really."

His face lit with relief and he grabbed the milk and ran to the fridge. Ah, the rapid mood swings of the young.

I stood more slowly. Eric regarded me warily, as well he should, then abruptly gave one of his resigned half-shrugs—the ones that marked him as supremely French—and I was pretty sure I knew what went down.

As a former *flic*, a cop, I thought I could trust him. Mostly. Plus, he had a thing for me. Or I had one for him.

Okay, we were attracted to each other.

But I was involved with Jason, sort of, despite the Dioguardi Demon thing. He left before we settled anything, and Eric had stuck to his vow that he wouldn't "poach." Very noble. And annoying.

As for trusting him in other arenas, well, just because he was an OPJ—*un officier de police judiciaire*—didn't mean he'd keep any promises he deemed "less necessary," such as not trying to break through to my nephew.

Geordi darted from behind the fridge door to grab the peanut butter, which my now-bruised veggies had cushioned. He ran back to the kitchenette while I scooped everything else up and followed. From across the room, Eric's emotions popped, hot with energy, but tempered by something cooler. Disappointment. Frustration.

Despair.

I couldn't stay mad at him, knowing how lonely he was with just me for company, and only at odd hours, while Geordi was asleep or in the other room.

When the groceries were tucked into cupboards or

the fridge, I said to Geordi, "I saw Monsieur Renaud at the market. He left something outside his door for you. I would've grabbed it, but my arms were full. Do you want to go see what it is?"

My rhetorical question earned a shriek of delight. He raced from the apartment and pounded down the hall to the flat at the end by the stairs.

I have few memories of my parents, who died when I was young, and none at all of any extended generations up the ancestral tree. Which is maybe why I have a soft spot for elderly men. Not in a creepy May-December way; in a simple, "I get along with Old Guys" way. Especially Swiss-French ones like Monsieur Renaud, whose grandson was Geordi's age, giving him insight on which books were *au courant* for a seven-year-old boy.

Geordi ran in, clutching a hardbound collection of Astérix comics. Grinning, he disappeared into his room and slammed the door. He reads fast, but I figured his new favorite anti-hero would occupy him for at least an hour.

I joined Eric at the window, where he once again stared pensively at the passersby below. The sun had slipped behind the clouds, and like it, I expected Eric to have cooled off. But if anything, he was more agitated. Often, when he got like this, small objects nearby began vibrating and sometimes flew across the room. I didn't see any loose scissors or paperweights, or anything else dangerous, so I waited silently.

After a moment, he spoke without looking at me. "*Ils ne me voient pas.* They cannot see me. I could stand before them, and they would pass through me as though I did not exist. And I would be powerless to stop them."

"Not entirely powerless," I said, thinking of the

flying objects. "Besides, at least you know who down there is alive. I can't even tell that for sure."

"It is not the same. You can touch them, dead *or* alive. They hear you, they speak to you. No one living speaks to me, and I can touch no one…except you, *mon ange*."

My angel, his pet name for me. But today the words sounded bitter, not teasing.

He said abruptly, "You are angry that I attempted to speak with your nephew."

"I'm not. Not really."

"Truly?"

Relief flared in his eyes, followed by a sudden heat, and I fought the urge to lean in. Sharing a flat without being together was like putting a diabetic in a candy factory. Not to mention I'm hiding him from Michael. As a devout Catholic, Eric *should* have been taken away moments after death. But since he was my only link between my current state of limbo and the afterlife, I wasn't anxious to lose him.

Well, that and other reasons.

"I admit I was angry at first. But I know how difficult this is for you."

His jaw hardened. "I do not want your pity. I want *you. All* of you. I want to drink coffee with you at the corner café while we read the paper. *Together*. I want to go for a drive, and *I* want to be at the wheel. Most of all, I want to help you, with your nephew and whatever absurdly dangerous thing you must do when *le saint Michel* returns. I want to *help*, and I cannot."

"You *do* help. I couldn't do half what I'm doing if you weren't here, keeping Geordi safe. Besides, the next rock probably won't be as hard to get as the last one."

That's part-two of my new job. The short version is that Satan destroyed one of Michael's sanctuaries, and now they're locked in a battle to retrieve the most rock shards from the fallout. If Michael gets more, all is well. If Satan does, he can harness Michael's energy from the rocks and escape Hell, or destroy the world, or do something equally fun. Guess he's still a *teensy* bit pissed about being evicted from Heaven. Go figure.

Eric shook his head in wonder. "*Tu vois?* This is what draws me to you: your ability to find the good in a situation. But…there is no good in my situation, other than that you are in it."

I opened my mouth to protest, and he leaned forward, eyes flashing.

"*Non.* It is true. Were I alive, we would be together. But I cannot ask this. Not when we cannot even speak in front of your nephew. I should have gone on. To Heaven or Hell, either would be better than *this*, being near you, *needing* you, but not man enough to treat you properly."

"Eric—"

I stopped because, really, what could I say? My choices kept him here. Not initially, but I'd been committing the sin of omission for months.

I exhaled. "Do you want me to call Michael down? I'm forever grateful for all you've done. But I can't ask you to stay when you're this unhappy."

We were so close, if he'd had breath, it would have caressed my skin. "*Mon ange.* Do you not understand that you are the closest to *happy* that I have ever come?"

His gaze dropped to my mouth. He made a noise low in his throat, of frustration, or desire, or both, and suddenly gripped my shoulders, fingers digging in, keeping me at arm's length. He felt so solid, so *real*. I brought my hands up to explore the hard muscles of his chest and shoulders, his smooth neck and jaw, and from there, slid my fingers into the thick waves of his hair.

He groaned. "*Mon ange*, were I not already dead, you would kill me."

I shook my head, denying I had power over him, and he brushed his knuckles against my cheek, then cupped my chin, lowering his mouth until only my own breath separated us.

"*Si, c'est vrai*. I am as surprised as anyone. But I am not afraid to say it: I am yours." His gaze flicked over my features as though memorizing them, and when he spoke, his voice was fierce. "*Et tu—t'es la mienne*."

His lips parted, eyes dark with desire. The cage of his arms relaxed, and I leaned into him. And then a *crash!* from the hall sent us jumping apart.

A deep booming voice I'd know anywhere said, "Hyacinth? Child? Are you in there?"

I stared at Eric, heart hammering, adrenaline and all sorts of other more pleasurable hormones racing through me. It seemed my new boss had arrived at last.

Chapter Two

The more we see, the more we are capable of seeing.

~Maria Mitchell, American Astronomer (1818-1889)

"Hyacinth?" Michael sounded impatient already. I should have been grateful he hadn't just appeared beside me, which was his usual habit, regardless of whether I was in the bathroom, or clothed, or anything else.

I mouthed to Eric, *Do I tell him*?

He hesitated, then shook his head. With a crackle of energy and a small *pop!* he dematerialized through the window onto the fire escape, leaving behind the sharp, sweet smell of nitric oxide. He went places without me, often with other dead folk who, for whatever reason, had also stayed on Earth. Atheists, or those with a non-afterlife belief system. So he wasn't without peers.

But he had a point about squiring me around town. It hardly made for a romantic dinner if the other patrons saw me talking to Mr. Invisible, and *le maître d'* booted me—us—out.

Geordi poked his head out. "Tata? Is it Uncle Michael?"

"Yes, sweetie, it is."

I took a cursory self-inventory. I'm no fashionista, but I wanted to be sure Eric hadn't *actually* sizzled my clothes off. Considering his look of frustrated desire as he left, it was a miracle either of us was still dressed.

I unlocked and opened the door. Sure enough, Michael stood on the other side. If anything, his beard was fuller and his mass of wavy dark hair was, well, more massive. Everything about him was oversized, from his muscled arms and tree-trunk legs, to his size twenty-wide sandaled feet. He'd exchanged his Ancient Warrior garb for something more modern, though where he'd found tan Chinos and a white dress shirt in an XXXL, I had no idea. Probably archangelhood came with a personal tailor, or maybe the magic to do it yourself.

In fact, he'd dressed much like Eric, except I doubt Eric would be caught alive *or* dead wearing sandals, except at the beach. Thinking of him made my face heat, though whether from residual lust or because I was hiding him from Michael, I wasn't sure.

"Tonton!" Geordi cried, running to him. Michael scooped him into a bear hug, then airplaned him in a circle until he giggled helplessly.

This wasn't the first visit Michael had paid us. In fact, he'd checked in about once a week since we left Turkey, so I'd thought it prudent to come up with a cover story, for Geordi's sake. It was Michael's idea to say he was my *tonton* on my mother's side, and therefore Geordi's Great Uncle. Since Geordi was starved for family connections and Michael had an easy way with children, this lie was a great success.

Today, though, I dreaded his visit. He'd been patient, allowing us to get settled. But last week, he'd heard rumors of a rock shard on the collector scene. If these had panned out, he'd tell me today, and I'd be officially launched on my unwanted career, restoring stolen items to their rightful owner.

As a former graverobber *and* high-end fence for the backstabbing Marseille elite, you can see how this would be a struggle for me.

Geordi squealed, "Stop!" and Michael let him slide to the ground, from where he promptly demanded, "Tonton, do you have any treats for me?"

Michael grinned. "Perhaps."

Geordi lunged for a cellophane-wrapped package bulging from Michael's shirt pocket. He came out with a bundle of apricot delight—"sugary slugs," his favorite treat—and bounced with happy anticipation.

"Don't eat them all at once," Michael admonished. "Now go. Your aunt and I have things to discuss."

"Will you play a game with me later, Tonton?"

"Of course, if there is time."

Geordi grinned, then made a show of wobbling dizzily back to his room, shutting the door behind him.

Michael said, "It is good to see him happy."

I nodded. *Yep. Absolutely. And did you notice? It's because he's with me.* He might still have nightmares, but how much worse would they be if he were left to the mercy of strangers?

But Michael had been clear from the start that our arrangement was temporary, and he expected me to find Geordi a "permanent home." Meaning, *not with me.*

As I've said, I have other ideas, but I wasn't about to telegraph those yet.

He moved to the eating nook and sat at the rusty metal-and-yellow-laminate table, the battered chrome legs of the ancient chair creaking like pins about to snap under his bulk. "Sit, child. We have much to plan."

"The rock?" I asked, joining him on a second chair. This one's legs were sturdier, but its seat cushion was nearly flat from years of use.

"Yes. It is one of mine."

I drew a shaky breath. *Think of him as just a client. You're a professional. This is merely another retrieval.*

Yeah, right. A retrieval of something Satan wanted. *Satan.*

Despite what I'd said to Eric, the whole prospect, with or without added demons, scared the crap out of me when I thought about it. So I tried not to.

Michael continued, "I think you will be pleased to learn it is close by, in Germany."

"Okay. That's good." Our lack of funds would make any travel a challenge, but at least it was only one country over. "But won't whoever has it go to Colossae to send it to Satan?"

Michael shook his head. "Another good thing. It is not in the possession of Satan's minions. Even if it were, there are many classes of demon, and many ways the rocks may be consigned to Hell." He made a *tsk*-ing sound. "Come, child, surely you have done some research by now."

"Erm. Been busy unfreezing my finances enough to buy food, and hiding my nephew from various members of the Mob."

His brown eyes twinkled. "Yes, yes, I suppose that would do it. But you seem to be succeeding at that last quite well. So perhaps for next time…?"

"Fine. I'll bone up on *God v. Lucifer*. But you said this time it doesn't matter? What *is* the situation?"

"This shard is in the hands of a harmless amateur rock collector, who most likely acquired it for its appearance. I believe if you go to him, perhaps offer some small payment, or another collectible in exchange, he will hand it over without complaint."

"Okay, sounds good. But about that whole payment thing… Obviously I can't go back to Marseille. And even if I get my money from the bank here, I'll eventually need an income."

Michael grinned. "I am an archangel, child. Money does not exist for me. However, I realize you are in a unique situation, and the work I ask of you will not garner a *monetary* reward." A reminder that being here at all should be reward enough. I forbore to comment, and he continued. "I will see what I can do. Perhaps I can supply you with funds taken from some of Satan's lesser demons before I banished them to live with their master."

"You can do that? Like the vice squad or something—you can take stuff from a raid and use it for the next job?"

His laugh roared, and Geordi stuck his head out. Michael dropped to a chuckle, waving Geordi back to his comics. "Go, my son. Your *tata* and I were sharing a joke."

When he was gone, Michael said, "Yes, something like that. Most demons came by their wealth in underhanded ways, even before Satan turned them. We make every effort to restore anything valuable to its rightful owner. If we do not know who that is, the items are donated or held in limbo, in case they may be of use in future operations."

I tried to picture Michael and his subordinate angels operating in such a mundane manner. So…bureaucratic. I suppose it made sense. He'd been around for thousands of years, so he'd need some kind of system. It just blew my mind to think of *angels* "busting up" a ring of demons, then donating their loot to the Salvation Army.

"In any case, I will reimburse your expenses for this trip, whatever they may be." He paused, holding my gaze. "As for your living expenses, what is in your bank account should be plenty for the time you will be here."

My heart pounded and I tried not to sweat. I'm cautious by nature, and this was *the* most important thing I'd ever do. "Fair enough," I said levelly.

He watched me for an intense moment, then sat back. "Speaking of your time here, I also expect you to begin sorting souls for me."

And there it was, the *other* moment I'd been dreading. I'd agreed to this, albeit under duress, but it was still a daunting prospect. "How? I mean, I can't exactly advertise."

"I do not think you will need to. It seems the newly dead find you on their own."

This was true. Besides Eric, there were at least three other occasions I knew of where I'd happened across a freshly minted soul before Michael showed up on scene.

"For now, I believe the simplest method would be to let them continue to seek you out. Then you will assess them, make a determination, and call me down."

"Will that really save you so much time, since you still have to lead them away?"

His dark eyes sparkled with renewed mirth. "Child. We have an agreement. And, yes, it will. Half my time with the Dead is spent determining their fate. You will shoulder some of that burden, so that I may operate more efficiently. Come, there will not be so many. Just those who believe in Heaven and Hell. Even a few here and there will help."

"But what if I'm wrong? What if I send someone up who really needs to go down, or vice versa?"

"That will be Saint Peter's problem. Or Satan's. Although I suppose *he* will not object to receiving an extra soul or two."

My jaw dropped, and Michael roared with laughter again. Luckily, Geordi ignored us this time.

Michael wiped his eyes, wheezing. "It was a joke, child. I will—what is the phrase?—double-check your work. At least, initially. In fact, though, I trust your judgment. This is one of your many gifts."

"Okay," I said slowly. What choice did I have? "I'll keep an eye out, and if a new soul crosses my path, I'll do my best. As for the rock…"

"I will tell you the man's name and location, so that you may start right away."

###

"Right away" turned out to be a relative term, but Michael didn't seem concerned. Unlike before, when two High Demons were sending the shard to Satan on a specific date, now I had no deadline, other than retrieving the rock before Satan noticed it.

Since the collector was a mere hobbyist with no religious connections, it was unlikely anyone from Hell would take note of him. And as I'm the only one Michael's ever met with the ability to sense his powers in the rocks, it was a safe bet the collector didn't know what he had. Still, I didn't want to squander my advantage.

But I did need to pay rent, buy train tickets, and take care of a few things. I'd gotten our passports in order when we arrived in Switzerland, made easier by the fact that I'd retained my French citizenship all these years, and Geordi and I share a surname. I probably should've faked our identities, but Jason was my expert in that department, and as noted, he wasn't around.

I could have used the IDs we'd had in Turkey, but I didn't know who knew us by those names. Jason had returned Geordi to me voluntarily and swore he didn't work for scumbag Nick's branch of *la familigia*, so it seemed likely he'd leave us alone for now. But the Dioguardis are good at "extracting information," probably even from demons, so who knew how long our reprieve would last.

In any case, we'd entered Switzerland legally. My theory on that ran something like this: Any sneaky Dioguardis would never believe we'd just wander around using our own names. Ergo, at least initially, they wouldn't bother to search for Hyacinth Finch and Geordi Dioguardi-Finch.

I knew I was on thin ice, but I really didn't know what else to do. I may be a grave-robbing former thief, but I'm a remarkably naïve one. Plus, I had to use my real identity to get funds from my bank account. Which, even so, was proving problematic.

Late that afternoon, I dragged Geordi back for another begging session with the bank manager, Herr Gutzwiller. Eric hadn't returned, but he couldn't help with this anyway. Still, as I sat in the now-familiar wood-paneled office, surrounded by expensive lemon-polished mahogany furniture and what appeared to be authentic, if not hugely "important," paintings from various seventeenth century artists, I couldn't help wishing for moral support.

The main bureaucratic difficulty seemed to be that the account was in both my name and Lily's, and without her co-signature, withdrawals were strictly limited. But while my own death hadn't impaired my ability to write, *her* death made a co-signature out of the question. Jason ensured she got a decent burial, but as a result, the Dioguardis had the paperwork. Not just her death certificate, but also her will, which named me as executor of her estate and as Geordi's legal guardian.

Technically, Nick had died first, about a minute before Lily and me. But was that long enough for custody to transfer to her, before passing to me? Or because she'd lost custody during their divorce proceedings, did the Dioguardis get Geordi now?

It was all a big, hairy mess, and Herr Gutzwiller wasn't inclined to help. He reminded me of Frau Blauch except with flawless English. He had the same tall, rectangular build, gray hair, and matching attire—in his case, a suit and tie—not to mention a wall-like resistance to my pleas.

"Listen," I began, leaning forward in my chair until I almost touched his über-shiny desk. His heavy brows drew together in distaste, but I pushed on. "Lily died in France. Her late husband's family isn't very, er, fond of me. I requested a copy of the death certificate from the Marseille City Hall, but it won't get here until next week. Isn't there *something* we can do? My nephew and I need to keep our apartment. Please."

Herr Gutzwiller's gaze flicked to Geordi, slouched in the chair next to mine, and his mouth turned down. I don't think he liked children much. I did a quick nephew-check myself. I was never sure if talking of Lily's death bothered Geordi. I'm pretty sure she managed to shield him from seeing Nick get shot, and Jason took him away before *she* died. But I doubt that made it less traumatic.

Still, he seemed okay for now. Bored, but okay.

"I am very sorry," Herr Gutzwiller said, his stiff tone contradicting his words. "Unless you can produce proof of your sister's death, you will only be able to withdraw…" He glanced at his computer screen. "One thousand euros."

Considering the balance was seventy thousand, this was a paltry sum. Rent was five hundred euros, so after food, we wouldn't have enough for the trip. I couldn't wait for the death certificate, which might be delayed even longer. Getting the rock should only take a few hours, but I had to allow a day for the train on either end, and at least one night in-between, for which we'd need a room, plus a way to get around.

I actually have a car, just not here. It's parked somewhere in the slums of Marseille. At least, I hope it's still there and not chopped up for parts by Jason's friend, at whose house we'd left it. He'd agreed to dispose of Nick's car for us, so after two months, why not throw mine in too?

It was a depressing thought. Geordi squirmed on his chair, and I wanted to join in.

My car.

I sat up, startling both Herr Gutzwiller and Geordi, and grabbed my purse off the floor, raking around until I found the large travel wallet containing our passports and other important documents. I pulled a paper out triumphantly.

"Here! This is the title for my car."

Herr Gutzwiller peered down his angular nose at me. "Madame. I doubt very much that your car is worth—"

"At least as much as the balance in my account."

He stopped, mouth open. I guess my thrift-store jeans

and nubby sweater did not say to him, "owner of a massively expensive car."

He closed his mouth and cleared his throat, then took the title from me and examined it, obviously regrouping. "Madame—this name here. The man who signed the car over to you…"

"A client, of my, um, antique shop. A very *grateful* client."

Ha. Now it was *his* turn to squirm. The car was a prototype, one of the first smart cars. Now that they were on the market, they didn't cost outrageously much. But this one, every part custom made, not off an assembly line, was worth a helluva lot. And the man who gave it to me was *very* wealthy and well-known, even in Switzerland. Probably not for stealing objets d'art from his peers, which is how *I* knew him, but what the hey.

Herr Gutzwiller rose, practically drooling. "Would you excuse me a moment?"

I inclined my head graciously. "Of course."

He came around the desk and hurried out the door.

I nudged Geordi. "I think we're in business."

He nodded solemnly, and I fought down a sudden ache. It must be so hard to listen to the adults, casually discussing his mother's death in terms of monetary gain. Losing her at all was impossibly awful. I should know; I was younger than him when my own parents died. Lily found a loving adoptive family, but I bounced around foster care until I aged out of the system.

I would *not* abandon Geordi to that fate.

Behind us, the door opened and Herr Gutzwiller returned, followed by a woman in a blue blazer, dark flowered skirt, and red heels, who I remembered seeing in the lobby earlier. She wore the vaguely distracted expression of one who crunches numbers on a computer all day and only comes up for air long enough to marvel that a world exists outside her office. Her brown hair was twisted up in a knot, a blood-red-and-blue night lily tucked jauntily into one side. It must have been fresh picked, because its rich, sweet scent wafted over me. She glanced at me, then around Herr Gutzwiller's office, as though it'd been awhile since she'd seen it.

He sat behind his desk, expression as close to beaming as it had probably ever been. "I have spoken with our director, and we are *most* sorry we have not taken better care of your financial needs to date."

That explained both the woman's presence and her distraction. Probably bank directors were rarely bothered with the day-to-day workings of their bank. I must be extra-special. Go me.

Herr Gutzwiller continued, "With your car as collateral, we are delighted to advance you as much money as you need, up to the full balance of your account, once the car is appraised. It is outside, yes?"

"Er, no. We walked." His expression headed south, and I added quickly, "I don't drive it often. I keep it in a garage, to protect it."

The beaming returned. "A splendid plan. It must be in very good condition."

"Practically new." This at least was true. Or would be if I could be sure it was still intact. I coughed delicately, but the bank director only gazed at a point above my forehead, seemingly unconcerned about the condition of my car.

I said to Herr Gutzwiller, "I have to leave town for a few days. Would it be possible to leave the title with you and make an appointment for the appraisal when we return? Say, two weeks from tomorrow? Meanwhile, if you could advance me a very small amount, just enough for rent and our travel expenses, I'd be very grateful."

He hesitated. Without an appraisal, I'm sure he wasn't supposed to advance anything beyond the original sum he'd quoted. However, the name on the car's title weighed heavily in my favor. I thought he'd confer with the director, but evidently her only job was to ensure I was "properly taken care of," not to interfere.

"Madame," Herr Gutzwiller said at last, "if this client of yours is so grateful, perhaps he could advance you the funds himself."

"He probably would," I said, startling Herr Gutzwiller, who, I'm sure, expected more hemming and hawing. But it was true. My clients *are* grateful, and generous, when possible. "Unfortunately, he's somewhere near the South Pole right now, but if you contact his assistant, he can vouch for me."

Gutzwiller chewed on that, then caved, and I resisted a celebratory fist-pump.

"Very well," he said, and began typing on his keyboard.

A few minutes later a sum was moved from the joint account to an individual one I'd opened when we arrived in town. The amount wasn't exorbitant, but it would make Frau Blauch do the happy dance. Of course, when we retrieved the rock and returned to Switzerland, I'd have to, somehow, produce my car for the appraisal. But I'd worry about that later. For now, it was enough to know we weren't entirely without resources.

During the whole process, the bank director stayed silent, occasionally peering over Herr Gutzwiller's shoulder, but mostly pacing the office. Several times, I felt her gaze on me, but each time I looked up, she glanced away.

Did she suspect I'd lied about the car? If so, why not call me out?

Geordi didn't notice. He'd taken out his stone scarab, given to him by a woman in Turkey. It was four centimeters long and shiny black, and he'd slid off his chair to make it "crawl" over the whorls in the carpet. He brought it out when he was anxious, bored, tired, happy—pretty much any time he needed a visit with his "friend."

When we finally rose to go, I thought I should at least thank the director, despite her standoffishness. I said to Herr Gutzwiller, "You've been extremely helpful." Then I turned to the director, who stood at the window, her back to me. "Thank you. I appreciate the bank's willingness to help in our unusual situation."

"It is nothing," said Herr Gutzwiller.

My gaze snapped back to his. "Actually, I was speaking to—" I gestured toward the woman, who finally faced me, her eyes sad.

She said softly, "*Il me voit pas*—he does not see me. I am not the director. I am dead. I am waiting to speak with you, at your convenience."

Well, hell.

Chapter Three

*Because I have loved life, I shall have no
sorrow to die.*

*~Amelia Josephine Burr, American Poet
(1878-1968)*

I said to Herr Gutzwiller, "Never mind."

Ignoring his funny look and praying Geordi hadn't noticed, I grabbed my purse and held out my hand. Herr Gutzwiller shook it awkwardly, like he wasn't sure what to make of me. I put on a bright, not-crazy smile, and asked, "Is there a WC?"

He nodded. "Allow me to show you the way."

I jerked my head imperceptibly at the dead woman, but she'd already caught on and fell in behind Geordi. Once in the lobby, Herr Gutzwiller gestured to a set of stairs near the entrance leading to the basement.

"Thanks," I said. "We've got it from here."

"Tata Hyhy?" Geordi said as we headed down.

"Yes, sweetie?"

"Is this the bathroom? I need to *faire pipi*."

Perfect. I knew he would. Even before becoming his guardian, I had experience with him "suddenly" needing to go potty. Now I regularly detoured off to the nearest restroom every hour or so, just in case.

We reached the bottom, and I said, "You go in the boys' room over there. I have to go too. I'll be out in a sec." He opened the door, and I added, "Don't forget to wash your hands, really well!" That should buy me an extra minute, at least.

Crossing my fingers that the WC was empty, I opened the door for the dead woman—thanks to Eric, I knew dematerializing took a while to learn—then let it shut behind us.

"I'm sorry we have to talk in here," I said once I'd determined that we were, in fact, alone. "I'm, uh, a little new at this."

"*De rien*," she said in that same soft tone. "It is nothing. But…I do not know what I am to do, or where I am to go. Can you help me? Something brought me into the bank, and when I saw you in the lobby, and knew that you saw me, I thought, well, it is worth a try."

Most of the newly dead I'd met were upset by the process, but she didn't sound distraught. Her fine-boned face only puckered in a small frown, as though she were mildly puzzled.

I took a deep breath and blew it back out. "Tell me your name."

"I am Lisbette Moucheron."

"You are *française?*"

"*Ouais*. From outside Paris, here on business. We went to a restaurant last night, my colleagues and I. It is likely I drank too much. I awoke at *un hôtel étrange*—not my own."

"And were you…?"

"*In flagrante delicto?* Yes. I do not recall much of the evening, but I believe I thoroughly enjoyed it."

She smiled like she knew a really good secret, and I found myself mesmerized. Suddenly, an impression *surged* through me. It wasn't that her life flashed before my eyes. It was more like…her essence was revealed to me. Similar to the gut feeling I'd had with other dead folk, but this was stronger. Almost tangible.

"How did you die?" I asked, mostly from curiosity. I already knew what my recommendation to Michael would be.

Her delicate eyebrows drew together in concentration. "As I say, I do not know exactly what happened. I awoke early and dressed, then walked down to the street. *La rivière* was so beautiful…there were lilies near the bank. I may have slipped. I am not certain. But I do not swim, much to the disappointment of *ma mère*. She was on *l'Équipe Nationale Française*."

"And no one tried to save you?"

"It was very early. I was alone."

I wasn't sure how to proceed, so I said, "Thanks for sharing." She gave a little half-shrug, reminding me of Eric—why do the French *do* that?—but didn't speak. I cleared my throat. "Uh, I'm not actually the one who guides you. But I can call him down. Before I do, just to check—do you believe in Heaven and Hell and all that?"

"Oui, bien sûr."

Okay, then. I didn't really think she'd ask where to go if she meant to stay here. Still, I didn't want any awkward situations if she was an atheist. I closed my eyes, concentrated, and thought, *Michael.*

When I opened them, there he was, dressed as he'd been earlier, except he'd exchanged the ginormous sandals for even bigger sneakers. Lisbette had already turned to him with that look of trust all Michael's souls wore.

He took her hand and gave it a reassuring pat, then faced me. "Well, child?"

"Lisbette Moucheron," I said promptly. "Up."

He considered a moment, then nodded. "Very good. You leave for Germany soon, yes?"

"Packing and buying our tickets next."

"Good."

An instant later, they were gone.

I hadn't realized how nervous I was until my adrenaline crashed and my legs started shaking. I made it to the sink, gripping the porcelain and bending forward until the nausea passed. My face in the mirror was white, like I'd been through the wringer. I had to get myself under control before Geordi saw me.

I could do this. I just didn't want to. It bothered me, having someone's fate in my hands, even after they were dead. It was hard enough caring for Geordi.

Speaking of whom…

I splashed water on my face, then dried my hands and left the bathroom. Geordi waited by the men's room, totally fine and not at all worried about me. So maybe I was projecting. Not necessarily a bad thing. The Dioguardis *were* searching for him, and I shouldn't leave him alone, even for a minute. This time, he didn't even have Eric watching him.

Strike one and two for Hyacinth-the-Guardian.

I grabbed his hand. "Let's go."

"Okay." He glanced at the bathroom door, then back at me. "Where did that lady go?"

My heart stopped then pounded like a jackhammer as my adrenaline spiked higher than ever. "What lady?"

"The one in the blue coat who wanted to talk to you. Where is she?"

"You…saw her?"

Geordi nodded solemnly. "I know Herr Gutzwiller

didn't. I heard her say she's dead. Did she go somewhere?"

I sagged against the wall, my skin icy-hot, my fingers numb in his grasp.

Oh God.

If Geordi could *see* the newly dead, and hear Eric, then his demon blood must be as strong as Jason thought. I fought down the bile souring my gut. I'd convinced myself there was only a little blood in him, a tiny drop, negligible. How could there be even a hint of Hell in that angelic person?

But if Jason was right, and demon powers only manifested before puberty when the blood was *very* potent, then I couldn't keep fooling myself. And at some point, I would have to talk with Geordi about it.

Not here, though. I drew a calming breath, wishing my heart wouldn't beat so loudly. "She's gone. And we've got to go too. Home to pack, and then to the train station."

Geordi perked up at that. He loves trains. And he didn't seem too worried about meeting a dead woman at the bank. I wish I was so blasé.

Usually, Jason had said, it's only Full Blood demons who can see the Dead, not half-bloods.

Which begged the question: Exactly how much demon blood did Geordi have?

###

The trains to Germany were more booked than I expected, given it was long past the summer tourist season. Even Oktoberfest had ended two weeks ago. I finally found us seats on the late train, departing Zürich at nine that night and arriving in Trier at five the next morning, after two connections. Unfortunately, this meant several hours of waiting at the station, but I found a bench and we hunkered down.

When I told Geordi we were off to Germany, it didn't faze him. After Lily snatched him off the courthouse steps in Paris and brought him to Marseille, and then I dragged him to Malta, Turkey, and finally Switzerland, it probably took a lot to surprise him.

Eric came home while we were packing. I didn't ask where he'd gone and he didn't say, but he was just as moody as before. I also didn't ask if he was coming with us as the question would only offend him. At least he didn't need to pack; the "dead" clothes he'd acquired in Turkey were all he had and, apparently, all he needed.

Our relationship so far was a modest one. I'd seen him naked during the ceremony where he became "full Dead," which was hardly a romantic interlude, and he'd caught me unawares once after a bath, but that was it. The details of his existence were a touchy subject, but I was partway down that road myself, and I admit to being curious.

As I sat on the bench between him and Geordi, something else niggled at me: If Geordi *saw* Lisbette, why had he only *heard* Eric? Maybe because Eric was "more dead" than Lisbette? If she'd stayed on Earth, no doubt she would also have gone through a ritual to "seal her deadness." But since she went straight off with Michael, presumably she'd…

Well, I didn't actually know what happened to souls who went up *or* down. I hate lack of information, but I now existed in a state of perpetual uncertainty.

Beside me, Eric said quietly, "They have called our train."

I started up. "Oh, thank—" I caught myself, and

turned to Geordi. "Time to go!"

He stopped kicking the bench—I probably should've stopped him sooner, in consideration of the other folks on it, but oh well—and jumped up with alacrity. "Can we sit by the window, Tata?"

"It's pretty dark out, but sure. I'll see what I can do."

This train wasn't totally full, but it was close. I found us a set of four seats facing each other, hoping that a woman travelling alone with a small child would discourage anyone from joining us. Plus, by putting Geordi and Eric both across from me, Eric and I could talk after Geordi fell asleep, and it would look like I spoke to Geordi instead. Unless anyone noticed he was asleep. But I couldn't plan for *every* contingency.

For about thirty minutes, Geordi kept up a steady narration of everything he saw outside. When we passed from the well-lit urban landscape into the dark countryside, he made up stories about what was *probably* out there. It was highly entertaining.

Then at minute thirty-one, he yawned, laid his head against the window, and passed out. I waited another five minutes, then said to Eric in a low voice, "He saw a dead woman today."

Eric's gaze snapped to mine, his hope heartbreaking. "Truly? *T'es sûr?*"

"I'm sure. At the bank. I didn't know he saw her until after I passed her to Michael."

"But how did you manage that without involving him?"

The heat rose in my cheeks. "I did it in the ladies' room, while he was in the boys'."

"*Mon ange*, you cannot leave him alone like that. You have become complacent. But his father's family are not stupid. Soon, they will learn of the Swiss account, if they have not already, and come for him…and you."

I shivered. I didn't need reminders of the Dioguardis' cruelty. That was why Lily'd taken Geordi in the first place, and the *raison d'être* for my bargain with Michael.

"I didn't know what else to do. Michael's leaving it all up to me, and I have no idea what I'm doing. None."

His glare softened. He leaned forward and rested a hand on my knee. "I am sorry. I have been selfish. I have not considered how this might be difficult for you."

His fingers were warm, one of the things that surprised me most about the Dead, and the heat radiated up my jeans to…*other* parts of me.

If he noticed, he made no comment. But he didn't remove his hand.

"It's okay," I said. "I just have to figure it out going forward. If Geordi sees them—you—now, it could make things…easier."

Eric quirked an eyebrow. "But you would prefer that it remain difficult, because the alternative suggests that the demon blood is already manifesting itself?"

I nodded, unable to voice my fears. But he understood and gave my knee a reassuring squeeze. "*Mon ange.* He is still your nephew, the same child as before. You must take every day as it comes. You must not treat him in a certain way now, when yesterday you would have acted differently."

I blew out a breath. "I know. It's just—Jason said—"

Eric made a derogatory noise and sat back. "I still do not like him. But even I must admit that his demon blood is not the reason."

"But he said it's *especially strong* when it shows up

this early."

Eric lifted a shoulder negligently. "We will have to wait and see. It does no good to borrow trouble."

He was right. And yet the fear remained, no matter how I tried to ignore it. But now we had other things to discuss. Quickly I outlined the details of the latest installment in The Quest for Michael's Rocks. He was as relieved as I that this one was a non-demonic, hopefully easy in, easy out.

"*Mais bien sûr*," he said cynically, "another shard will no doubt turn up soon, which *is* in the hands of Satan's helpers."

"You just said not to borrow trouble!"

A smile spread across his face, and I lost my breath. It happened so rarely. His life hadn't been exactly carefree, and his death wasn't much better. But every now and then, a flash of joy broke through, and it made me want to *make* it happen more often.

"*Mon ange. You* must not worry. I, on the other hand, may worry as much as I like."

I opened my mouth to cry *not fair*, when the doors to the next car opened, and two men stepped through. We'd just pulled out of the station in Basel, Switzerland, where we'd added yet more passengers. The first man was some sort of train official, with epaulets on his black uniform and everything. He strode down the aisle toward the back of the car. The second man was middle-aged and heavyset, with a florid complexion and dark hair graying at the temples. He wore jeans, sneakers, and a floral Hawaiian shirt that rode up over his beer gut. He had to be a tourist as he lacked the self-assurance of a local.

He glanced around the crowded car, and I noticed he had a nasty bruise blossoming on his left temple. He met my gaze and stepped closer.

"*Occupé*," I said, indicating the "empty" seat next to Geordi and the one next to me.

He shook his head. "Do you speak English?"

I considered lying, but he seemed harmless enough, and we were surrounded by people. "Yes. But I'm afraid these seats are taken."

His gaze travelled over the seats in question, boring into the one Eric occupied. Eric's own gaze swept over the man, and then met mine.

"*Mon ange*, perhaps you should let him sit. I can go elsewhere for now."

I shook my head slightly. I should've put a sweater or a book on Eric's seat, to make the lie more convincing. But I didn't like doing that to him. He could pass through solid objects, but it wasn't easy. Whenever possible, I left his seat clear and opened his doors, small things to try to help. Unfortunately, I think that contributed to his feelings of dependence, but I didn't see a way around it.

In this case, maybe sitting on a sweater would be a small price to pay for avoiding a bigger intrusion.

To the man I said, "I'm sorry."

"You're American?"

I frowned. The Dioguardis have branches in the US, as well as Western Europe. Plus, I'm naturally reticent. I wasn't about to give personal details to a stranger, no matter how "harmless."

"These seats are taken."

"Yeah, right. Then tell me where to go."

I twisted around, craning my neck to view the seats behind us. He was right; they were all full, and we had a few more stops before our connecting train. In fact, a woman was heading up the aisle toward us. She must have entered at the far end, meaning the next car down was also full.

She assessed the situation and made a beeline for us. She was of medium build, with light hair cropped short and spiked on the ends. It was a young style, for maybe a middle-schooler, but she had to be in her twenties. She wore black shorts and thigh-high leather boots, a sleeveless white blouse, and several long bead necklaces. Her bare arms were tattooed with interlocking rose vines, and she wore so much perfume, it suddenly smelled like we were in a florist's shop.

"*Puoi aiutarmi?*"

My Italian was rusty, but I did my best to explain. "*Questi posti sono occupati.*"

She frowned. "You are *inglese?* Perhaps *il bambino* could be moved next to you, and one of us could sit?"

Clearly she expected the man to do the gentlemanly thing, but his expression soured. "I was here first."

"*Signor*, I am sure this *woman* would prefer to help a lady instead."

He glared harder. "I was here *first.*"

Never mind that I didn't want to help either of them. I wasn't much of a gentleman myself.

Eric, by contrast, was. He stood, regarding me seriously. "*Mon ange*, you must help them. And I must not be here when you do."

And then it clicked. *Tell me where to go*, the man had said, while the woman had asked, *Can you help me?*

I turned to them, shaken. "You're dead? Both of you?"

"But of course they are," Eric said quietly. "Why else would they argue over a *single* vacant seat, when to the rest of the passengers, it appears there are two?"

Chapter Four

*I am ready to meet my Maker. Whether my
Maker is prepared for the great ordeal of
meeting me is another matter.*

*~Winston Churchill, British Prime Minister
(1874-1965)*

This was getting old fast, and it was only my first day on the job. Michael was right when he said the newly dead were drawn to me; they jockeyed for position. But I've had pushy clients before, and two childish souls didn't faze me. I could even deal with them popping up awkwardly in the midst of the Living when we had nowhere to talk.

What I feared I *couldn't* learn was how to tell them *from* the Living. So far, I was zero for seven on that score, not even counting the hundreds of souls I must have unknowingly encountered since dying. I'd even done the opposite once, thinking a live woman was dead.

Eric didn't have the same problem. Maybe being more dead gave him the ability to… What? Sense them? See an aura I missed? To me, it was like being blindfolded and asked to sort a bouquet of roses by scent. I couldn't tell one from another, and it made my head hurt.

"Look, you'll both get your turn," I said quietly, mindful of Geordi and the other passengers. Now that we'd left Basel, the main lights in the car were dimmed. Many people slept, read, or worked with individual lights. Eric had dematerialized into the next car so he wouldn't run into Michael. I knew he had to go, but I missed his support.

I stood and glanced around the car. No one paid any attention to me or my "guests," so I sat again, this time by Geordi. No way would I let them anywhere near him.

"Sit," I said, pointing to the two empty seats.

My tone must have conveyed my irritation because both souls appeared chastened. I did notice that the man slipped in before the woman, taking the window seat. She frowned, but squared her shoulders and took the aisle seat without complaint. Points for her, while my dislike of him increased. For one thing, he'd put himself across from Geordi. I'd much rather the woman was in that seat, but it was silly to make them switch.

"Now," I began, "tell me—"

"I'm dead," the man interrupted. "But then you should know that already, shouldn't you?"

My temper spiked, and I forced it back down. "I'm sure this isn't easy for you—"

"Well, duh. Some asshole mugged me in back of the train station. Took my wallet, then when I threw a punch at him, he bashed my head in with a board."

Now that he sat across from me, I saw his bruise was larger and more serious than I'd originally thought. Still, it was hardly my fault he'd stupidly attacked his mugger.

"You should've let him go," I snapped, "and reported it to the police later."

"Typical woman. What the fuck would the cops here do? They don't give a shit about Americans until they need us to blow up one of their neighbors."

He sat back, smirking, and I resisted the urge to tell him off. No wonder Americans have a bad rep abroad. I wanted to consign this guy to Hell just on principle.

I took a deep breath and blew it out. Maybe I should do the woman first. I didn't see anything physically wrong with her, so I asked, "How did you die?"

"*Non lo so*—I don't know. Maybe I was mugged too. I just woke up *morta*—dead—and saw this train. I thought, perhaps I should get on."

"Hey!" The man leaned forward, stretching across her to get in my face and coming way too close to Geordi. "You can't do that—it's my turn!"

"I can do this however I want! And if you don't back off, I won't do you at all." The woman looked smug, so I added, "*Either* of you."

Okay, that sucked. I'd stooped to their level. He might be a jerk, but she was lying. She knew exactly how she died, she just didn't want to say, and had copied his story.

"Fine," the man growled. "Ladies first."

He sat back, glowering out the window, and I faced the woman. "I don't believe you. That's not how this works. You tell me the truth, because if you don't, my boss will know, and you don't want *him* finding out you lied."

Her stony expression wavered, showing a hint of fear. I had no idea what Michael did with the mildly dishonest. I mean, super bad folks went to Hell, but I didn't think skating around the truth qualified. You had to lie *and* do other terrible things.

At least, as a perennial truth-skater myself, that's how I *hoped* it worked.

"*Bene*. Okay," she said finally. "I took something,

qualche droga. I don't know what. I found them in my boyfriend's coat. I fed some to his pet rat, and it fell asleep. I was tired, so I took some myself. The next thing I know, I'm dead."

I stared. Even the man twisted around to gawk at her.

"You killed your boyfriend's rat," I said, "then took the same crap yourself?"

She scowled. "No, *stupida.* You couldn't kill that thing with rat poison. Besides, I only gave it *un pochino.* I figured since I was bigger, I should take more."

I couldn't argue with her logic. Plus, both boyfriend and rat were better off without her.

I said to the man, "You go. But make it fast."

"I already told you, I was mugged."

"I know. But this is your one shot to tell me something—anything—to sway me."

"To do what?"

The woman turned her scowl on him. "To send you up instead of down, dumbass."

He glanced from me to her, then back. "*You* decide that?"

"What did you think?" the woman demanded. "She's here to write your fucking eulogy?"

"Sorry," he mumbled. "You just don't...I mean..." He reddened and wisely trailed off.

"Deal with it." No need to mention that Michael could reverse whatever decision I made. I was damn tired at this point. It was past midnight, I'd had a long day, and apparently, I didn't even get to set my own office hours. "So, anything to add?"

For a second, I thought he would actually grovel, but instead he said, "Fuck that. I don't got nothing to say."

"Fine. Great."

I sat back. Beside me, Geordi was still zonked out, and watching him sleep gave me a moment to recover. Upon reflection, neither the man nor the woman was all that bad. But it still took some searching before I got the sense that they should both go up.

Okay, then.

Michael.

The car's doors opened and in he walked. "Hyacinth. It is good to see you again so soon."

He eyed the two souls, who gaped at him. And no wonder. He'd swapped his earlier duds for a royal blue train conductor's uniform, including shiny gold epaulets, a bright red fez, and for unexplained reasons, a monocle.

"This is—" I stopped, realizing I'd never gotten their names. I hurried on. "Anyway. Neither of them's a prize, but they should go up." I'd also forgotten to ask if they believed in Heaven and Hell, but it was too late now.

Michael grinned. "And why do you think that?"

"Aren't you in a tearing hurry?" I asked testily.

"Child. I told you before that while a soul is in limbo, we have space in which to work. Many souls die at once. Without that cushion, I could never be with all of them."

"Still. No reason to wait, right?"

He laughed, holding his normal roar to a chuckle so no one around us would notice. "Very well. If you wish me to take them away, tell me your reasoning."

I sighed. He had said he'd check up on me, so this was probably fair.

"She's a drug addict," I began. "She stole from her boyfriend, then OD'ed, but I don't think she did anything bad enough to merit Hell. I mean, doesn't Heaven have some kind of rehab or atonement program or something?"

Michael grinned again. "And him? What is your logic there?"

"He's a jerk. But last time I checked, that's not a mortal sin."

"No, it is not." Michael faced the souls, who stood, expressions of trust softening their features as they awaited his guidance. "Come, my children. Follow me."

I wasn't sure why he always said that since it didn't seem like any following was involved. Instead, they all just vanished, and I drew a shaky breath.

What a day. It would be morning soon, when I had to embark on the next phase of my *other* new job. Geordi stirred, and I put my arm around him, resting my head on his. Even if Eric came back, I had no energy to talk.

In a minute I was asleep, and I didn't wake until Eric touched my shoulder to say we had to change trains.

###

When we arrived in Trier the next morning, the station was as crowded as our trains had been. Briefly I wondered if some of the folk I saw were dead, but when I asked Eric about it under my breath, while Geordi was bent over a drinking fountain, he shook his head.

"They are alive. Maybe five or ten are dead, but no more." He saw my panic and added quickly, "Do not worry, *mon ange*. They have chosen to stay on Earth and are full Dead. They will not ask for your aid."

I sighed with relief, then frowned at the crowds. "I don't get it then. Why are they all here?"

"I do not know. I speak German, but I have not spent time here."

"It's my first visit ever."

Most of the archaeological digs I'd been on, and ergo, the graves I'd robbed, were farther south: Turkey, northern Africa, Greece. Apart from France, Northern Europe was not a region I knew much about.

With that in mind, I grabbed a guidebook from the convenience desk, and we left the station, heading for the nearest hotel in my price range. As we walked, I read tidbits about the area aloud to Geordi, mainly for entertainment, but also to impart possibly relevant info to Eric. Not that being a ghost destroyed his ability to read. He just couldn't easily manipulate a book's pages. An argument for e-readers if I've ever heard one.

Geordi was accustomed to his Tata Hyhy's obsessive interest in ancient history and listened with half an ear, throwing in the occasional seven-year-old question. For instance, when I mentioned that, in its heyday, Trier was called the Second Rome, he wanted to know where the first one was. Or when I read about the Porta Nigra—the "Black Gate"—the largest extant Roman city gate north of the Alps, he asked why its stones were so dark.

"I don't know, sweetie," I said, scanning the guidebook. "Maybe just because they're eighteen hundred years old. It was built in the second century."

He thought about that. "But other rocks are older than that and they don't go black."

Eric caught my eye and quirked an ironic brow, but before I could come up with an answer, Geordi switched gears. "Do they have different bugs in Germany?"

"Not different, exactly, except that maybe the crickets sing in German."

He giggled at that, a carefree little boy, and I marveled at his resilience, though it was only two months since his mother had died. And then a pernicious thought slithered into my heart, splitting it with a sudden, cold fear. After dying and coming back to life, I now healed more quickly. Could Geordi's demon blood be why he'd bounced back from tragedy so fast?

Eric saw my face and put a hand on my arm. "*Mon ange*, remember what we discussed. You cannot dissect every little thing he says or does, or it will eat at you like a swarm of locusts, until nothing remains but fear."

I drew a shaky breath and nodded. Geordi regarded me curiously, then turned in Eric's direction. Which wasn't reassuring.

I pretended not to notice, returning to the guidebook. "Oh look, sweetie. They have Roman baths from the fourth century. Underground heating and all. I bet if we took a tour, you'd see some bugs down there."

Geordi's face lit, and I showed him the color photo in the book. Eric also peered over my shoulder and murmured, "*Et puis, la Cathédrale de Trier.*"

Without thinking I said, "The cathedral? Really?"

He gave a Gallic half-shrug, this one self-deprecating, and Geordi said, "What's a cathedral?"

Crap. I didn't know if he'd heard Eric first, but option two—that he'd heard me talking to no one—wasn't much better.

"It's a really big church. This one's the oldest Catholic church in Germany."

"Are there bugs in it?"

"Probably."

I ignored Eric's snort of amusement, and we walked in silence. Now that I wasn't reading, I examined the scenery. Trier has, unsurprisingly, a Bavarian feel. Tall houses with pointed roofs, decorative woodwork, and multi-paned windows; narrow brick streets with the occasional sidewalk further cramping them; and an endless parade of cafés, with enough outdoor seating for an army of tourists.

Then, just to be contrary, a Roman-era building pops up: warm yellow brick, arched doorways and windows, and a completely different vibe from the surrounding structures. Despite my tiredness and the need to find Michael's rock, I itched to explore, to enter even the most mundane of these ancient holdovers and let all that history bathe me in its cool impermanence. To think about the men and women who walked before, what they did, how they did it, and where they all went.

Not that there were undiscovered artifacts at this point, but the urge burned in me nonetheless. I am what I am, and with a sigh, I pushed any sightseeing off to the "after work" timeframe where my fun usually gets relegated. Which today, shouldn't be far off. If all went according to plan, we'd find the rock by early afternoon and have plenty of "fun" time after that.

At the first hotel that fit our budget, we found they were booked up. It was tiny, though, so I didn't think much of it, until the next one we tried was also full. When we arrived at the third, with the same result, I feared we'd be sleeping on a park bench.

"Please," I said to the concierge. "Can you tell me *anywhere* that might have a room?"

I'd given up on finding more than one. Eric would have to sleep on the floor, or find the local Dead hostel, or however it worked.

The concierge's English was as dicey as my German and thickly accented—I felt like we were in a World War II drama—but his meaning was clear. "I am sorry. Vee haf no *Logis.*"

"But why?" I asked in frustration.

"You do not know? You are not here for *das Fest?*"

"*What* festivities? Oktoberfest ended weeks ago!"

"*Ja, normalerweise.* But avhile ago, it vas ze two hundredth anniversary of ze original Festival, and of *der Geburt*—birth—of Karl Marx, who is from here. Zese dates haf passed, but vat are a few extra years *unter Freunden*—among friends? Also, Martinstag—*das Fest des* Saint Martin—is in two veeks, as is ze beginning of Carnival in nearby Cologne. Vee in Trier haf taken all zis as reason to celebrate somevat longer zis year."

Beside me, Eric started to laugh. "We have come to Trier, in the midst of a six-weeks' celebration, expecting to find a room, without advance reservations."

I would have elbowed him in the ribs, but I didn't want to look any more foolish. Besides, Geordi again frowned in his direction. Surely nothing drastic would change with his demon blood in the next few days. But when we returned to Switzerland, I'd track Jason down and make him explain it to me.

The prospect sent mixed emotions through me: anxiety, excitement, anticipation, and yes, lust. But also anger, because he'd lied and then deserted us, along with gratitude for what he'd done to save us. Even Eric, despite their mutual dislike.

Meanwhile, it was already midmorning, and if we didn't find a place soon, we wouldn't make it to the rock collector's home today.

I said to the concierge, "Is there an Airbnb nearby or a flat? Anything at all?"

He eyed me, then Geordi and our small carry-ons. "Von of ze live-in managers has gone to tend her sick *Mutter*. She vill be back in a day or two, but you can haf her room tonight. I am sorry. It is ze best I can do."

I blew my bangs out of my eyes. "We'll take it."

###

Half an hour later we'd stowed our bags in the tiny top-floor room and were back in the lobby. Forget sleeping on the floor; between the bed, the bureau, and a writing desk with chair, there was barely room to walk. I couldn't discuss it with Eric, but he lifted a brow speakingly at the bed, and heat flushed my face and throat, down to my breasts. Not that anything could happen with Geordi sleeping next to me, but hey.

Luckily, it was only one night. We could probably even hop the late train home tonight, but I didn't want to count on it. Better to have a room, just in case.

We hadn't eaten since dinner at the train station last night, so I asked the concierge for directions to the nearest vegetarian café. This being the land of hamburgers and sausage, he couldn't think of one that served no meat at all, but he recommended a place that might suit, and we headed out.

I've been a vegetarian since I was Geordi's age. One of my foster families introduced me to the idea, and it stuck. Of course, *I* didn't stick with them. I never stayed with any family more than a year. Not because I was a terrible child or they were terrible families. It's just how the system works. Unlike Lily, no one adopted me, so every year I got switched out and went somewhere else.

For the most part, I don't mind. I've been therapized enough to know what has and hasn't wrecked me emotionally. And the care coordinators made sure Lily and I stayed in touch. Without that, I probably would've turned out much worse. That is, if you don't put *robbing graves, lying for a living, and retiring to fence stolen goods* in the "worse" column.

Anyway, I've been a vegetarian most of my life. At

least…I still think of myself that way.

We stepped into the café, and I was assailed by the smell of spices and warm cheese and…*Blutwurst*.

Blood sausage. My mouth watered, and I grabbed a nearby chair for support.

Ever since Michael brought me back to life, I've *had* to eat meat, and the redder, the better. No chicken breast or turkey bacon for me. Even pork wasn't great.

Steak. Hamburger. Beef sausage.

My body demanded them, and nothing my brain said shut off the cravings. I'd worked out a system where one day a week, I consciously ate a serving of red meat, while the other days I stuck to my veggie guns. Today wasn't a meat day, though.

Geordi saw my reaction and came to the correct conclusion. "Tata, you need the meat today, don't you?"

"I'm fine, sweetie. I just need *some* food. It doesn't have to be meat."

Geordi's blue eyes narrowed, his expression so reminiscent of Jason, my heart ached. "If Jason was here, he'd get something with beef and make you eat it."

Have I mentioned that, for a seven-year-old boy with the usual superhero-and-cartoon obsessions, he's remarkably astute? Obviously, he doesn't know I'm dead. But he *does* know what makes me tick, better than I do myself sometimes.

We found a table by a window, and I surreptitiously pulled out a chair for Eric. He sat, also regarding me thoughtfully. "Your nephew is right. You need the meat, even if it is not your 'regular' day."

Drat them both. I focused on Geordi, holding his gaze in case he'd heard Eric and was about to "out" him. "Fine. I'll order eggs and sausage. But that's it. No more until next week."

Geordi grinned at me. But when the waitress came, he did order an extra side of bacon. I knew he meant to give it to me, and I hid a smile. There were worse things in life than him wanting to help me—or be like Jason.

We were halfway through the meal, Geordi and I barely able to chew fast enough, Eric reading the paper I'd laid out on the table for him, when Geordi suddenly asked, "Tata, why are those people staring at us?"

He pointed with his fork at a group of half a dozen folks in varying degrees of casual-tourist-business dress, hovering near the door and watching me expectantly.

The greasy sausage abruptly lost its appeal. "I'm sure they're just waiting for a table."

Except the café was half empty. The waitress walked right past the group, but I already knew she couldn't see them. And yet…Geordi could. That didn't mean anything, though. He'd seen Lisbette, so this wasn't a big change and didn't mean his demon blood was getting stronger.

Eric said, "*Mon ange*, I believe you have more souls to sort."

"What does that mean?" Geordi asked.

"What does what mean, sweetie?" I asked as the first soul in line made eye contact and started toward us.

"What the invisible man said."

My gaze snapped to his. "*What?*"

"The one at the table. There." He gestured at Eric's chair.

Eric froze, and my heart dropped to my stomach, where the slimy sausage now seemed determined to climb back out. "Can—can you see him?"

Geordi said scornfully, in the way only children can,

"Of course not. He wouldn't be *invisible* if I could."

"Of course not," I managed weakly. My heart jackhammered, and I looked to Eric. What was the point in *not* doing so, if Geordi already knew he was there?

Eric raised his gaze slowly to mine. There was such hope in it—such desperation, to find that another of the Living might hear him—might someday see and touch him, as I did. Something had kept him here, and though he'd been made full Dead, it was the Living he craved.

Part of me *so* wanted him to exist in my world. But was that selfish? It would be easier for *me* if Geordi saw him. But despite my lack of a moral compass, I'd had misgivings all along about keeping him here. He was a person, breathing or not, and "because I need him" wasn't a great reason to keep him from wherever he should have gone.

Before I collected my thoughts, the dead man arrived at our table. "Excuse me," he said in German-accented English. "I belief you may know vhere I am to go?"

I sighed and set down my fork. "Take a number." He stared blankly, so I said, "Never mind. Tell me your name and how you died."

While he spoke, I noticed that two new souls had joined the queue. When the man finished, I didn't bother to hide what I did from Geordi, just said to Eric, "You might as well wait at the park across from the hotel. This could take a while."

"*Bien*," he said and stood, and Geordi pointed a finger roughly at his face.

"Don't get lost," he said with another fierce Jason expression. "Tata needs you."

Did I ever.

Chapter Five

*Dying is a very dull, dreary affair. And my
advice to you is to have nothing whatever to
do with it.*

*~W. Somerset Maugham, English Writer
(1874-1965)*

"If nothing else, it's restoring my faith in humanity,"
I told Michael thirty minutes later. "Sort of."

"And how is that, my child?"

He sat across the table from me, next to Geordi,
who'd been given a crash course in Tata Hyhy's new job
and Tonton Michael's role in it. I didn't go into details,
just explained that the newly dead needed help on their
journey, and Michael and I gave it to them. I left out the
part where Michael was an archangel, in lieu of getting
into the whole God-and-Heaven thing.

Geordi appeared neither surprised nor concerned by
any of this. I guess I underestimated the capacity children
have to accept the incredible. I mean, if you believe in
the Tooth Fairy and Santa Claus, what's so weird about
your aunt sorting the slushpile of the Dead?

Maybe he wasn't wrong on the other stuff too. Until
I died and started seeing the Dead, I never believed any
of *this* was possible. Why shouldn't Santa Claus be real?

As for how and why Michael was in Trier, I let
Geordi fill in his own gaps. I think he assumed Michael

also took the train, but at a different time. Like this was a business trip—essentially true—but Michael came at the last minute.

"So far," I said, answering Michael, "I haven't met anyone who should actually go *down*. There's a lot of losers out there, but apparently the world isn't all bad."

He chuckled and sipped espresso from the ridiculously tiny cup he held. Or rather, the *tasse à espresso* was perfectly normal-sized. It's just that his hands were so massive—*he* was so massive—that even a coffee mug would be lost in his grasp.

Today he'd tried for tourist garb: extra-large jeans, sandals with socks, in deference to the autumn chill, and a gray bedsheet-sized t-shirt that read, "Jesus Saves: Have You Invested Your Life In Him?" But no matter what he wore, he'd never look "normal." He might as well have stuck with his warrior gear, except all the weaponry would probably get him arrested.

The waitress didn't notice his odd get-up, or else she didn't care. She took his order and brought his food like he was any other customer, so maybe it was just me.

"Child," he said, "I have very little time, as you well know. What is it you wish to discuss?"

In short order I'd sorted the dozen or so souls who'd lined up in the café, then called him down, requesting he return after delivering them. Luckily, they were all straightforward: no jerks, whiners, or odd cases, just a rash of fatal illnesses, a car accident that took out four of them together, and two elderly women who'd died of "natural causes," otherwise known as "getting old."

"It's just that now there's a lot of them lining up wherever I go. And—" I hesitated.

As far as I could tell, Michael knew nothing of the

demon blood running through the Dioguardis. He'd said often enough that he wasn't omniscient, but this seemed like an even bigger "miss" than not knowing about Eric. His *job* was to keep Satan in Hell and prevent his minions from running amok on Earth.

Geordi was occupied with his scarab, crawling it around the sugar bowl and through the unused utensils. What the hell. I didn't have to tell Michael the demon-blood part yet. Or maybe ever.

I asked point blank, "Why is Geordi seeing the Dead now too?"

Michael paused, then lowered his cup. "I am afraid I do not know. Some children just…do. They are more imaginative, more open to the truths adults have learned to suppress. Or perhaps it is this time and place."

I raised an eyebrow. "Oktoberfest?"

"Autumn. We are nearing the ancient fire feast Samhain, the eve of All Saints' Day, followed by All Souls'. The veil between the worlds of the Living and the Dead is thinner now than at any other time. And Trier is a very old city. The conditions are ripe for anyone who is receptive to see the Dead more often."

"Is that why I'm seeing so many of them now too?"

His eyes twinkled. "Perhaps. But I do not think so. In your case, I believe it has more to do with you opening yourself up to them. Your abilities appear to be a side effect of your…situation."

"Okay. Thanks. That helps."

In truth, I was relieved. Maybe Geordi seeing the Dead had nothing to do with his demon blood. If other children saw them, ones with no trace of the blood, why couldn't he? Besides, Eric hanging around and me being a magnet for the Dead had to increase Geordi's exposure.

The more he was near them, the more he'd pick up on their presence.

Michael stood to leave. "I am afraid that, as I mentioned, I do not carry any money…"

"I've got it. Some boss you are. You're supposed to treat *me* when we have a business brunch."

Geordi said, "Bye, Tonton. Will we see you again?"

"Soon, my son."

"But not *too* soon," I cut in. "I still have my *other* job to do."

"Of course. I expect a full report when you are done." He exited the café and I sagged in my seat.

"Here, Tata," Geordi said and scraped his extra side of bacon onto my plate.

I ate it without comment.

###

We paid the bill and walked toward the park. Knowing Geordi likely heard Eric thanks to possessing the innocence of a normal child, not because *he* was possessed, made the idea less bothersome. I took his hand as we wove through the crowds. Worrying about the Dioguardis and Satan was all well and good. Losing Geordi through inattention would be beyond stupid.

"So," I said once we'd left the business district for the more residential area where our hotel and the park were, "do you have any questions about what Michael and I said back there?"

He squinted up at me. "No."

"You're sure? That was a lot all at once."

He shrugged and we walked in silence for half a block. Then he said, "Who's the Invisible Man? Is it Jason?"

"Oh, sweetie. No. It's a man named Eric. I met him

after he…died."

No need for details. Geordi might accept all this, but I wasn't ready to get into Eric's life as a cop and how it related to Geordi's scumbag father. Plus, I didn't want him questioning why his parents weren't still around.

"Oh," he said in a small voice.

We'd stopped at the corner across from the park playground. I didn't see Eric yet, and I thought it might be good to have more alone time to sort some of this out.

Finally he said, staring down at his feet, "I knew the Invisible Man was dead. I thought maybe…Jason was dead, and that's why he went away."

"Oh, *sweetie*." I dropped to my knees and pulled him tight. If I'd had the power, I would've consigned Jason to the Last Circle of Hell then and there for the pain he'd caused my nephew.

Intellectually, I knew Jason had good reasons for running off. Like, that he'd stolen High Demon powers to save us, making him a liability to a woman hiding a young demon from their shared clan. Plus, if he'd stayed, he'd be openly flaunting the Dioguardis, who he'd already defied by helping us escape them.

I couldn't explain any of that to Geordi, though. From his perspective, the first positive male role model he'd had, who'd loved him and played with him, and taught him to skip rocks and take care of his Tata Hyhy, had abandoned him without a word. I could see how Ghost Jason was preferable to being ditched on purpose.

Pulling back, I smoothed Geordi's bangs and wiped a tear off his cheek. "I know you don't understand. I don't understand it all, either. But Jason had to leave, to keep us safe. Something…happened to him, while you were with your cousin Paolo. Jason wasn't sure what it would do to him, so he *had* to go. Otherwise, he would never have left."

Geordi snuffled and wiped his nose on his sleeve. "Is Eric your friend?"

"Yes."

"Is he staying with us?"

I hesitated. I didn't want to scare him or lead him to too many other questions—like, what was our sleeping arrangement, or did Eric ever walk through us—but I've always felt honesty is the best approach with children.

Yeah, I know. The irony of it all. With children, yes. With adults, not so much.

I said slowly, "Yes. He's been with us since we left France." I paused, but Geordi just regarded me solemnly. "How do you feel about that? Is it okay?"

He shrugged again. I'd started to realize he did that when he wanted to ask a hard question or tell me something difficult. He said, "When we were on the boat with Jason, I heard someone talking to me. Was it Eric?"

Honesty, right?

I sighed. "Probably. He—" Oh, what the hell. "He's wanted to talk with you for a while. He'd very much like to be your friend too."

"Will I ever be able to see him?"

"I think so. I can see him and touch him, just like I touch you. He's solid to me, and I think someday, he'll be that way for you too. I don't know when, but it seems like you're hearing him more clearly, right? So maybe it will be pretty soon."

"Oh. Okay."

It wasn't a squeal of delight, and I thought that when we got back to Switzerland, a few sessions with a child psychologist might be in order.

On the other hand, who could blame him if he needed time to ponder? He'd always been a "mental" child. Not that he didn't roughhouse and play with the best of them. But at the end of the day, he needed his down time to process his experiences. So did I, for that matter.

I said, "He's waiting for us at the park. I know he'll be happy to learn you know more about him."

We crossed the street, aiming for the playground where I assumed Eric waited. It was then that I realized if Geordi heard Eric on the boat at the end of August, it debunked Michael's theory about this time of year making him more receptive.

And it destroyed my theory that length of exposure made it easier. Because our time on the boat was right after I met Eric, and I'd barely learned I could see the Dead myself. But Geordi hadn't heard him much since then, so maybe it did have something to do with the dead person's "freshness." Eric died about a minute before I met him; it didn't get much fresher than that.

We found him sitting on a bench by the playground, which was considerate given he wasn't particularly "kid-oriented." Unlike Jason, Eric treated Geordi sort of…distantly. He rarely used his name, referring to him instead as "your nephew," and while concerned intellectually that Geordi could be part demon, he lacked the aunt-slash-parent gut terror about it that I had.

His gaze zeroed in on Geordi, who peered at the bench—not *at* Eric, but in a general way—and then at me. "Is he here?"

"*Oui!*" Eric leaned forward until he almost touched Geordi. "*J'suis ici.* Do you hear me?"

I don't know who watched Geordi more closely, me or Eric. However, he gave no indication he'd heard anyone but me.

"Yes," I said to him. "He's on the bench."

"What happens if I sit on him?"

As always here lately, I wasn't sure whether to laugh or cry. Way to go for the practicalities, in a completely surreal situation. "Eric will move if you get too close."

"What if he's not fast enough?"

"Uh…"

I'd never thought about that, and from Eric's frown, neither had he. In theory, Geordi would pass through him like he wasn't there, same as when other live folks got in his way and he couldn't dodge them. He said it felt like a sudden chill that dissipated once they were through.

By contrast, Eric was completely solid for me. We'd bumped into each other constantly back at our small apartment, forcing me to stifle my *oomphs* in front of Geordi.

But for Geordi, Eric was only partially real so far. He didn't even hear him all the time, as if Eric were a radio station with poor signal strength. So, what *would* happen if they came together?

"I don't know, sweetie," I said at last.

Eric tensed. "I could try to touch him now, if he would like to find out…?"

I hesitated. The hope was clearly agony. If Geordi felt him, it would mean so much. But if he didn't, the despair would be devastating.

"Oh," Geordi said. "Can I go play?"

Eric slumped, and I blew out a breath. "Sure. Just stay where I can see you."

Geordi ran off, and I sat next to Eric. He was silent, watching Geordi and the other children playing. More benches surrounded the circular play area, with various adults on them, but none were close by.

After a minute he said, "I would like to go to Mass."

I stared at him. "*Can* you?"

"*Quoi?* You think I will burst into flame if I enter a sacred structure?"

"Not exactly. I keep telling you I know less about this than you do."

"Of course. I apologize." He took my hand, twining our fingers, then lifted it to his lips. The light kiss sent all kinds of heat through me, and from the glint in his eye, he knew exactly the effect he had on me. "It is just that, when I was alive, my faith was strong. I have told you that I went to Mass every week, but I have not been to confession nor taken communion since I died. I realize I cannot take it now. But I would like to be there, to share as much as I can in the service." His voice was husky. "It is something you would not be doing *for* me. We could share in it together."

His eyes burned with the intensity of his feelings, and I drew a shaky breath. I was born Catholic and made it through the basic early sacraments, despite an eclectic mix of foster-family cultures and faiths. The care coordinator who kept Lily and me close also ensured I was exposed to the religion of my parents.

But after striking out on my own, I only went to Mass when Lily and I were together on a weekend. So before I died, faith wasn't a big part of my existence. And *since* I died, I'd avoided thinking about it. No matter how much you believe in the concept of God, the thought of actually meeting Him—or Her—is freaky-scary.

And yet… Eric had so little influence in my world. Would it be such a sacrifice, if it meant so much to him?

Plus, as the care coordinator had known about my

parents, I realized this was something Lily would want for Geordi. I was even his godmother, sworn at his baptism to raise him in the Catholic faith should no one else be around to do it.

I was pretty good at being Fun Aunt. I'd had seven years of practice at that. Responsible—and therefore Religious—Guardian was a whole new role.

I squeezed Eric's fingers. "Okay. I'll go to Mass with you."

His smile was filled with relief. "*Merci*. There is one tonight, *à dix-huit heures et quart*."

"*Tonight?*" It came out as a squeak, and he laughed.

"*Mon ange*. I do not believe crossing the threshold will cause *you* to explode in a ball of fire, either."

"Of course not! I just thought, you know, we'd go after we get home. Like, next week, or next month, or…something."

He closed his hands over mine, every aspect of his frame, his expression, the gentle way he spoke, telling me how important this was to him. "We are in Trier, the oldest city in Germany, at the very site of its first Catholic church. And it is Saturday. We will have time after we retrieve Michael's rock. You were not planning to leave before tomorrow, anyway."

He had me there. It was still early, and as I kept reminding myself, getting the rock shouldn't take long. The collector lived just outside of Trier, so it was a matter of finding his house, working out the payment, and returning here. Probably in plenty of time for Mass.

"Fine. Tonight, then."

"*Merci*," he repeated and gave my hands a final squeeze before sitting back on the bench.

I sat back too. What had I gotten myself into?

It wouldn't kill me to go to Mass. Probably. I mean, I was already dead. Sort of.

Gah.

But was it wrong to attend church, not from needing to be close to God, but because a hot dead guy asked me to? That had to be some kind of sin. Even *thinking* about sex in conjunction with church was a sin, wasn't it?

And what would happen when the priest called down the Host? I saw dead people. Jesus was dead.

What if I saw *him*?

What if I didn't?

It was way too early in the day for this much theological debate. But not to get the rock. For once, just *once* since I died, I'd get to do something easy.

I stood. "Let's get started. If I'm going to church later, I need time to prepare."

"*Mais oui*. Anything to ensure you do not explode."

I ignored him. On the other hand, maybe we'd burst into flame together.

I suppressed a shiver of anxiety. Surely Michael would've told me if I was prohibited from entering a church. Or maybe this was one of those side effects he didn't know about. Only one way to find out. Unless I managed to stall at the collector's house.

Somewhat cheered, I called Geordi over from the playground. Who knew what the day would bring?

Chapter Six

The stroke of death is as a lover's pinch,
Which hurts and is desired.

~William Shakespeare, English Playwright
(1564-1616); Antony and Cleopatra,
V.II.295-296

As most of the tourists had come to Trier to drink, not sightsee, we had less trouble renting a car than we'd had finding a room. The concierge helped us out, and within the hour, we were on our way in a cute little Peugeot 107 that was still huge compared to my car. Geordi and I just fit in the front, with Eric crammed in the back. You'd think an advantage to being a ghost would be the ability to fit into small spaces, but apparently not. Or at least, not without more energy than Eric wanted to expend.

The country outside Trier is hilly and forested. Lots of evergreens, so not much fall color, but beautiful nonetheless. It was cool and cloudy, the flashes of sky between the trees a dull, lowering gray. It almost felt like snow, but I didn't think it was *that* cold. Still, the drive was dark, if short. Thirty minutes, tops.

Michael had given me the address, so all we had to do was drive to the house and knock. Or rather, to the mansion.

When we got to the turn, I thought the navigation app

was wrong. It showed a road, where clearly this was a driveway. Then I realized the driveway *was* the road.

My stomach twinged. If he was this wealthy, he might not be amenable to giving up his trinkets. Back in Marseille, I'd had plenty of truck with the über-rich, who were my main clients. In a constant game of one-upmanship, they hired my former partner, Vadim, to steal each other's best pieces. Then they hired me, in my capacity as a fence, to negotiate complex deals back and forth, until their collections were evened out.

None of it made sense, but it netted me some hefty commissions, and one absurdly valuable car, and gave me insight into the minds of people who lived in ginormous mansions. Namely, that they liked their stuff, liked getting their own way, and did *not* like anyone interfering with either of the above.

Then again, this was "just" a rock Herr Burke found in Turkey. If he liked money, maybe he'd sell it for a price. A small one, since that's all I could afford.

I pulled over by the side of the drive, across from the mansion. Geordi, Eric, and I got out and stared at it.

Mansion was an understatement. Castle would be more apt. It was huge. Royalty huge. Great-big-stone-pile, impossible-to-heat-in-the-winter but nice-and-cool-in-the-summer huge. I was clearly underdressed. I have all kinds of Visiting the Rich clothes, but I didn't bring them to Turkey, and I hadn't bought any new ones since landing in Switzerland.

I glanced down at my jeans and sneakers, and the ratty hooded Shetland sweater I'd dragged on in deference to the weather. Then I examined Geordi. Apparently, Fun Aunts skipped baths. It must've been two or three days since he'd washed more than his hands.

Plus, I'd forgotten to make him change his clothes, which he'd slept in on the train.

Eric said, "*Mon ange*, it is just a house, and he is just a man."

"Easy for you to say," I said. "You're invisible."

"*Eh bien*. But it is still true that you have nothing to worry about."

His gaze travelled over the appropriate parts, and he gave me a slow, wicked smile. I would've swatted him, but, well, it *was* flattering. And…there was still a touch of sadness in his eyes. He wouldn't believe me if I said his deadness didn't matter to me, but before I could figure out what to say instead, he shuttered his expression.

"Perhaps he is not even the owner," he continued. "Perhaps he merely works here."

"I suppose that's possible," I said doubtfully.

Geordi regarded me curiously. I didn't think he'd heard Eric since this morning, but we were pretty much talking openly in front of him now. If nothing else, it might make the adjustment easier when Eric did "break through," or whatever happened.

Bending down, I did my best to straighten Geordi's clothes. He twitched and squirmed in typical seven-year-old fashion, balking completely when I tried to run my fingers through his hair. I gave up and switched to picking at the worst of the pilled yarn on my sweater.

Eric said, "Come. You are stalling. You will not escape Mass that easily."

I threw him a look. "I'm only thinking of you. I'd hate for you to vanish in a puff of smoke."

"Is Eric going away?" Geordi asked.

"No, sweetie. He just wants us to go to church with

him."

That piqued Geordi's interest. "Ghosts like church?"

"This one does."

He thought about that. "And you think he might get hurt when he goes in? Because he's not supposed to?"

Smart kid. I sighed. "I'm a little worried. But I'm sure it's fine." I didn't bring up my concerns for myself. Geordi didn't need *that* adding to his nightmares.

"*Mon ange*. I have already been inside a church."

"You have?"

"Not to Mass, but to see if I could. There are not so many places I can go without finding myself in someone's way. Most churches are open all day, but empty. They are an excellent place to sit and think." One side of his mouth quirked up. "Even for disreputable ghosts such as myself."

Geordi now watched the place where Eric stood, listening intently. I was about to ask if he'd heard Eric or could see him, even partially, when across the drive, the castle's mahogany double-doors were flung open with a muted *thud!* and a woman stepped onto the spacious entablature that served as a "porch."

"Can I help you?" she called out in English.

Tall and willowy, with long blonde hair falling in loose waves down to her waist, I pegged her at about my age, so somewhere around thirty. She wore a sleeveless white t-shirt, cinched at the waist by a braided red belt with long tails and a circular black clasp surrounded by twelve sun-like rays. Her skirt was of some diaphanous material in shades of blue, green, and purple, and ended just above her ankles.

She came down the steps, stopping on the last one, and I saw her feet were bare, her toenails and fingernails painted black, a jarring effect when paired with her light coloring and pale pink lipstick. She'd probably seen us from inside and got tired of waiting. She didn't seem impatient though, just curious. And non-threatening.

I crossed the drive. "Sorry to bother you. Is Herr Burke available?"

She examined me, then Geordi. A warm smile lit her face, and her green eyes sparkled. "Well, hello there. What's your name?" Her English was flawless, but she had a slight accent I couldn't place. Not German. Canadian, maybe?

Geordi stared at his feet shyly, and she said, "That's okay. You don't have to talk to me. But I promise I don't bite!" To me she said, "I'm Heinrich's wife. Is there something I can do for you?"

I did some mental arithmetic. Either Herr Burke was ultra-wealthy *and* damn young, or she'd married an older man. Michael'd been pretty scarce on the details. I didn't even know who'd told him Herr Burke had the rock in the first place. But there weren't a lot of young guys with this kind of wealth, unless they'd inherited it.

I said to Frau Burke, "I really need to speak to Herr Burke. I understand he has an extensive rock collection?"

She rolled her eyes: the long-suffering wife. "Heavens, yes. It's the most ridiculous thing. He finds them everywhere—in rivers, on the road, behind pubs. I really don't understand it." Her sweeping gesture encompassed the vast structure and grounds behind her. "We have all this, and his greatest joy is finding pretty pebbles. He has cases of them, all over the house."

I warmed to her. Despite the eye roll, she spoke of her husband with affection and amused tolerance. She could be an ally if he refused to sell.

She straightened. "My goodness! Where are my manners? It's freezing out here. Please, come in."

It was cold, worse than when we'd left Trier. I don't know how she'd stood there this whole time, with bare arms and feet, without shivering. Eric frowned as she ran lightly back up the stairs, but when he met my gaze, he merely said, "*Après toi.*"

Geordi squinted in his direction. "Tata, did Eric say something?"

Frau Burke paused between the columns in front of the doors. "What did you say?"

"Nothing." I took Geordi's hand and gave it a warning squeeze. *Not* the best time for this.

We followed her up and inside, Eric slipping in as she slammed the heavy doors shut behind us. The marble entry was as impressive and austere as you'd expect, done in shades of green that complemented Frau Burke's eyes, and I wondered if it was coincidence or a deliberate homage to her beauty.

Either way, she appeared unaware of it, neither glancing left nor right as she led us down a long, wide hall. She seemed an oddly carefree spirit to inhabit such a "heavy" home. The side tables and cases along the walls were made of dark woods like mahogany and cherry, the numerous paintings had heavily gilded frames, and the floor-to-ceiling emerald-green drapes were thick velvet. Much of the statuary was either green marble or jade, but occasionally, a splash of blood-red appeared: a vase of stunningly perfect roses, or a soft Persian rug to warm the marble floors.

Speaking of which, I was right about the castle's heating challenges. Frigid air emanated from the open doors we passed and up from the floor, and I wondered anew at Frau Burke's lack of footwear. It didn't seem polite to ask, though, so we followed in silence as she guided us to another short hall, and from there, through a doorway into the library. Or should I say "a" library, for who knew how many this place had?

"Here we are!" she said cheerfully, waving us toward an ornate sofa covered in pale green silk and squatting on polished wooden claw .00feet. "Have a seat. Would you like anything to drink?" She eyed Geordi conspiratorially. "Hot cocoa, maybe?"

He perked up at that, but I said, "No, thank you, we're fine. If we could just speak with your husband…?"

"How silly of me! I forgot to say he's out. He'll be back soon, though. He went down to the property line. There's a creek. It always overflows this time of year, and he doesn't trust the boys to fix it."

"The boys?"

"Men, actually," she said, busying herself at a sideboard sporting an espresso machine, a selection of tins, and an insulated pitcher, probably of milk. Evidently we were getting drinks after all. "My husband's…retainers, I guess you'd call them. It all sounds so medieval, doesn't it? But they've worked for him forever, and before that for his father, and so on, for ages." She turned, and her brow puckered. "Sit. Didn't I ask you to sit?"

"Sorry. I didn't think we'd take so much of your time."

"Don't be silly. The cocoa's almost done."

I sat and Geordi followed suit. I admit to enjoying a bit of hot chocolate myself. Eric, meanwhile, paced the room, examining the books lining the walls. He crackled with agitation, but obviously I couldn't ask why.

Frau Burke poured the milk into a smaller metal pitcher in which she steamed it, using the wand on the espresso maker. She poured it into the mugs, stirred industriously, and brought them over on a silver tray.

"Thanks," I said, taking one. "You really didn't have to go to all this trouble."

"It's nothing." She twisted Geordi's mug so he could take the handle and smiled when he thanked her politely. To me she said, "You're probably wondering why I didn't just ring for the maid to do this, but the truth is, I like doing it myself. They have enough work already, keeping this giant cavern in order." She sat on the other end of the sofa with Geordi between us. "Now, tell me your names and why you need to talk to my husband, and if I can't help you, I'll make sure he does."

I was liking her more and more. But I'm cautious by nature, so I was torn. There wasn't any reason I could see to lie. And yet…

Eric stood by a case displaying some of Herr Burke's rock specimens. The frown on his face deepened, and I felt his tension, even from far across the room.

We'd always had a connection, an undercurrent of emotions running between us that ebbed and flowed in intensity. I hadn't experienced it much since we left Turkey, but it was in full force now. Something had upset *him*, a cop, who'd probably seen more of Marseille's underbelly than I cared to imagine.

If he was anxious, I should be terrified. But of what?

Frau Burke waited expectantly, and I sipped my cocoa to cover. It was amazing, creamy with a hint of peppermint, and it warmed me from the inside so that I relaxed somewhat. Eric's natural suspicions were probably just on overdrive. I set my mug on a nearby table, then leaned back into the sofa.

"I'm Hyacinth, and this is Geordi. Leclerc." Old habits. Geordi'd use my real name regardless, but revealing our last names—mine *or* his—didn't seem prudent. And if Frau Burke asked for our IDs, I still had the fake passports Jason had procured, proclaiming us to be Madame Leclerc and her son Geordi.

A puzzled frown creased her brow. "You're French? Your English is perfect."

"So is yours. Some people adapt to languages and customs more easily than others."

The frown vanished, and her lips curved up. "Forgive me. I didn't mean to imply anything. I was only surprised, as I thought you might be American."

"Like you?"

She shrugged and sipped from her mug. "I've lived here so long, I hardly know what nationality I am anymore."

I couldn't argue with that. I'd lived abroad for over fifteen years and didn't really feel American anymore. But though I was a citizen of France, I'd never truly be *French*.

"Now," she said firmly, "what do you need from my husband?"

Eric had moved to a glass case behind the sofa, so I could see him without facing away from Frau Burke. He met my gaze, and I no longer needed to *feel* him to know something was wrong. He opened his mouth, then his gaze flicked to Frau Burke. She watched me, her expression mildly curious but open, and not at all like she had anything to hide.

I wasn't sure what to do. I had to ask about the rock,

but maybe I should wait for Herr Burke. Eric lifted a shoulder resignedly before moving to the next case, which I took to mean that, whatever had upset him, I could still proceed.

"Well, as I mentioned, it's about your husband's rock collection. I have a client. He's interested in rocks from a specific region in Turkey."

I paused. Despite my nefarious business practices and extensive client base, I have limited experience with hobby collectors. Want me to retrieve a stolen Egyptian urn and broker the deal with someone far away from the original owner? Sure. Got a hot Degas on your hands? No problem, I can sell it. In my world, the collections were catalogued and coveted not only by their owners, but by everyone in their owners' circles as well. Hobby collecting was a whole other matter, and I didn't know how commonly one collector might ask after, or even know the contents of, another's collection.

Taking a breath, I dove in. "I've heard your husband's collection is extensive. I thought he might have pieces from that region, which might be of interest to my client."

"I suppose you'll receive a big commission from your client, for finding these pieces?"

"Something like that. He's...eccentric. He has a fondness for Turkey."

"What area?"

My own internal antennae started to twitch. Something I'd said had made her cool off dramatically. She wasn't angry, but I was definitely rebuffed. Still, I might as well answer truthfully if I had any hope of getting the rock.

"The southwest. Near Denizli."

From across the room, Eric swore loudly. Geordi's head snapped in that direction, and Frau Burke glanced at him—Geordi, not Eric—sharply.

"Did you hear something outside?" I said quickly to Geordi, and she shifted her penetrating gaze to mine. Her expression was no longer curious, it was more…thoughtful.

"Perhaps it is my husband. Will you excuse me? I will ask him to join us." She rose and set her mug on the sideboard, then left, shutting the doors behind her.

Eric turned to me. "*Mon ange*, we must leave here, *tout de suite*."

Motioning Geordi to stay put, I hurried over. "What is it?"

He pointed to a case that held a dozen or so black rocks, each supported by jade pins piercing a red velvet lining. Some shards were shiny, others dull, and they ranged from smoothly rounded to sharp and jagged. Nothing about them seemed to merit his ashen face.

"What? Do you think one of these is Michael's?" None of them "spoke" to me like the previous rocks I'd found, but maybe he knew something I didn't.

"No. But I have been near one of these rocks before."

"You mean you've *seen* one *like* it before?"

"*Non*. I have *been near one of them* before. That one, there—the shiny one with the sharp edges." His gaze flicked to mine, an anguish in his eyes I'd only seen once before, on a dark hill at Colossae, Turkey, after he'd put himself in unspeakable danger to help me.

"Tata?" Geordi called from the sofa. "I think Frau Burke is coming back."

Footfalls came from the hall, and Eric put his hands on my shoulders and said hurriedly, "*Mon ange*, the place where I *know* this piece originated—it was in the Plutonium."

His grip tightened and he crackled with energy. I knew what he was about to say, but his words still shook me.

"That rock came from the doorway to Hell—perhaps from Hell itself. I do not know why the Burkes have it, but we *must* leave *now*."

"Here we are!" Frau Burke came through the doorway, followed by a surprisingly young man with thick black hair. "I'd like you to meet my husband. Heinrich, this is Hyacinth and her lovely son, Geordi. I've just been giving them some cocoa."

Chapter Seven

It cost me never a stab nor squirm
To tread by chance upon a worm.
'Aha, my little dear' I say,
'Your clan will pay me back one day.'

~Dorothy Parker, American Writer
(1893-1967)

Herr Burke was forty at most, with winged black brows, delicate, aristocratic features, and a slim build. He wore an expensive black suit, shiny leather shoes—also black, and probably Italian—and a white dress shirt that had to have a thread count in the thousands.

Eric still crackled away, but I couldn't see how being rude would help us achieve our goal, so I put my hand in Herr Burke's and let him kiss it. I half expected to shudder with revulsion or pick up on some evil energy, justifying Eric's tension, but it was just a polite hand-kiss. His touch wasn't overly warm, which would suggest demon-ness, and when I checked, his eyes were a soft brown. Then again, I didn't know that all demons had blue eyes. But the ones *I'd* met did, so I let myself be reassured.

Maybe Eric was mistaken. Maybe the rock in the case came from somewhere near the Plutonium, not in it. No living creature can survive the poison gases inside the cave, and the Turkish officials walled off all the entrances long ago. They don't know it really is a gateway to the Underworld; they just know they don't need a lot of dead tourists on their hands.

Or maybe if the rock was from the cave, it was small enough that ground or air movement brought it to where an animal dragged it out. Or Herr Burke could have acquired it elsewhere, instead of finding it himself.

A niggling voice in my head said, *If this rock did come from the Plutonium, it's a huge coincidence*, but I ignored it and withdrew my hand from Herr Burke's.

"I'm very sorry to intrude like this."

His friendly smile widened. "Don't be absurd. We get so few visitors this time of year. It's a pleasure to meet you. I trust the cocoa was satisfactory."

His English was excellent, almost no German overtones, but with a slight British inflection, and I wondered if he'd lived in the UK.

"It was delicious. Thank you." I nudged Geordi, and he added his thanks.

"*Mon ange*," Eric murmured. "I do not like this. Something is wrong, and we must go."

Geordi peered up at him, a worried frown pinching his small face, and I thought, *Crap*.

Herr Burke said, "Rachel takes great pride in her cocoa."

She positively glowed, and he seemed to think this reflected well on him also, so I said, "Frau Burke has been very kind while we waited to speak with you."

"Ah, yes. My rock collection, was it?"

His wife rolled her eyes again, then smiled. There was a lot of smiling happening. Friendliness and good cocoa shouldn't be suspect, but I couldn't totally dismiss Eric's concerns. And yet, I needed Michael's rock. If I didn't ask about it now, I might miss my chance.

"Yes. Frau Burke says—"

"Please," she broke in. "You must call us Rachel and Heinrich."

"Okay. Thanks." I continued to her husband, "I've heard you have a large collection, including pieces from Turkey."

"Rachel would say *large* is an understatement."

"Yes. Well. In any case, I have a client—"

"Client?"

The smile stayed put, but his eyes narrowed. The niggling voice niggled louder, but really, he had a right to be curious.

"I own an antiquities shop. I don't deal in rocks per se, but one of my regulars collects them. He heard of your collection and wanted me to ask about any pieces you might have from Southwest Turkey, near Denizli."

Heinrich studied my face. His expression was still open and guileless, but I couldn't help feeling it was a mask. Or maybe Eric freaking out had messed up my radar. Signal interference or something. Of course, if I'd been almost sucked into Hell, and later found a chunk of the cave that did the sucking, I'd freak out too.

"I do have a few stones from that area," Heinrich said. "Is your client searching for something specific?"

I hesitated, but caution won out. "No. But I know his tastes. Perhaps I could take a look, and if I see anything interesting, we can work out a deal…?"

Heinrich seemed put off by this, and it occurred to me that Rachel also had cooled when discussing my "commission." Probably money talk was gauche to them.

Heinrich merely said, "Of course. This way, please."

Rachel led us through the door. I gestured for Geordi to follow and as he stood, he glanced right at Eric.

Perfect. Good timing. Trouble with both the men in my life at once. Or all four of them, counting Michael's sending us on this "easy errand," and Jason's continued absence. *Hyacinth and Men* was officially more trouble than it was worth.

Heinrich closed the library doors behind us, Eric just squeaking through, and we trooped back down the short hall to the long one, and from there, to another hall, this one with no windows. A couple of turns later, and I was thoroughly lost and trying not to show my nerves.

We were just viewing a case of Turkish rocks, right?

I didn't examine the paintings or *objets d'art* we passed this time, but I did notice that the farther in we went, the colder it got. That was something, anyway. All the demons I'd met so far either emanated heat or surrounded themselves with it.

"*Mon ange*," Eric murmured in my ear, startling me so that I jumped.

Heinrich frowned, and I tried to laugh it off. "Almost stepped on Geordi, but we're fine."

He smiled and sped up to walk next to his wife.

Eric's lips pursed. When he spoke, he kept his voice low, as though they might actually hear him. "I do not trust them. Did you not take note of his attire?"

I said under my breath, "His clothes seem appropriate for a man of his wealth."

Geordi heard me—maybe he'd heard Eric too—and whispered, "Tata, didn't Frau Burke say Herr Burke was out in the yard?"

I almost missed another step. Some skilled observer I was. Rachel *had* said that. Not just "outside," but down in the presumed mud of an overflowing creek. Or at least, close by. If he was still out when we arrived, he couldn't have come in, showered, changed, and made it to the library in the short time we waited there. Flood-prevention must involve sandbags and hard labor, so even if he'd supervised from a distance, he should have had traces of mud on his pants and his shoes.

Heinrich and Rachel led us through double doors at the end of the corridor into a large, dark study. Hefty desk with black leather blotter and stud detailing, and an even heftier leather chair behind it. More green velvet drapes, closed against the gray drizzle, and a smattering of statues and other art pieces. But instead of books, the walls here were lined with floor-to-ceiling glass cases, displaying an impressive and diverse quantity of rocks.

Geordi took one look at them and went to sit in a black horsehair wing chair.

It was then I had my second Big Realization of the day: Michael pegged me for this job because I can sense shards from his sanctuary. It's why the Rousseaux killed me and Eric went to the brink of Hell. The degree to which I sense them depends on size and proximity, but the entire time we'd been here, I hadn't detected even a trace of Michael's energy. Not a single vibration—nada. Surely if one of these was his, I'd pick up on *something*.

Eric's gaze flicked over the rocks, then met mine. He lifted an eyebrow, and I shook my head slightly. But I couldn't tell Heinrich I saw nothing of interest to my "client" without examining at least a few specimens.

"Over here." He moved to the far wall and pulled a set of keys from his pocket, unlocking a case and sliding its doors apart. "This is my best collection from Turkey."

"I'll just be over here," Rachel said cheerfully and

sat in the matching wing chair near Geordi, stage-whispering, "My husband *loves* rocks. But I bet you have more interesting tastes." She pretended to think, then said, "I bet you like bugs!"

Geordi dug in his pocket and produced his scarab.

Rachel's eyes lit with excitement, and she held out a hand. "Wow. That's cool. Can I see it?"

Geordi nodded shyly and handed it to her, and I suppressed a stab of jealousy at his ready acceptance. Telling myself it was good to see him happy, I faced the rocks.

Heinrich gestured to the top row. "These are from northern Turkey, the ones in the middle are from the central region, and these down here are from the south."

"Okay," I said, examining them with as much enthusiasm as I could muster. There were certainly a variety of shapes and textures, some similar to Michael's shards, but I didn't get a peep off of any of them.

After a suitable amount of time, I said, "Thanks very much, but I don't think any of these are quite what my client prefers." At least the disappointment in my voice was genuine.

From the other side of the room, Rachel said, "My sweet, did you tell her about the rest of them?"

He looked displeased at her interference. And here I thought my real clients were over-protective. Sheesh.

Still, he said to me, "My wife is correct. I have more rocks from Turkey."

"Oh?"

Rachel did yet another eye roll and gave the scarab back to Geordi, before rising to join us. "What Heinrich means is that this is barely a tenth of his Turkish collection."

I would've been more excited by this if I'd sensed the rock anywhere nearby, but I tried to sound peppy. "Wow, that's a lot of rocks. Can we see the others?"

"We'd be happy to show them to you," Rachel said, "but they aren't here."

At that I did perk up. "Really? Where are they?"

Heinrich said, "In a vault. There are hundreds more. Perhaps if you could describe what your client wishes to find, I could retrieve a selection for you to examine."

Beside me, Eric crackled even more. "Do not tell them too much."

While I agreed with him on principle, I *had* to get the rock before Satan heard about it. If it was buried in a vault in the cellar or offsite somewhere, that could explain my not sensing it. And if Heinrich locked his collection up *that* tight, he'd never let us browse on our own. So unless I told him something, we were at a dead end.

Misinterpreting my hesitation, Heinrich said, "If you can't describe the type of rock, perhaps you can tell me why that region of Turkey appeals to your client?"

I thought about that. It wasn't like these were secret archaeological sites. Quite the contrary: The Turks had fenced them off, spiffed them up, and advertised them, attracting crowds of tourists every year. Probably I was over-thinking it, my anxiety influenced by Eric's suspicions, which in turn were the result of his natural cynicism and his former profession.

I said, "My client is a...religious man. He wants rocks from Colossae because of its significance in early Christianity."

Rachel appeared only mildly interested in this, and Heinrich's expression remained neutral. "I do have pieces from that area. Perhaps not of Colossae itself, but from the riverbed nearby."

My heart raced. "Wonderful. Is your vault here?"

"Unfortunately, no. But I have time later today. Perhaps you can return tomorrow morning? If you leave us your cell number, Rachel will call you."

This time I did have to hide my disappointment. "That would be fine. Thank you so much."

The drive back to the hotel was silent. Eric and I needed to talk, but even though he was breaking through for Geordi, this discussion wasn't appropriate for a young boy. Hell was an abstract concept for Geordi. Knowing it was real and that his new ghost friend feared the Burkes had a connection to it wouldn't help his nightmares.

The weather'd gotten worse, dark, rainy, and windy, but it hadn't dampened the post-Oktoberfest, pre-Martinstag festivities. As we entered Trier, people still crammed the streets, and since it was afternoon, many more had either begun drinking or were already drunk.

Was I ever that carefree? Maybe due to the lowering clouds, I suddenly felt isolated from those alien beings. They laughed raucously and stumbled through life, arm-in-arm with their friends, their reality unreal for me.

For the first time, I experienced a pull *away*. From them. From Life. How easy it would be to fulfill my promise and find Geordi a good home, then slip through the veil to the afterlife.

No. I shook my head hard, gripping the steering wheel, an anchor against a thought too horrifying to contemplate.

I was just antsy. Unsettled. I wanted to park, go to

our room, and lie on the bed in utter silence. Geordi's a pretty quiet child and Eric, well, he's a ghost. Not exactly Mr. Intrusive. But it felt like forever since I'd been alone with my thoughts. Before I died, I flew solo most of the time. Even Vadim traveled a lot, acquiring stolen items for me to fence, and we only met up sporadically.

Now, I needed time to process, but I kept not getting it. And today was no exception. When we got to the hotel, there was nowhere to park. Evidently a side street off a side street wasn't far enough from the beer tents. Revelers spilled from the sidewalks, impeding our progress, and I honked repeatedly to get their attention.

"Perhaps we should go directly to the church," Eric murmured.

I'd forgotten about *that*. I checked the clock on the dash. "It's only three. Mass won't start before five, will it?"

Okay, I was stalling. I admit it. Even though Lily was younger than me, she absorbed more of our parents' faith. Or maybe because I'm older, I understood more and resented a God who took my parents at such a young age. Lily also being taken, from me *and* Geordi, hadn't changed that opinion.

"*Mon ange*," Eric said patiently. "It may be easier to park over there, and we can walk back here after Mass."

On a good day, I'm no fan of crowds. Trier during the Party of the Century really wasn't working for me. I saw a break in the revelers and gunned it around a corner to circle the block once more. Eric gave a resigned sigh, with added Gallic half-shrug, and sat back in the seat.

"Look, Tata," Geordi piped up suddenly from the back. "That looks like your car."

I followed his gaze and sure enough, a bright green

Peapod was parked under a tree half a block down. I squinted. Not just any bright green Peapod—*my* bright green Peapod.

"Watch out!" Eric shouted and I hit the brakes, narrowly not-hitting the man and woman staggering down the middle of the street in front of me.

"Move!" I whaled on the horn, but they barely noticed, and I wondered what Michael would do if *I* killed the next two souls he had to transport. Then we'd truly be a full-service operation.

After an excruciating length of time, they stumbled onto the opposite sidewalk, and I double-parked next to my car. Ignoring the motorists who now honked and shouted at *me*, I got out and peered through the window.

Eric said, "*Mon ange*, what are you doing?"

"This is my car. *My car*. Here, in Trier."

"You are certain?"

"Positive."

Geordi looked from me to Eric, but Eric didn't notice, and for once, I had bigger things to worry about. I ran to the driver's side and tried the handle. Locked.

A million thoughts crowded my mind. I couldn't quite believe it, but I'd know my car anywhere. Like I said, it's a prototype. There are others on the road now, but none of them are exactly like mine.

Besides—my heart pounded halfway out of my chest—on the floor of the backseat was a square of canvas: one of the very pieces covering the first of Michael's rocks I'd found. It lay where I'd dropped it after the Rousseau brothers forced me to retrieve the shard from my safe, before killing Lily and me.

The last I'd seen either of them—car or canvas—was parked on the street near Jason's friend's place just after

I met Eric. Had Jason's friend sold it? It'd been two months. I couldn't blame him for wanting to get rid of it and make a profit besides. But even so…

I shook my head in disbelief. "How in the world did it end up *here?*"

"Well, it wasn't easy," said a rough voice behind me.

I whirled, not knowing whether to laugh, cry, scream, or faint.

Geordi had no such dilemma. He flung open his door and rushed to the sidewalk, hurling himself at breakneck speed past me.

"*Jason!*" he shrieked and barreled into him.

"Oof! Yep, kiddo. It's me."

He hugged Geordi back, but it was me he regarded searchingly over the top of Geordi's head, his blue eyes dark with emotion.

And then Eric dematerialized from the car so fast, it rattled. "I will kill him."

"*NO!*" Geordi said directly to Eric, Jason's arms automatically holding him back while he fought to free himself. "You leave Jason alone! He's my friend, and Tata's too!"

"I guess he can see you now," I said to Eric. Then I sank onto the curb to keep from passing out.

Chapter Eight

In Heaven, all the interesting people are missing.

~Friedrich Nietzsche, German Philosopher (1844-1900)

"He can see Eric?" Jason demanded. "*Already?*"

If it stunned my own personal demon that my nephew saw dead people, then who was I to pretend it was okay?

"Yes," I said, because sitting on a crowded German sidewalk, having a friendly conversation about demons and the Dead, with Jason of all people, wasn't any weirder than the rest of my life. "It's been coming on gradually. But today's the first day Geordi's really seen and heard him."

I don't know why I didn't mention Geordi seeing other dead folk too. Maybe because, even after everything we'd been through, I didn't trust Jason. I knew he'd never hurt Geordi. But he had his own code of ethics about the whole Dioguardi Demon thing, and who knew what effect that might have in the long run.

Jason knelt in front of Geordi, pulling up his eyelids and peering at his irises, which were the same changeable blue as Jason's own. None of the revelers passing by paid any attention, and suddenly, I was glad of the crowds. Safety in numbers. Or just reassuring that

Life went on, regardless of our own problems.

"They've never gone black," I said. "Believe me, I've been checking."

I saw the relief in Jason's expression and suppressed another shudder. This would be okay; it *had* to be okay.

"Thank God," Jason said, and pulled Geordi back into his arms. Geordi used his full strength to hug back, holding on for dear life to the first man who'd loved him and treated him with respect. Tonton Michael was nice and all, but for Geordi, Jason was *it*.

Unfortunately, other people saw it differently.

Eric's fists were clenched at his sides, his crackling energy dark with frustration. For the first time, I could *see* him killing someone. When he spoke, his voice was tight with control, and I caught myself leaning away.

"*Mon ange*, I made a promise to you. If you wish him to leave, I will make it happen."

Jason ignored him, eyes closed while he clutched Geordi tight. I made a *hold on a sec* gesture at Eric and said to Jason, "What about you? Can you still see Eric?"

Jason's eyes opened, and his gaze flicked to mine. It was a touchy subject, because if Jason *could* see Eric, it was partly my fault.

Okay, it was all my fault.

"Yep," Jason said, and my gut clenched.

He gave Geordi another squeeze, then tousled his hair before coming to sit by me on the curb. Having him so close, after so long, was bittersweet. I didn't know if I wanted to kiss him and be held the way he'd held Geordi, or if, like Eric, I wanted to kill him. Of course, Eric's reasons were different than mine. Even I knew I was mad because Jason left, not because of what he'd done before that. But I *could* be mad about that too.

On the other hand, he was more demon now than when I met him because of me. So maybe we were even.

"I'm sorry."

"Hyacinth." The quiet way he said it sent sadness and loss and *want* shuddering through me. "I've always been…what I am. It's not your fault."

I shook my head. "You said yourself that what happened—what *I* asked you to do—it's why you can see Eric now, when you couldn't before."

"True, I've changed. But…you've changed too."

My head snapped up, heart hammering. He *couldn't* know. I'd never told anyone my secret, except Eric. Jason had to mean "changed" in the general sense.

Geordi watched us, while Eric moved to stand by my other shoulder. I was so grateful for his presence and his support.

Jason gave a lopsided smile. "We've all changed."

"I need a drink," I said to no one in particular.

"Here, take mine," said a portly man passing by, and he thrust his full stein at me.

What the hell. I was already dead, my nephew was a demon, my not-quite-ex, not-quite-boyfriend—also a demon—had just showed up with my missing car, and my *other* not-quite-boyfriend—a ghost—was offering to commit murder on my behalf.

What were a few germs between friends?

I took a swig, then another.

God, it was good.

###

"So what's new?" I said brightly a half hour later.

I sat on a park bench next to Jason, while Geordi played on the climbing structure and Eric stood a respectable, if tense, distance away. He didn't *want* me anywhere near Jason, but he recognized we had stuff to sort out. Even Geordi went to play without complaint.

Not that we could do it all now. In fact, I'd rather not do *any* of it, ever. More beer sounded like a better idea, but the stein was long empty.

Jason leaned forward, elbows on his knees, watching Geordi play. "I missed him so much."

My heart cracked, although I noticed he didn't mention missing me. But then, I hadn't expected him to. And I certainly wouldn't admit to missing him.

"Why are you here?" I said, when I wanted to ask, *Why did you leave?* Then I added, "And how did you find us?"

Brunch was hours ago and the stein was big. I wasn't thinking clearly, or I would've been more concerned that if Jason found us so easily, anyone could. Probably. I had trouble connecting the dots, but it seemed logical.

Jason opened his mouth, then shook his head. "It's a long story." His eyes were dark, but with emotion, not the black of demon energy. "How've you been?"

"Oh, you know, the usual. Demon nephew, invisible roommate, dead people at every turn. What have you been up to?"

His eyes narrowed. "Do you see all the Dead?"

Oops. Guess he hadn't known that. I forgot he'd only seen me talking with Eric. "Uh, maybe. I really don't know. We're getting off-topic here."

"Hyacinth..."

I hurried on. "It was nice of you to bring my car all the way here, but you could've just called and told me where in France you'd moved it."

"Fine. You don't want to discuss your abilities." He searched my face. "If I called, would you have come?"

"No." Maybe it was the beer, but it just popped out, and I saw the hurt in his eyes.

"For God's sake, after all this, you still don't trust me?"

I swallowed, unable to form an answer, and he sat back, jaw clenched so tight it startled me when he spoke.

"I couldn't stay away."

"What?"

His expression was unreadable. "You weren't supposed to see me. I only came to drop off your car."

Now *that* penetrated my beer-induced haze. "Drop it *off?* Like you dropped Geordi off in Turkey?"

"I gave him back to you, didn't I?"

"That's not the point. You dumped him and ran. And you just admitted you were about to do it again."

"I *had* to run in Turkey. I'd just stolen High Demon powers. I was like a tiny piece of metal, with Hell being the biggest magnet you've ever seen."

"You could've at least said good-bye instead of ditching Geordi like that. He has nightmares, and at least some are because he thought you might be dead."

That got to him, and he pinched the bridge of his nose. "I'm sorry. The last thing I wanted was to hurt Geordi. Or you. But I couldn't stay. Not with the Rousseaux's powers fresh in my system."

"Fair enough. But you didn't explain any of that, and you didn't get in touch. Not once, in *two months*."

His mouth quirked up. "Well, it did take a *little* work to find you."

"I thought you might be dead too." I hadn't meant to say that either. Damn the beer.

"Is that right?"

He was close. Too close.

Ten blocks was too close.

He reached for my hand, and I leaned away on the bench. "What have you been doing?"

His arm dropped, regret in his eyes, though whether it related to our immediate situation or the long-term loss of whatever relationship we'd had, I couldn't say.

"Cleansing myself of the Rousseaux's powers."

"Did it work?"

"No."

I stared, not sure I'd heard right. I've studied enough cultures to understand the basic *wounded hero goes away to heal, then returns stronger and more heroic* myth. If I'd thought about it, I'd assumed that's how it would be with Jason. He'd go wherever "good" demons go to regroup, and when he came back, he'd either be the old Jason or something more: bigger, better, stronger.

The problem being that I kept forgetting this wasn't a myth.

"Are you saying you still have the Rousseaux's powers in you?"

"That's one way of putting it."

"Or…?"

"You could say that now they're a part of me. Or I'm a part of them—whichever." He paused. "Permanently."

Oh, God. I wished I'd worn a coat, even though my chills were internal. "But they're in Hell. Aren't they?"

"For now."

"I thought they got sucked back in or whatever and were stuck down there with Satan."

"Hyacinth. Satan doesn't grant High Demons their powers so they can sit around Hell, shooting the breeze. They'll be back."

"When?"

"I don't know. You took a lot out of them when you stole that rock. But it's not the physical damage they care about. You hurt their pride. They won't forget that."

I shuddered. "Geordi…"

"We have some time. If they tried, they could sense him. But for now, it won't occur to them to check."

There was so much I needed to know, about what to expect, and how to protect Geordi and myself. Any problems I thought I had earlier, like dealing with weird rock collectors or hordes of dead people, paled with the realization that High Demons had it in for me.

But that wasn't all.

Eric approached us. "*Mon ange*, it is late. We must leave now or we will be late for church."

Jason's eyes widened. And then he started to laugh.

"Shut up," I said.

He only laughed harder, finally wheezing, "This I've got to see."

"You are welcome to join us," Eric said hospitably.

"Why thank you," Jason said with equal politeness. "I think I will."

As pissing matches go, it didn't *look* very spectacular. But a ghost who was in no way, shape, or form in a state of grace, daring a partial demon with High Demon powers in him to go to church, could cause serious fireworks as they passed through the door. That is, if the whole building didn't spontaneously combust when I got near it.

Or maybe it was me who'd burst into flame, not the building. That was a comforting thought.

###

I was relieved to learn that "church" meant Saint Matthias' Abbey, not Dom Saint Peter. Since the

Cathedral was the oldest church in all of Germany, I assumed that's where Eric wanted to go. However, as a renowned museum and pilgrim destination, the Dom was open all day, but only offered services in the mornings. Fortunately—for Eric, not me—Saint Matthias' was near the hotel and held Mass at six-fifteen on weekdays.

It was almost dark as we trucked back to the hotel. I was still too much in shock over Jason's reappearance to ask where he was staying, but he waited downstairs with Eric while Geordi and I got cleaned up.

While we were alone, I asked Geordi about seeing Eric, and he shrugged, fiddling with his scarab and avoiding eye contact. "I just looked and saw him."

"At the Burkes' house?" I said, and he nodded, head still down.

I've been on the shrink's couch myself, so I thought for a minute, then asked the question I always hated them asking me. "How do you feel about that?"

He shrugged again, and I decided not to press him. He's a great kid—the best—but he can be touchy at times. He'll go from uproarious giggles to fierce frowns faster than I can adjust. Lily used to say his wires got crossed when she pushed him about the Big Stuff, and at seven, he's had more than his share of Big Stuff. Like his Mommy needing a restraining order against his Daddy, and then losing both parents in one day. Not to mention the whole aunt-who-sees-ghosts, now-he-does-too thing. If he needed space to process, well, I could relate to that.

But I couldn't totally leave him hanging, either. I tilted his chin so his serious gaze met mine. "I know all this is…weird. But I want you to know, Eric's our friend. He helped us a lot in Turkey." I almost said he'd saved my life, twice, but decided it might worry Geordi more to know my life had *needed* saving.

"Okay," he said. Then he asked in a small voice, "Is Jason leaving us again?"

Ouch. I couldn't begin to answer that. Who knew what Jason's plans were, or if I even wanted him to stay. I hadn't figured out where Eric fit into my feelings, and Jason coming back made that harder. But if Geordi had demon blood in him, I needed help, and Jason was the person to provide it.

I sighed. "I don't know, sweetie. I wish I did."

We went downstairs, and I tried not to notice Jason's eyes cutting to me right away. Geordi hung back at my side; he might be glad Jason was back, but it *had* been a while, and after an awkward moment or two, we made it outside and headed for the church.

I held Geordi's hand as we wove through the crowds, with Jason on his other side and Eric by me. At least, when we weren't dodging the beer drinkers. In a couple of blocks, though, we left most of them behind. Saint Matthias' is on a wide street, just far enough from the center of town to give it a semblance of peace.

Folks trickled inside—more revelers were out tonight than worshippers—and as we neared the doors, a new worry assailed me. I slowed, and Eric and Jason both threw me looks.

"Just a sec." I dropped to my knees in front of Geordi. He'd only turned seven in June, so I was pretty sure I knew the answer to this, but I asked anyway. "Have you gone through First Eucharist yet?"

He frowned. "What's that?"

All righty then. Just to be sure, I clarified, "At Mass, do you take the wafers—the bread—and drink the wine?"

He shook his head and crossed his arms over his chest, as I'm sure Lily had taught him.

Jason and Eric still regarded me intently, but their expressions had changed. Eric's was now filled with a longing so sharp and painful, my heart ached. Likely not for me or Geordi, but for the simple act of taking communion, now denied him. Attending church without fully participating might be as bad as not going at all.

For his part, Jason managed to have no expression at all. I'd never seen anyone so neutral. He was like the Switzerland of demons.

I stood. "What?"

"Nothing."

"Tell me." He opened his mouth, about to blow me off, so I rested my hands on Geordi's shoulders. "Whatever it is, we have a right to know."

"Fine. It's just—" His gaze dropped to my nephew and softened. He ruffled Geordi's hair, then said to me, "He might have…trouble…with the sacraments."

My grip tightened. Geordi squirmed and I forced myself to relax. "Trouble how? Concentrating in class, or…?"

I couldn't say, *Or bursting into flame when the body and blood of Christ pass his lips*, but Jason understood. Unfortunately, his answer wasn't reassuring.

"I'm not sure." He checked for eavesdroppers, but most of the churchgoers were already inside and in the dark street, none of the other passersby paid us any attention. "Most of us—the Dioguardis—we go through first Communion not even knowing we might be…"

He hesitated, and I supplied, "Special?"

He nodded, grinning at Geordi. "That's us, kiddo. We're special." His gaze flicked back to mine and sobered. "But the…specialness…for most of us, it doesn't come out until five or ten years later. After we've been taking communion for a long time."

I waited, and when he didn't continue, started to ask what he meant. And then I got it. "Are you saying you've built up an *immunity* to the *Eucharist?*"

"Not exactly. Maybe. I go to Mass, Hyacinth, and I swear, nothing's ever happened. But the blood's weak in me. It didn't manifest until I was almost seventeen. When it shows up at Geordi's age, it's very strong. And when things like this happen"—he tilted his chin at Eric—"even before the blood manifests, it's possible starting the sacraments could be too much at once."

And here I was worried about me, Jason, or Eric vanishing in a shower of sparks when the Holy Spirit appeared. Instead, I had to decide if I should bring Geordi up in his mother's faith or keep him away from church entirely.

Eric said, "*Mon ange*, if you have changed your mind, I will understand."

I shook my head, surprising even myself with my vehemence. "No. Let's do this. It's what Lily would want, and for today, it's what I want too."

Jason regarded me with a measure of respect. "That's very…brave of you."

Great. Just what I wanted to hear. Most parents at church were being brave by hoping their kids would behave and not destroy the church. Me, I got the kudos because the *church* might destroy my *nephew*.

I took a deep breath and led the way inside just as the entrance hymn began to play. None of us imploded, exploded, or otherwise ceased to exist.

On the other hand, the night was young.

Chapter Nine

*Life is a great surprise. I do not see why death
should not be an even greater one.*

*~Vladimir Nabokov, Russian-American
Novelist (1899-1977)*

In the event, nothing happened.

Well, stuff happened, but not anything bad. In fact, it was all rather normal. The stern priest shouted the homily in energetic German, only some of which I caught, as my vocabulary consists of useful phrases like "Where is the bathroom?" and "How much does that cost?" Biblical stories and their meanings went over my head. Geordi's too. He squirmed, alternately bored or uncomfortable, neither of which struck me as demonic.

Eric, however, appeared to get a lot from the service, and surprisingly, so did Jason. The priest called down the Host and we lined up for communion, and as he'd claimed, Jason took the bread and wine just fine. I know I should've believed him, but it still surprised me that he didn't sprout horns and a tail, and instead, simply crossed himself and returned to our pew.

I herded Geordi in front of me, his arms dutifully crossed, and was even more surprised at how glad I felt when the priest blessed him. Not just relieved. It went deeper than that, but I didn't have time for analysis as in the next moment, the priest lifted kindly eyes to me.

95

"*Der Leib Christi*," he intoned and placed the communion wafer in my hands.

I murmured, "Amen," put the wafer in my mouth, and crossed myself. Then a man holding a crystal goblet offered me, "*Das Blut Christi*," after which I, too, returned to the pew, where I knelt and bowed my head.

It all happened so fast, and so much by rote. It took a moment to realize that, though I was dead, and never a regular at Mass anyway, I must still be in a state of grace with the church. Or maybe that was all bunk, and God could really give a rip about who took communion.

I glanced to where Eric stood, his face expressionless as he bowed to the altar, lips moving in prayer. Okay, not *everyone* could receive the Eucharist.

He crossed himself and came to kneel beside me, and a short while later the Mass ended and we filed back outside. The earlier coolness had become a biting cold, and I wished we'd brought one of the cars. Which reminded me we had an extra person tagging along.

I said to Jason, "I guess I should ask where you're staying?"

"I've got a room."

"Where?"

He just looked at me. Some things never changed.

"Okay, then."

I turned to go, and he touched my arm, frowning. "That's it? You're leaving?"

"Yeah, pretty much." Geordi was asleep on his feet, and I wasn't far behind. "It's been a long day."

He held my gaze. "You never told me why you're here."

Eric placed a hand on my shoulder, leveling a hard stare at Jason. "The same could be said of you."

Something had changed about him. Attending Mass without fully participating had to be bittersweet, but even so, it clearly had a positive effect on him.

"I brought her car," Jason said evenly.

Eric pressed his lips together. "Anyone could have done that. Or you could have waited until she returned to France. I believe you are here for something else." He bent his head subtly toward Geordi.

My blood froze. I said to Jason, "We're going now."

"Hyacinth—" He stepped closer, hand outstretched.

"No. We're not discussing this. Ever."

He took another step, but Eric blocked his way. After an intense moment, he said, "I'll see you tomorrow."

I started to say something childish like, *Not if I see you first*, but he'd already walked away.

Eric frowned. "*Mon ange*, you are exhausted. And you need to eat."

"In the morning. I'm not hungry."

"Frau Burke's cocoa was really good," Geordi said.

"There you have it," I said. "The cocoa was a meal all by itself."

"That was before lunch. It is half-past seven now."

I really wasn't hungry, but I hadn't noticed until he mentioned it. We'd had breakfast at the café, and cocoa at the Burkes', and nothing else all day. Except my beer.

"Maybe it's the weather."

Or maybe it was that pull I'd felt earlier, that sudden, inexplicable desire to leave the Earth and its cares behind. I shuddered and shoved the thought away.

Eric frowned some more but let it go.

By the time we got to our room, Geordi practically snored as he walked. He was too big for me to carry, and I saw Eric's frustration mount at his inability to help.

Along with missed baths, Fun Aunts who were emotionally and physically spent also skipped tooth-brushing on occasion. I steered Geordi to the bathroom, lifted the toilet seat for him, and left him to go potty.

Five minutes later he hadn't flushed, and upon opening the door, I saw why: He'd done his business, then decided the floor was good and lay down on it. When I tried to move him, he had that Gravity-Plus-Sleeping-Child thing where they spontaneously gain a thousand pounds. I gave up and brought him a pillow and blankets. If he was uncomfortable, he'd wake up and move. Who was I to meddle?

When I came out of the bathroom, Eric leaned against the desk, watching me seriously. "Thank you."

"For what?"

"For tonight. For going to Mass with me." He came to stand before me. "I believe I owe you an apology. I have not been the most pleasant companion of late."

"Oh. Please. You have nothing to apologize for. I'm grateful you've been here for me. And for Geordi." The words sounded lame and inadequate. I hoped he knew how sincerely I meant them.

His gaze travelled over my face before meeting my eyes again. "*Mon ange*, I have told you little of my life before. It was not easy, nor good, in the way that you are good. But it was my life, and it ended. Instead of embracing my new circumstances, I have fought them. But at Mass tonight, I realized something."

For a rare moment, his face was open and cynicism-free, and my pulse pounded and my breath quickened. A slow smile curved his mouth, as though he were fully aware of my response to him. It had been a long time since I'd felt truly connected to him in this way.

In an effort to bring things back down to normal, I asked, "What did you realize?"

"That I became full Dead in Turkey, but I have not been fully dead, as it were." He brushed my cheek with the backs of his fingers, making me shiver. "*Mon ange*, I have wanted you for a long time, but I did not believe you could want me. Less even than half a man, *un fantôme*, insubstantial."

I wanted to tell him just *how* substantial he was to me, but he now stroked the curve of my neck, and the shiver rocketed to shuddering hot *need* in nothing flat.

He continued, "At Mass, I discovered I am still part of this world. For whatever reason, God wished me to take a different journey than my peers. I do not yet know why, but I know this: By holding myself back, I am flinging His gift away in contempt."

His gaze lingered on my mouth. "You are part of that gift, *mon ange*, and I should not have hesitated. But…perhaps I am too late."

The hint of a question was in his voice, that soft, low rumble that washed over me and tickled my senses, even as his fingers teased my skin. My brain had no energy for thinking—my blood had rushed to other parts of my body—but I understood what he meant: Now that Jason had reappeared, would I go back to him?

I would've laughed at the irony of choosing between a demon and a ghost. But Eric was close, and there was nothing funny in the way he watched me, awaiting my answer. The problem being that I didn't know how to respond.

Well, my body gave off all kinds of responses to him—very positive ones. But as noted, my brain hadn't caught up, either to Jason's presence or Eric's deciding the wait was over.

I spoke, and what came out surprised me as much as it did him. "I'm not fully dead either. I have a body; I walk and talk with the Living. But I'm not one of them. And yet I'm also not one of the Dead. Sometimes, I feel drawn to them. And then I think, I *can't* leave Geordi. I just… I don't know where I belong."

Seconds ticked by. His hand rested on my collarbone, neither of us moving apart, but not coming closer, either.

"*Mon ange*," he finally said, his mouth hovering over mine, "you belong in both worlds. You…*belong*."

If I'd had doubts about how his ghostly lips would feel, they vanished at the first brush of his kiss. I moaned, and he slid his tongue into my mouth. Every part of me liquified with heat and I grabbed his shoulders. He cupped my head with one hand while the other stroked my back and side, then found my breast.

I gasped and he pulled me tight. He was hard. Not just in the expected place—he was hard *everywhere*. Not sensing him? Not a problem. He filled me, filled my mind and body, and yes, even my soul. He tasted like the iron in blood, the salt of the sea, the Earth's minerals, and something subtler that I couldn't name.

Once, in Turkey, he'd *pulsed* his desire to me when we weren't even touching. He did it again now, and melded together as we were, the sensation intensified to the point I wouldn't need the physical act of lovemaking to feel, er, more than satisfied.

He broke the kiss, murmuring, "*Mon ange…*" and then trailed his lips over my eyes, my cheek, the sensitive curve of my throat.

"Eric!" I gasped, my fingers digging into his scalp.

His hand slipped to the waist of my jeans. Somehow,

they were undone, sliding over my hips, his fingers pressing into my underwear—*there*—

I shuddered once, twice, and then I was over the brink, falling down the other side, holding him close, barely able to stand as the ache he'd created deep inside roared to the surface and exploded in heat and need and wave after wave of sheer release.

"Oh…God…" I managed.

He let me go, a satisfied smile on his lips.

"You're not going to gloat, are you?" I asked, and he laughed, then kissed me. Lightly at first, then deepening to greater urgency. His hand covered my breast, pulling my sweater and bra across the nipple so that the ache started anew.

"*Mon ange—*"

"Stop calling me that. I don't feel very angelic right now."

His smile went just a bit smug. Then he sighed, all lightheartedness gone. "This, what we are doing now— it does not change our situation, and perhaps it complicates it more, as you have feelings still for Jason."

I tried to protest, but he placed a finger over my lips.

"Do not deny it. He is tied to your nephew, *bien sûr*. But also to you. When, together, the two of you pulled me from my prison at the Rousseaux's, the tie deepened. Intensified. It is in part why I have been acting as I have, because I do not share that connection with you."

I shook my head, and one corner of his mouth lifted in his habitual, cynical half-twist. "*Si, c'est vrai*. But another thing I learned tonight: I cannot change the world around me. I can only choose how I will inhabit it. I choose *this*"—he pulled me tight—"and I choose making you forget *him*, if only for a while."

"You can't possibly be for real," I said, and he dropped his mouth to mine.

"*Mon ange*, let me show you how *real* I am."

It actually wasn't hard—ha!—to believe in this aspect of his "realness." All the right parts were doing all the right things, and he obviously wanted me.

He fit our forms together, his mouth covering mine in a way that, pardon the cliché, made me forget my own name, let alone my mixed-up feelings for another man. I slid my hands over his back, tugging his shirt free from his waistband.

And that's when my brain kicked in. I'd touched his face and hands before, but now I experienced a disconnect. It was like, extremities? I can accept those. But a whole body? Feeling solid and warm, when I *knew* it wasn't there? Even the concept of ghost clothes suddenly seemed odd, no matter how I tried to ignore it.

Eric frowned. "*Mon ange*, where did you go?"

I shook my head, not wanting to hurt him, but he figured it out and kissed my palm.

"Do not worry, and do not think so much. I understand. But I promise you, another thing I have learned tonight: I am very much a man still, whatever form I may be in."

He undid his pants then recaptured my fingers, bringing them down *there*. I automatically gripped him, his hard heat filling my hand, and he groaned. He *was* real. Solid, natural, and obviously turned on.

Over-thinking went out the window as quickly as it had come. He thrust into my palm, his mouth covering mine, his tongue, every inch of him sliding into, over, around me. Then he pulsed his thread to me, and I wanted to say, *See, there are ways we're connected that I don't share with Jason.* But it all felt too good, so instead, I pulsed back at him. He got the message. His own thread grew brighter, stronger, his movements more purposeful.

Though he wasn't inside me, he took me, and I took him right back. He was in my hand, my mind. He thrust once, then again and again, the urgency of his mouth matching the rhythm of his hips as he closed his hand over mine, wrapping my fingers tighter, until with a final hard thrust he climaxed, his low groan proving beyond a doubt that, ghost or no, he could still, er, get the job done.

He stepped away and discovered the bed behind him. He sat, then fell back, eyes closed, clothes disheveled, looking for all the world like a man who'd just had sex.

Go figure.

"*Mon ange*, if that is the way your hand feels…" A shudder of his heat echoed through me and a slow smile curved his lips. "Next time."

I slipped my jeans off, then joined him on the bed. Making one of us sleep on the floor now seemed ridiculous.

I stared at the ceiling. "Did you mind?"

He lifted himself up on one elbow to gaze down at me. "Mind? *Mon ange*, surely you can tell whether a man is…happy…with lovemaking or not?"

I glared at him. "Not *that*. I get that you, uh, enjoyed it. I meant, did you mind that it was just my hand?"

The question was absurd, but he'd given me a great gift by not expecting more. For an arrogant, cynical, full-Dead OPJ, he was being awfully considerate.

The smile spread to his eyes, and he brushed the hair from my face. "There is no *just* where you are concerned. I did not know what to expect. I have never done this, dead. You proved that not only does everything still work, it works *very* well. It was a good practice run." He pulsed once more in my mind, then withdrew. *"Next time…"*

Hoo-boy.

Of all the things on my list of This Shouldn't Happen, sex with Eric was pretty high up.

He lay back down, pulling me close and settling me against his chest. As I drifted off, I remembered something. When we were trapped in the Rousseaux's villa, I'd been unable to sense Eric, until I touched Jason.

What if I experienced Eric now, more intensely than I had in weeks, because Jason was back?

Was I linked to Jason—his demon powers, or just him—in some way I didn't understand? Or was it my guilty conscience? Nothing was resolved when he left. If he'd stayed gone, I could accept that as an end. But Eric was right to question his reappearance.

You weren't supposed to see me…

Why? Because he planned to snatch Geordi? Or something less sinister, like observing us from a distance, in case we needed him?

The first reason would make me hate him. The second, well, it was the other side of that coin, and I couldn't put the possibility into words. It was too raw, especially in light of recent developments.

Beneath my cheek, Eric slept, more peaceful and content than I'd ever seen him. I wrapped my arms around him, reassured by his solidity, wondering if I'd just aligned myself more with the Living or the Dead.

And wondering, long-term, which was the better bet?

Chapter Ten

Dying is a wild night and a new road.

~Emily Dickinson, American Poet (1830-
1886)

"Tata Hyhy?"

I shot up, the blanket slipping off my chest, and squinted at the clock. Barely seven. I lay down again, about to tell Geordi to go back to bed, when two things struck me: One, we were not, as I'd first thought, in our Zürich apartment. We were in the manager's room at an overbooked hotel in Trier, Germany. And two, I wasn't alone in bed. A fact that Geordi'd noticed before I did.

"Why is Eric in bed with you?"

Merde.

I scooched away from Eric and pulled the covers tight around my legs. At least I'd slept in my sweater. A quick scan showed Eric still wore his shirt also, and if memory served, his pants. Although those were likely down around his ankles by now. Thank God for blankets.

"Well, sweetie, there's only one bed, and you fell asleep in the bathroom."

Truth was, Geordi had a seven-year-old's understanding of adult sleeping arrangements anyway. As far as he knew, Eric was my "friend," and friends sometimes had sleepovers.

As though reading my thoughts, Geordi piped up,

"Like when you and Jason slept in the same bed before?"

Oops. We had fallen asleep together in Turkey a few times—nothing happened—but I thought Geordi hadn't seen us. He must have gotten up to pee in the middle of the night and wandered into our room.

"Uh, yeah." Then I saw Eric was awake, watching me with a gimlet eye. My face heated. "It's not like that."

He broke into one of his full-watt smiles and stretched before sitting up. "It would not matter to me if it was *like that*. We both have our pasts, *n'est-ce pas*? What interests me is the present."

I noticed he didn't say "the future." But maybe I read too much into it. Who knew what my own future held?

He pulled his pants up, then kicked off the covers and padded barefoot to the bathroom. Whatever passed between us last night had changed him even more than attending Mass. He was less tightly wound. Not carefree—he'd never be *that*—but less care*worn*.

I didn't know what last night meant to me. But…what if it meant a lot to him? I couldn't even pretend it was just a "physical release." How could it be when he had no body? No matter how real he felt to me.

I ran a hand through my ratty hair, then eyed Geordi. "Shower. You. Now."

"No."

"Hot cocoa at breakfast if you do."

He thought about that. "I'm not hungry."

That gave me pause. I still wasn't hungry, either. Our last meal was nearly a day ago. Even with the Burkes' cocoa and my beer, I should be starving by now. After I died, I couldn't eat fast enough, particularly when gorging on meat. But though Eric wore ghost clothes and had other "trappings" of the living, I'd never seen him eat a ghost meal or imbibe a ghost drink.

Was I becoming more dead, despite my best efforts?

No. I was still breathing. I had a body that needed food. *I* needed food. I just…didn't want any.

Besides, Geordi wasn't dead, so that didn't explain his lack of appetite. And from what I'd seen of Jason, demons, even partial ones, could happily eat their way across multiple continents. So that wasn't it either.

Stumped, I said, "Okay. But you do have to shower." He opened his mouth to refuse, and I added, "Do it, or we go back to church this morning."

Bribes may not always work, but certain specific threats do. He caved and went to knock on the bathroom door. Eric invited him in, and once the door had shut, I slid out of bed, retrieved my jeans, and tugged them on over clean underwear. My sweater wasn't too bad, so I left it on, then brushed my hair into a ponytail.

A few minutes later, I'd tidied the room, and we were ready to go. We had nowhere to sleep tonight, but maybe we'd have the rock by then and could head home.

As we trundled out the door with our suitcases, my cell phone rang, an unfamiliar number on the screen. I answered and was greeted by Rachel's cheerful voice.

"I'm sorry, I just noticed the time. Did I wake you?"

"No, not at all. We're just on our way to breakfast."

There was an odd pause. Then she said, "Wonderful! I'm glad I caught you. Henrich got *all* his Turkish rocks from the vault." She sounded amused. "Really, he could've just brought the ones from Denizli, or taken pictures to show you. Anyway, they're all here, and we thought you could come for dinner tonight to see them."

I hesitated. It was a generous offer, and they'd gone to a lot of trouble. But I didn't relish finishing late at their place and having to go home tomorrow instead.

"That's very kind of you. But could we possibly come earlier? We planned to leave town before dinner."

Hopefully, I hadn't offended her, or getting the rock from her husband would be even more difficult.

She paused again, then said, "Of course. Is lunch better?"

"Are you sure? We don't want to cause you any—"

"Nonsense. It's no trouble. Besides, I have a special treat for Geordi."

The weird stab of jealousy hit again, but I'm a big girl, so I pushed it away. "Okay. Thanks."

"See you at one o'clock."

We hung up, and I told Geordi and Eric the plan.

Eric frowned. "I still do not feel right about this—about them."

Geordi looked from him to me. "Why?"

And here we were, back in the soup. At least when Geordi couldn't hear Eric, we didn't have to watch our words in front of him.

Eric pursed his lips. "It is nothing, I am sure."

"Is it because of the Plutonium rock?"

Eric's brows rose. If he hadn't realized by now that Geordi was a perceptive kid, he'd better learn fast.

Geordi continued, "My scarab is from there."

"It is?" I asked.

"That lady said so when she gave it to me."

He fished it out and offered it to Eric, who started to reach for it. Then his face fell, and he withdrew his hand. Geordi frowned, clearly about to ask why Eric couldn't hold the rock. I considered stopping him, but what the hell. They had to figure out their own relationship now that Eric was, so to speak, out in the open.

Geordi said, "Why can't Eric hold my scarab? He can touch people, right? People who can see him?"

He poked Eric's side, and Eric scowled. "*Hé!*" Then his expression changed to shock. "You can feel me?"

I don't know why we were both so surprised. If Eric and I could touch each other—a memory of last night washed through me, and I fought down a blush—then why wouldn't it be the same for Geordi?

"Of course!" Geordi poked him a second time, and Eric swatted him, then stared at his hand.

"And I can touch him." Kid person or not, he dropped to his knees and dragged Geordi into a tight embrace.

"Hey!" Geordi squirmed and pushed him away, and Eric laughed and stood, beaming at me. If I thought last night wrought a small change, this transformed him.

Geordi, never one to lose sight of what mattered, said, "If he can touch people like us, why can't he hold the scarab?"

Eric, too distracted by the joy of connecting with another live person, didn't answer, so I said, "Maybe it has to do with living creatures versus inanimate objects. Stuff that can't move by itself." In the spirit of full disclosure, I added, "He can push things around sometimes. But he can't grasp them the way we can."

Eric tuned back in and said, "Your aunt is correct. It is difficult, but I can move things if I must."

Geordi said, "You mean like magic?"

"You may call it that, if you like."

"But my scarab's magic. The tomb lady said so."

"Sweetie—" How could I explain that adults sometimes said stuff like that without really meaning it?

"No, it is!" He grabbed Eric's hand and dropped the scarab into it, quickly taking his own hand away. "See?"

Eric's fingers automatically closed over the scarab, and we both realized at the same instant that *he hadn't dropped it*. I stood, frozen, while Eric slowly opened his palm. The scarab sat on it, just as you'd expect it to rest in someone's hand. Eric raised his stunned gaze to mine.

"*Mon ange*, it is true. I am not using any of my energy to keep it aloft. *I am holding it.*"

My mouth was suddenly dry. I stepped closer, unsure what I expected to learn, but needing to see nonetheless. The scarab appeared the same as ever: shiny, black, and about the size of a large prune.

"Is it—" I hesitated.

"From the Plutonium?" Eric supplied. He turned it over, examining it from all sides. "I cannot tell. It is not like the others I have seen. And yet, there is something different about it, else how could I do this?"

He tossed it into the air, then deftly caught it, his expression making it clear he hadn't expected the demo to work. "*Incroyable.*" He returned it to Geordi. "*Merci beaucoup.* Thank you for showing me this. Keep it safe."

Geordi nodded solemnly and repocketed the scarab, and I drew a shaky breath, abruptly realizing we still stood on the tiny landing outside our room.

"Okay, then. Let's get our bags down to the car."

"*Et puis*," Eric said as we started down the stairs, "breakfast for you, *ouais?*"

"Er," I glanced at Geordi, then behind me at Eric. "We're not hungry."

"But you have not eaten in a day."

"We'll have lunch at the Burkes'. It will be fine."

"And what will we do until then?"

"Sightsee?"

It was a weird concept, to be honest, in the midst of

all this other stuff. But I used to do a lot of it in my grave-robbing days. Back then, I called it "market research," treating it as part of my job, but that didn't make it less fun. I'd never been to Germany before, and while my tastes lean more toward ancient artifacts than medieval relics, I admit I was curious about the Porta Nigra, and even Dom Saint Peter and the Diocesan Museum.

As we entered the lobby, I remembered that while dealing with "all this other stuff," I'd forgotten one of the biggest things I had to worry about. Literally, very large.

Jason spotted us from the chair he sat in near the wall and rose to his full six-foot-six-inch height. He regarded me thoughtfully before dropping his gaze and grinning at Geordi. "Hey, kiddo!"

"Jason!" Geordi dive-bombed his stomach, and I wondered if they'd ever tire of the ritual.

Jason hugged him hard, and I thought, *Probably not*.

Over Geordi's head, Jason narrowed his gaze at Eric, and I tried not to think in excruciating detail about what had happened between us last night. What was wrong with me? Jason and I weren't "together" anymore, if we ever had been. But though it'd been two months, too much lay between us, and I felt guilty, plain and simple.

At least Eric wasn't advertising our "adventure." True, he was relaxed, almost happy even. But Jason didn't know him well enough to draw conclusions from his lack of cynicism. Good, since the last thing we needed was a demon-ghost showdown in the hotel lobby.

"What are you doing here?" I asked as Jason patted Geordi on the back and released him.

"Waiting for you."

"Oh. Er, we were just checking out."

"I see that."

Geordi said eagerly, "Tata, can Jason come with us?"

"Oh. I don't think… That is…"

"I'd love to, kiddo. Where are we going?"

"Sightseeing!"

He made it sound like the most exciting adventure ever, and I experienced another *I'm not Lily* moment. Married to a rich mobster—not that she knew it at the time—Lily was a full-time mom, who spent her days taking Geordi to museums and other fun places around Paris. Since she'd died, I hadn't taken Geordi anywhere "fun." Just Turkey, Switzerland, and here.

While I wallowed in guilt, Geordi moved on to the next salient point. "Then we're having lunch at the Burkes'. They live in a castle and they have the best hot cocoa ever. You have *got* to try it." He turned to me. "Please, Tata? Please-please-please can Jason come?"

Eric made a face, but gave one of his Gallic half-shrugs, communicating that it was my decision.

"Why don't we start with breakfast?" Jason said.

Geordi said, "We're not hungry. Are we, Tata?"

"Not hungry?" Jason gasped dramatically. It showed a hint of the man I'd known—theatrical, flamboyant, mercurial—before I learned he was a lying Dioguardi Demon with evil designs on my nephew.

Okay, maybe not evil. Maybe he even thought he knew what was best for Geordi. But anything that took Geordi from me was evil in my book, so I clung to that.

Jason pretended to peer around. "Where's the real Geordi? The one I know was *always* hungry." Geordi giggled, and Jason tousled his hair. "Have you been making your aunt eat meat?"

"Yes," Geordi said, chest puffed with pride.

"Good. Let's go make her have bacon for breakfast."

I cleared my throat. "Really, I'm not hungry, either. We'll be fine until lunch."

Jason frowned and moved closer. I would've backed up but I didn't want him to see my reaction. Then he sniffed me. Just once, and he wasn't obvious about it, but I glanced around anyway. Fortunately, there weren't many other guests up yet, and those that were seemed too hungover from last night's revelries to notice us.

"Stop it," I said under my breath. "Save your demon crap for when we're alone."

A slow smile curved his lips. "And when will that be?"

He leaned in, and God help me, I breathed him in too, for different reasons. For him, the scent thing had something to do with being a demon. But for me it was purely a response to his nearness. And hoo-boy, did he smell good. Familiar and strong and *right*.

It was then it hit me: I couldn't smell Eric. Last night, I'd tasted him and had every inch of him pressed against me. But I hadn't smelled him since he'd had his decaying wound, before he became full Dead. Now, Jason's scent filled me, clean and spicy. It made me feel disloyal to Eric, as though the reawakening of a sense I hadn't known was lacking was somehow my fault.

I stepped away. "I didn't mean—oh, never mind." To Eric I said, "Let's get out of here."

He frowned and said to Jason, "I do not like you—"

"Ditto."

"—but there is something you should know. Hyacinth and her nephew have not eaten since breakfast yesterday. And yet they are not hungry."

Jason's gaze snapped back to me. "You haven't eaten in twenty-four hours? Either of you?"

I blew out a breath, wishing I'd sat on one of the lobby couches. "Not exactly. We had cocoa at lunch."

"Cocoa's not enough."

"And beer—I had that beer last night."

One side of Jason's mouth quirked up. "Well, then, you're all set. But *Geordi* didn't have beer, did he?"

I tamped down my irritation. "I'm just saying it filled me up. It's no big deal. Anyway, since when are you the nutrition police? We're not hungry. Period. No breakfast equals more time for sightseeing."

Geordi said, "Yay!" and jumped up and down. At least one of them was on my side. Then he said, "More time with Jason!" and I decided it was a conspiracy.

Proving my point, Eric continued to Jason, "You see? She will not listen. Perhaps you can make them eat something."

Jason's eyes narrowed. This was absurd. They were bonding over a mutual desire to make me overeat. I grabbed my suitcase and took Geordi's hand, marching us to the lobby desk.

"I'd like to check out, please," I said to the clerk.

Eric and Jason hung back, chatting and frowning in my direction. No one near them noticed Jason talking to our Invisible Friend, which should've been a relief, but I was so aggravated, I half wished they'd *both* vanish in a puff of smoke and leave me and Geordi in peace.

Just for laughs, I asked the clerk if anyone was checking out today, but he shook his head.

"I am wery sorry. Most of our guests are stayink through ze veekend at least."

Oh well. We could always snooze in the car. At least that way, I wouldn't be tempted to get naked with Eric.

I glanced at him, conspiring with Jason, and thought,

well, *that's* a turn-off. But also touching. Which would have brought it back to being a turn-*on* if I'd let it.

Get the rock, then deal with the demon and the ghost.

I grabbed the suitcase and Geordi's hand and headed for the door, assuming Jason and Eric would follow. In my current mood, I wouldn't care if they didn't.

Then the very fact that I was *in* a mood gave me pause. I have my off days—I'm no princess. But I'm not usually flat-out grouchy. Especially when both Jason and Eric were just concerned because I hadn't done something normal people did several times a day.

I might not *feel* hungry, but I was acting hungry. Or rather, hypoglycemic. It was hard to focus, and I just didn't care *what* happened next. Yesterday, I blamed it on the beer. But maybe it was really my empty stomach.

Being dead takes a physical toll on me, and I'd almost come to terms with not being a vegetarian anymore. Would I now have to force myself to eat at all? And how did any of this relate to Geordi?

I looked down at him. He looked up at me.

I said, "They're right, aren't they?" He nodded, and I sighed. "I'll eat bacon if you get eggs and milk."

He thought about that. "And sausage, or I skip the milk."

"You drive a hard bargain." Jason and Eric hurried up, and I said, "You win. Take me to your chef."

"*Merci à Dieu,*" Eric said, but Jason just got more thoughtful. He obviously suspected something, which might've scared me more if I'd been able to focus.

Good thing I couldn't.

I faced the door, but a pair of teenagers blocked our way. The girl was shorter than me, about fifteen or sixteen, with straight dark hair and pale skin. She wore a black miniskirt over ripped fishnet tights and a ratty white t-shirt with enough holes that her red bra showed through. The boy was probably eighteen and about my height, wearing torn jeans, a faded black skate-punk t-shirt, and a carefully gelled "mussed" hairdo.

"Excuse me," I said, and tried to step around them.

The girl said something in German, sounding both scared and mad. The boy glared at her, then spoke angrily to me, gesticulating at the door, or maybe the street, behind them. She said something rapid-fire, but I didn't need a translator to know she was telling him off.

Geordi watched in fascination, but I couldn't tell if it was because of their fight or just that they were "cool" teenagers. I was pretty sure he knew some French swear words but hadn't gotten around to the German ones yet. Which, given the boy's tone, was a good thing.

"I don't suppose you speak German," I said to Jason.

He looked from me to them, then to Geordi, and frowned. "Hyacinth—" he began at the same moment that Eric stepped forward.

"*Mon ange*, I think I have finally found a way to help you." He spoke quickly in German to the two teens.

I was about to tell him it wouldn't do any good if they couldn't see him, when it struck me that they *could*. The boy responded by launching into a passionate discourse on something incredibly important to him, while the girl grabbed his arm and repeatedly interrupted as he tried to shake her off.

"Tata Hyhy?" Geordi said. "Are you going to ask them how they died, and call Tonton?"

Jason folded his arms over his chest. "Something you want to tell me?"

Merde.

Chapter Eleven

*There is no man so blessed that some who
stand by his deathbed won't hail the occasion
with delight.*

*~Marcus Aurelius, Roman Emperor
(121-180 CE)*

We stared at each other for a long moment.

Finally, I said, "No," and faced Eric. "What's he saying?"

The boy grabbed his arm, shouting insistently. The girl, in turn, grabbed the boy's arm, and he let go of Eric and shoved her so violently, she crashed through the glass door onto the sidewalk.

Except of course she didn't crash, she dematerialized, but not with the *crackle* and soft popping noises Eric made. It literally sounded like shattering glass, though the door remained intact. The girl's face crumpled, and she clutched her ribs as though they'd all been stabbed through at once.

Eric's face went white, and with a murderous glare at the boy, he slipped much more easily through the door and knelt beside her. I reached for Geordi's hand, and found Jason already held it. He regarded me evenly.

"Not a good time for this," I said.

"Never a good time." He moved with Geordi to the door and pushed it open, and I had no choice but to follow, rolling our suitcases out to the sidewalk.

Eric helped the girl to a sitting position, his arm around her shoulders. The dead boy still stood in the lobby, regarding the glass panels nervously. He hadn't thought to slip through with me, and the girl's experience clearly rattled him. Cautiously, he touched the door, then snatched his hand back and glared sullenly out at us.

The pain and anger in Eric's face made it clear he'd love nothing better than to kill the boy. Difficult, since he was already dead.

"What happened to them?" I asked.

Eric spat. "*Him*. That is what happened." The girl spoke urgently, and he scrubbed a hand over his face, then rose. "*Mon ange—*" He eyed Geordi and Jason. "It would be better if we spoke privately."

I stepped a few paces away and he followed. Jason wasn't happy about that, but he and Geordi sat on the curb next to the girl, who now huddled into herself, her head on her knees. Geordi got out his scarab and showed it to her, and she smiled tentatively as I faced Eric and waited for him to explain.

"He raped and strangled her," he said without preamble. His voice and expression were devoid of emotion, but I saw the effort it took him to not shatter.

"I understand."

I touched his arm. He didn't pull away, but his rigid tension didn't dissipate, and I dropped my hand.

He cleared his throat. "I am sorry. I—"

"Don't be. I've lost a sister too."

A wave of grief ravaged his features. "She was only fifteen," he said, and I knew he meant the dead girl, for his sister had been a police officer when the Dioguardis raped and murdered her before his eyes.

I hesitated. While he had that whole French-passionate-lover thing, he also had a strong Distant Cop vibe, and wasn't exactly touchy-feely. But he needed someone—needed me. He'd helped me repeatedly, and even if he hadn't, I'd still want to support him now.

Screw it. Our relationship could survive a mistake or two. I touched his wrist, and after a moment, he took my hand, gripping it tight, not saying anything. I felt Jason's eyes on us, but I ignored him. Screw it again: it was none of his damn business what Eric and I did.

At last, Eric drew a ragged breath and murmured, "*Merci*," before releasing my hand.

"Don't thank me. It sounds too…polite. I didn't do it out of duty. I…care…about you."

His lips curved up, and the barest hint of the familiar irony sparked his eyes. "*Mon ange*, there is no need for words. I am grateful, that is all."

"Okay." I gestured toward the girl on the sidewalk, and the boy in the lobby. "Can you talk about it?"

"*Ouais*. It is disgusting. She is—was—fifteen. Him, eighteen. He drugged her and forced himself on her. She thought he loved her, but he only wanted the sex. Not just with him—he—the others—"

His voice broke, and he refused to meet my eyes, so I said quietly, "Forced prostitution—sexual slavery?"

He nodded. "It is what they would have done to my sister, if they had let her live." He met my gaze, eyes dark with pain. "I have never forced myself on a woman. *Never*. And I never will. *Mon ange*, if ever you wish me to stop, or find my lack of a body repulsive, or—"

He was shaking, and I grabbed his other hand, fighting back tears for the boy he'd been at sixteen, and the man he'd become, before dying too young.

"It's okay. I know you'd never hurt me, and you don't repulse me. You must know that by now."

Fresh tears glistened in his eyes, then he dragged me close, clinging to me while his silent sobs racked us both.

"*Mon ange…*" He murmured it over and over, until gradually the tension left him.

A throat cleared behind us, and Eric released me, turning to get himself under control. Jason stood a few feet away, while Geordi still sat by the dead girl. The day was getting underway, but the nearby pedestrians didn't appear to find anything odd about a young boy seated alone on the curb, playing with a toy scarab.

I sent a questioning look to Jason, who inclined his head toward the hotel door. "That kid is stuck."

Eric turned sharply back and I followed his gaze. Sure enough, the dead boy's hand was sticking through the door, while the rest of him remained in the lobby. From the way the hand twisted and pulled, he was obviously—and unsuccessfully—trying to extricate it. Even at this distance, I read the panic in his expression.

A slow smile curved Eric's mouth. It wasn't nice.

He moved toward the door, and I ran to catch up. "What are you doing?"

"*Rien.* Merely helping him get out."

"Eric…"

"You can help as well. Take his hand, and try to pull him through."

"Eric!" But he was gone, dematerializing into the lobby. The boy saw his face and went white, then looked frantically at me, yanking harder at his hand.

He might be a murdering creep but I couldn't just leave him stuck in the door, and I was desperately afraid of what Eric might do. I grabbed the boy's hand, slippery with ghost sweat, and pulled. When that failed, I tried pushing him back through.

Meanwhile Eric bent near his ear and said something, a conversational expression on his face. The boy's gaze snapped to Eric's and he froze, then shook his head violently. Eric gestured at me, mouthing, *Move back.*

There was a glint in his eye, and God help me, I let go of the boy's hand and returned to Jason, who frowned disapprovingly. "Hyacinth…"

I raised my hands. "He's stuck. Sooner or later, someone—a live person—will push the door open. We can't just leave him there."

"But Eric—"

"Will get him out."

I knew he would. I just didn't know *how*, and I wasn't at all sure it would be pleasant for the boy. On the other hand, did a murdering, raping, pedophile pimp deserve "pleasant?"

Before either of us could do anything, there was a loud *crash!* and the boy flew through the door, his momentum sending him far past the girl into the street. He hit so hard, he bounced. Then he lay there, stunned.

"He is out," Eric said, coming through the door to stand on my other side.

"Yes."

We stared at him for a moment. The street was empty now but would be filled with cars soon.

"Shouldn't we—"

Eric squared his shoulders. "I am not a monster. I just gave him a little…push."

He went into the street and hauled the boy up by his arm, then dragged him to a spot on the curb away from the girl, who eyed him balefully and scooted closer to

Geordi.

"Okay, then." I looked at Eric, then Jason. "You should probably leave for a few minutes. Both of you."

Jason's eyes narrowed. "Why?"

I blew out a breath. "Because I have to do something, and you can't be here for it."

Eric said to Jason, "Come. She is right. We will take Geordi to the park, and she will join us when she can."

The muscle in Jason's jaw worked overtime.

Please, I prayed silently. He had to leave. If I was worried about what Michael would do with Eric, a ghost who should have gone to the afterlife, I *really* didn't want to learn what he'd do with a demon. His whole *raison d'être* was keeping Satan locked in Hell with his minions, so I doubted he'd let Jason run around loose, no matter how "good" a demon he was.

Actually, he'd met Jason once in Turkey, but that was before Jason took the Rousseaux's powers and made himself more demonic. Either way, I couldn't chance losing both of them at once.

"Come," Eric repeated quietly.

Jason's lips compressed, but he said, "For Geordi." He walked over, knelt, and said something to him. Then they both stood and headed in the direction of the park.

My gut clenched, and I swallowed. *Jason isn't stealing him, he's only doing what you asked him to.*

I said to Eric, "Thank you."

He lifted a shoulder. "He is important to you. I will leave now too."

"Wait. How did the boy die?"

He made a face. "Auto-erotic asphyxiation. While forcing himself on the girl and strangling her, he had a belt around his neck, tied to the bedframe, to increase his…pleasure. He fell off the bed, and it hung him."

Ouch. And—ick. "Thanks. I think."

He left, and I faced my charges. With the boy so close, the girl trembled. I'd better get this over with.

I thought, *Michael*, and a second later, there he was. I almost wished he was less speedy. This wouldn't be easy, and when the occasion merits, I'm not above sticking my head in the sand and hoping it all goes away.

Except it never does.

Michael had donned another jeans-and-t-shirt combo, with today's slogan reading, "When God made me, He was just showing off."

He eyed the girl and boy, then me. "You called?"

I gave myself a mental shake, then a physical one for good measure, like an athlete getting ready to compete. "These are—well, actually, I don't know their names."

Merde. If Michael discovered I didn't speak German, he'd question how I got their stories. So far, the souls I'd dealt with all spoke either French or Italian, the former of which is a no-brainer, and I can at least get by in the latter. But it'd be hard to explain how I knew where these two should go, when I couldn't get their most basic deets.

Even if I made it past this hurdle now, it would likely come up again. Evidently souls sought me out, regardless of my ability to communicate with them.

I hurried on. "Anyway. He murdered her. He's a real bastard, but I don't think she did anything worse than getting taken in by him."

Michael waited. I suppose I'd known all along it would come to this, but that didn't make it easier. When he first demanded I assist him, my immediate reaction was that I didn't want the responsibility. It was too much.

This was too much.

But I'd made a bargain, and I had to stick to it.

"The girl should go up. The boy—" My throat closed over the words.

"Yes, child?"

There was sympathy in Michael's eyes, an odd camaraderie, and I suddenly thought how lonely this job must be for him. Maybe my *capacity* for the work wasn't the sole reason he'd tapped me to assist him. Maybe, after millennia of going solo, the prospect of sharing the load held an emotional appeal I hadn't considered.

I sighed. "He should go down. He really should. I wish it was different—I don't want to do this—but—"

Michael nodded slowly. "The difficulty, child, is that Heaven cannot exist without Hell."

He said nothing more, facing the girl and offering her his hand. The trust-look softened her features and erased her anxiety, and she let him raise her to her feet. Then he turned to the boy, who eyed him nervously.

"Come, my son. You made your choice."

He spoke in English. Or maybe I *heard* English, but the boy heard German. Either way, his meaning was clear, and the boy nodded unhappily. However, as soon as he placed his hand in Michael's, he, too, relaxed, even though he wasn't headed for the Happy Place.

Michael said to me, "You have done well, my child. I am…sorry."

Then they were gone, and I sank to the curb, putting my head between my knees. Did it ever get easier?

From Michael's expression, probably not.

###

When I got to the park, Eric sat alone on the same bench as yesterday, while Jason played with Geordi on the climbing structure. Jason being so tall, this mainly consisted of him making encouraging noises while "swinging" from the monkey bars with his feet on the ground. Geordi seemed happy, though, so I sat by Eric.

Now the crisis had passed, he'd returned to his normal moody self. I guess it was naïve to think his spirits—ha!—would skyrocket, just because he'd had a ghost orgasm. At the same time, I was oddly relieved. I wouldn't know what to do with Chipper Eric. Cynical Eric was at least familiar.

After a minute, he said, "You should tell him."

"Who? And—what?"

"Him." He indicated Jason with a nod of his head. "That you are dead."

My jaw dropped. When I could speak, I latched onto the one coherent question I could come up with: "*Why?*"

"Because though I do not trust him, he knows things that may help you." He leaned forward, elbows on his knees. "I do not like that you have not eaten. There was a time when you ate everything, even meat, with abandon. This is too sudden. Your friend, I believe he knows why, or at least, has a guess. I cannot help you with this, but perhaps he can."

"I'm fine. I don't need help—his or yours." I saw him gearing up for battle and cut him off. "You're right not to trust Jason. He's a demon." *Part* demon, my conscience piped up, but I ignored it.

"*C'est vrai*. And yet, has he killed anyone?"

I opened my mouth, then closed it. He meant Jason was a demon, but as far as we knew, not a violent one. Whereas he, Eric, was a cop with a temper.

He took my hands in his, the ironic twist of his mouth at odds with the earnest look in his eyes. "*Mon ange*. I said I had not forced myself on a woman. This is true.

But I have done many other things as *un OPJ*, for which I make no apology. At the time, I believed those involved got what they deserved. As, in the end, did I."

He said it so simply, and I wondered again who he was in Life. Of course, cops had to do unpleasant things, including kill. And some cops did it more willingly than others. But could I hold Eric accountable for past actions, when his present ones were—mostly—above reproach?

"Great," I said. "You have your own code of ethics. I get that. But Jason's a demon *and* in the Mafia."

Eric shook his head, hard. "*Non*. He is not in the Life, I could swear it."

"But he's a Dioguardi."

"Perhaps. But was your sister not also a Dioguardi?"

"Not by birth, and she didn't know at first."

"Perhaps," he repeated, regarding Jason pensively. "But is everyone born to a family destined to follow that family's code? Again, I do not like nor trust him. But I do not believe he is a member of, shall we say, *le cercle rapproché des* Dioguardis." He hesitated. "In part, this is because of something his cousin said the night I died."

"Paolo?"

Jason had dozens of Dioguardi cousins, but he'd told me Paolo was in Marseille that night. It wasn't a big leap to think he was nearby while Jason was getting our fake passports and arranging the disposal of Nick's car.

"*Ouais, c'est lui.* As I said, I heard on my scanner that the Dioguardis were near. So I called in to *le commissariat*, then went to investigate. I had been following Paolo's actions. It is why all along I thought I had seen your *friend* before, because they are so alike."

"But doesn't Paolo live in Paris? And you live— lived—in Marseille."

He gave a half-smile at my faux pas. "*Ouais*, Paolo is from Paris. But he spent much time in Marseille, ever since his cousin, your friend, came to stay. I knew of Jason, *bien sûr*, but it fell to another officer to watch his actions. We found nothing suspicious."

He sounded peeved. Meanwhile, I already suspected Jason was sent by the Dioguardis to spy on me. Sister of the woman trying to steal their only grandson? I'd spy on me too. And it made sense that Paolo would visit every now and then for an update, before flitting back north.

Eric continued. "I saw Paolo and his men talking, nothing more. But then two more came. They had weapons drawn, but they lowered them and hailed Paolo as friends, asking if he also searched for your sister's husband. Suddenly, one of Paolo's men fired, killing one of the newcomers, before the other killed him. Then *les flics* came. The men ran—Paolo straight at me. I could not hide in time, and he recognized me. He said..."

He frowned, remembering. "He said, 'If you arrest me, the Dioguardis will find out about us.' I believe he meant that he and your friend were involved in something of which *la familigia* would not approve."

My brain whirled. None of it made sense. Why would Paolo Dioguardi's men shoot Nick's father's goons? I'd assumed that whatever their goals, Jason and Paolo worked *for* the Dioguardis. Was it possible Jason wasn't with them? That Paolo was his lookout, while Jason escaped with me and Geordi?

But...why?

"There is another thing," Eric said quietly. "I do not think Paolo meant to kill me." His expression was troubled. "My gun, it jammed. I think he expected to be the one who died, and when he did not...I cannot explain it, but I could swear to you, he was disappointed."

"I don't understand."

Paolo wanted to die? I'd only met him once, at Lily's wedding: a typical twenty-something guy, flirting with all the women, myself included. Not at all depressed or ready to off himself in a suicide mission. But then, what did I know?

"It was as though he were…tired. When I did not kill him, he said he was sorry. Then he lowered his gun to shoot me in the leg." His mouth twisted ironically. "He tried very hard only to wound me."

"What happened?" I asked, so engrossed in the story, I'd forgotten everything else.

"Nick's father's man—he had chased Paolo and shot at him just as Paolo shot me. The force of his bullet caused Paolo's arm to jerk up, and for all his efforts, he shot me through the heart after all. I believe he then killed the other man, but I do not know for certain. I was not myself for a time. Not until I found you."

I blushed at the implied compliment, but let it pass. "So, Paolo tried to die, and didn't. Then he tried not to kill you, and did."

"*Ouais*," Eric said with an ironic smile.

"But what does any of this have to do with telling Jason I'm dead?"

"*Je n'sais pas*. It is just a feeling. Whatever your friend is doing—whoever he works for—it is not the Dioguardis. And I do not believe he works for Satan, either. When you did not tell him the truth before, he came to believe you were a demon. The choice is yours. But I think if you do not tell him soon, he will *encore une fois* draw his own conclusions. And that could be bad, for you and your nephew both."

Chapter Twelve

Who never caused others to die
Seldom rates a statue.

~Unknown

Believe it or not, a morning spent sightseeing in the midst of all this madness was just what I needed. Eric had given me lots to think on, and it helped to have something to occupy everyone while my mind sorted the possibilities.

The first conclusion I came to was that I couldn't tell Jason anything until I knew why he was here. Eric's instincts might be spot on, but he had no concrete evidence to back them up. Maybe Paolo was referring to someone else, and he didn't even know what Jason was up to. Jason could be a double-double-agent demon-mobster, or—whatever.

I searched my memory for anything Jason had said about Paolo having demon blood, but drew a blank. A "recessive gene," Jason called it, which came out during puberty, or, in rare cases like Geordi's, sooner.

I'm not sure why it mattered, except it was another piece of the puzzle, and every tiny bit helped me to help Geordi. The worst part was I couldn't ask Jason himself without revealing the direction of my thoughts. We'd been so close; I hated not trusting him. But he'd admitted he came for Geordi, and if that meant he planned to take him, he had another think coming.

However, he did know things I didn't. About demons, and what Geordi would need as he grew up, and maybe even about what had happened to me.

I blew out a frustrated breath as the three of them strode ahead of me. While Saint Matthias' was a ten-minute walk south of the hotel, Dom Saint Peter was twenty minutes north, with the Porta Nigra another five past that, so we decided to start there and get breakfast later. We could've taken one of the cars, but it felt good to stretch my legs. I'm not rabid about it, but after an extended lack of exercise I feel like a slug. So, after storing our suitcases in the Peapod, we were off. With the crisp end-of-October air—no rain, thank God—walking was just the thing.

As I've said, my religious education was both spotty and multi-faceted. Meaning I was born Catholic, but my foster families subscribed to a variety of belief systems. However, since being brought back to life by an actual archangel, I admit my interest in early Christianity had grown. And after surviving our stint at Saint Matthias', I felt pretty non-combustible about entering Saint Peter's.

But first we hit the Porta Nigra, aka the Black Gate. According to the guidebook, it's the largest surviving Roman city gate north of the Alps. Originally made of gray sandstone, it blackened over the years from exhaust fumes and is now closed to cars. Of course, there's still a major thoroughfare right next to it, but what the hey.

I have to say, it's impressive. Four stories high and carefully restored in all its stone glory. The sense of history is amazing. That's what I loved most about my "research": the connection to something so old, that's survived for so long, in the face of humankind and our penchant for destroying everything in our path.

But as we approached it, I noticed something odd. The closer we got to the gate, the more…*alive*…I felt.

Awake.

Aware.

Every nerve tingling.

In fact, I felt the way Eric sounded when he dematerialized through things: crackling with energy. And the feeling intensified to the point that when I stood under the original arch, I…electrified. My hair stood on end, from the roots on my head, to every last fine hair on my arms and legs, and my fingernails were…liquid, *melting* with heat.

I stepped back, panicked. The sensation wasn't exactly unpleasant, but I *was* on sacred ground. Maybe Saint Matthias was a fluke, and I was destined to flame out after all.

Eric and Jason, who'd stopped in the square outside to examine the guidebook, shot me matching looks of concern, and I tried to laugh it off.

"It's nothing. Just a breeze or something. It startled me."

Eric seemed unconvinced but forbore to comment. Jason didn't have that problem.

"Hyacinth, what in God's name—"

"It's nothing," I repeated, tilting my head meaningfully at Geordi, who played in the square, hopping from one paving stone to another, getting ever nearer to the arch.

He saw me and gave one of his best and brightest smiles. Then he made a giant leap and landed dead center under the arch. I couldn't help it—I stepped forward, ready to snatch him back, only—

Nothing happened.

I don't know what I thought *would* happen, except that maybe he'd feel the heat too. If he did, he gave no sign. He grinned again, then examined the arch's architecture above, rotating under it to get a better view.

Well, that was good. Wasn't it? I mean, I hardly *wanted* him to be uncomfortable. And yet, it was one more way in which we were different. I wiped the sweat off my face, then noticed the men still watching me.

"Must've been my imagination."

"*Mon ange*," Eric began, mirroring Jason's frown, and I blew out a breath.

"It's *fine*." To prove my point, I went to stand with Geordi under the arch. The warm tingle returned, but it really wasn't unpleasant. I followed Geordi's lead, rotating while gazing up. The intensity varied based on my position. I stepped back, and it got markedly cooler.

Then Geordi said, "If you stand right here, it's the warmest."

I stared. "You feel it too?"

He nodded, smiling. "It's cozy!" Then he frowned. "You know what else, Tata?"

"What?" I asked cautiously.

"It makes me hungry."

He was right; suddenly I was *starving*, like my body had finally caught up to the fact that I hadn't eaten in a day. My stomach growled loudly as Jason and Eric joined us.

Jason glanced uneasily around. "It is kind of…warm."

Eric frowned. "I do not feel it. But then, temperature does not affect me."

So maybe the heat had nothing to do with me *or*

Geordi, if Jason felt it too. The few other tourists who, like us, were out before nine o'clock, either didn't notice or didn't care, as none seemed to be commenting on it.

"Can we go eat now?" Geordi asked, and Jason and Eric both looked at him in surprise.

Then they looked at me.

Great. More bonding.

I said, "Sure. Let's take a quick tour of the cloisters and the museum, and then we'll find a café." To Jason and Eric, I admitted, "Yes, I'm hungry too. Besides, Saint Peter's will be celebrating Mass at nine. We might as well wait to see it until after the services are over."

In the event, there wasn't much more to see at the Porta Nigra, after the gate itself. The cloisters were small and made of stone, as was the museum, which was housed in the former monks' quarters next door. Its display cases held a selection of historical artifacts but surprisingly few religious ones. I suppose most folks got their faith fix around the corner at the Dom.

As we wandered through, I did notice something else, though. Certain parts of the structure, usually the older ones, made me feel warmer and hungrier. I would brush close to a wall, or duck my head under a low lintel, and abruptly realize my skin was burning.

Not painful, just…hot.

Geordi's experiences mirrored mine, but on a lesser scale. He noticed the heat, but wasn't as affected by it.

I asked the curator about the building, and she explained in accented English that the sandstones weren't joined with mortar as was typical of this type of construction. Instead, they were connected by iron rods, some of which were the original pieces dating from the late second century, when the gate was built.

I thanked her, and we left to seek out breakfast. Geordi and I made good on our promises to each other—he ordered eggs and milk, and I got bacon, sausage, eggs *and* waffles—while Jason and Eric watched us with varying degrees of relief and concern.

As I ate, I decided the heat could have had something to do with the iron, particularly if the connector rods were very old. I was pretty sure my meat-eating thing related to iron consumption, because eggs also helped. But they weren't as good as steak, sausage, or bacon.

So, internally, something in me needed meat. But externally, maybe elemental iron affected me in some way I didn't yet understand?

In deference to Geordi, Jason and Eric refrained from questioning me, for which I was grateful. When we were all as stuffed as we could be, I paid the bill and we trooped back outside. Jason tried to give me some cash, but I fobbed him off. He'd paid my way all through Turkey, and I didn't relish being further beholden to him. Especially given our new and even more tense situation.

The café was on a triangular route between the Porta and the Dom, so five minutes later we arrived at the cathedral. We bypassed the main church and headed instead for the jumbled group of attached structures to examine the art and artifacts, and to see the tombs below.

I have to say, it's even more impressive than the Black Gate, both inside and out. It even feels more like a fortress, perhaps because the entire building was preserved, as opposed to the Gate's single wall. The cathedral is also stone-built, but connected with mortar, and I didn't experience any waves of heat as we entered.

Inside, the quantity and quality of the artwork is amazing, and I couldn't help drooling. Jason gave me the side-eye. He knows some of my past, and maybe suspects the rest, but I ignored him and moved farther in.

Geordi was more subdued than earlier in the day. Not in a bad way, exactly. He's not loud under normal circumstances, but now he was even quieter. He followed us around, looking dutifully at gorgeous medieval paintings and holy relics without complaint, until Jason finally took him to play in the square outside.

Every time they went off alone together, I suffered a pang of anxiety. So far, so good. But it made me antsy not having Geordi with me, and I hurried through the rest of my tour, then found Eric near the religious pieces, listening to a docent and frowning slightly.

"*Mon ange*," he said on seeing me, "I believe we should return to Saint Matthias'."

"Um, okay." I bit my lip, and he shot me a self-deprecating smile.

"*Ne te fâche pas*. I am not so anxious to be in the presence of the Host again."

"Then why?"

"Because the remains of Saint Eucharius are there."

"Okay. And we like him because…?"

"Part of the crozier of Saint Peter is buried with him—the staff Eucharius used to restore the life of his companion, Maternus, after he had been dead and buried for forty days."

It *was* an interesting idea. Of course, as a child, I'd listened skeptically to biblical stories of mystical healing and folks being brought back to life.

But now…why should I be the first?

I'd also assumed Michael went under the table, so to speak, in resurrecting me. But if there was a precedent—if it was more common than I'd thought—that changed things. It might even provide leverage in my quest to remain on Earth permanently.

"Thank you," I breathed. "Let's go."

As it happened, we couldn't go just then. By the time we got outside, it was past noon. We needed twenty minutes to find the car, with another thirty to get to the Burkes'.

Predictably, Jason insisted on tagging along.

"Don't you have anything else to do?" I asked testily.

"Nope. Nothing's more important than Geordi Time."

Geordi grinned happily, and I gave up.

"I am glad," Eric murmured while I held the car door open for him.

"Why?"

"Because he will know if the Burkes are demons. And even if they are human, he will be better able to protect you, should anything go wrong."

He had a point. I'd forgotten that demons could sense other demons, at least the unshielded ones—whatever was involved in that. I still didn't know. But having Jason with us meant I had someone at my back—someone big and strong, and able to throw a punch, or run like hell, carrying Geordi.

We took the rental car instead of the Peapod. For one thing, it was roomier. For another, the Peapod still had French plates, albeit different ones than *I'd* had, and I didn't want the Burkes questioning why I'd had two cars in two days. Keep it simple.

I started the engine, then faced Jason and cleared my throat. "Um, if you notice anything…unusual…at the Burkes', will you tell me?"

He glanced at Geordi, then back at me. "Aren't we just having lunch with friends?"

"Not exactly. I mean, I'm sure they're perfectly harmless. I'm hoping to get a rock from the husband, for a client." I could see he was about to ask, *What the hell for*?—boy was he not up-to-speed—so I flicked a glance of my own at Geordi. "Just, please—be careful. But, you know, if anything leaps out at you…"

He blew out a breath. "Fine. I get it. I'll shield myself, but keep my antennae up."

I chewed my lip. "You have—"

"Figure of speech."

"Oh."

I pulled away from the curb, and we drove in silence. Geordi watched the scenery, which was even prettier in dry weather, while Eric stared moodily out the other side.

I was also lost in thought when Jason finally spoke. "Another rock?"

I considered not answering, but he did have some right to know. I nodded.

"From the same place as the last one?"

"Yes. They're…special."

"I got that. Care to tell me why?"

"No."

He was silent so long, I thought he'd dropped it. Then he asked, very low, "Does Eric know?"

My gaze snapped to his, and I caught the flash of hurt in his eyes before I jerked mine back to the road.

"I see," he said.

"I'm sorry. It's just…" How could I explain? I didn't want to hurt him, but it seemed I already had.

"You don't trust me."

"Would you? If you were in my position?"

I felt him watching me, and I gripped the wheel tighter. Finally, he said, "I would never hurt Geordi. Never. I'm here to help him. He needs things—training, information, support." He paused meaningfully. "Shielding."

Duh. He'd told me, long ago, that young demons couldn't shield themselves. An adult had to do it for them until they were old enough, or they learned the skill, I wasn't sure which.

There was so much I didn't know. Could I let my pride get in the way of something so important? I might be pissed at Jason, but he was the only "good" demon I knew. What else could I do? Waltz up to the Dioguardis and beg a referral to *their* preferred Demon Mentor?

"I'd like to help you too," Jason added, leaning forward. "Whatever it is, Hyacinth—whatever happened in France, and then Turkey—you can trust me."

"Yeah. Right. You're a demon *and* a Dioguardi."

"It's because of those things that you *can* trust me."

Seconds ticked by before he sat back in defeat. "Have it your way. But think about it: not all the Dioguardis are bad, and you *know* in your heart that I'm not like the Rousseaux. I'm taking a big risk, just being here. And…I didn't come only for Geordi."

Somehow, I kept my gaze on the road. There was enough ambient noise that I didn't think Geordi or Eric had heard us. If I ignored them all, maybe I could get the tears under control before we arrived at the Burkes' and I had to face Cheerful Rachel again.

Chapter Thirteen

*When a man dies, he does not just die of the
disease he has: he dies of his whole life.*

~Charles Péguy, French Poet (1873-1914)

When we parked and got out, Jason eyed the Burkes'
castle. "Interesting friends you've got."

"Tata?" Geordi asked, waiting politely for Eric to
slide across the seat and out of the car, before closing his
door. "Will there be more hot cocoa?"

"I don't know, sweetie."

Jason shot him a thoughtful look.

"What?" I asked under my breath as Geordi ran up
the steps, intent on using the giant metal knocker in the
shape of a sunburst, similar to the one on Rachel's belt,
which he'd missed last time, thanks to her coming out to
meet us.

"I'm not sure." Jason examined the castle, which
appeared oddly more impenetrable in the weak sun than
it had in the glowering clouds. "But it was after drinking
the cocoa that you both lost your appetites, wasn't it?"

"What? Magic cocoa?"

"Maybe."

It wasn't the answer I expected. On the other hand,
dying, being reborn, magic rocks, and solid dead folks—
not to mention demons, archangels, and the existence of
Heaven and Hell—weren't exactly "expected" either.

We were almost on the landing, and the whole thing felt silly. "Coincidence. Or maybe she used whole milk. I use nonfat, so her cocoa probably filled us up more."

Eric, walking close behind, said to Jason, "You will keep your eyes and ears—your demon senses—open, *ouais?*"

"Of course. But—" Jason hesitated, but Geordi didn't seem to be listening. "If they were demons, they would've noticed Geordi immediately."

My chest was suddenly tight. Geordi'd already banged the knocker. We only had a few seconds or a minute before the door would be answered.

"What are you saying? When it was the Rousseaux, you said even if they sensed him, they'd figure he was just a child and not important enough to worry about."

"That was before. You're missing the point. It's likely they *aren't* demons. That's a good thing."

"But it's bad that other demons can sense him now. Isn't it?"

He clearly didn't want to answer, but finally he nodded.

Rachel chose that moment to throw open the doors. "You're here!" She beamed first at Geordi, then at me. Then her gaze landed on Jason and her eyes widened. "Why, you must be Geordi's father. The resemblance is amazing. Monsieur Leclerc, I presume?"

Jason's gaze slid to mine and my face heated. But then I jumped into the fray. Keep it simple, right?

"Frau Burke, may I present my…husband, Jason."

If she noticed the slight hitch in my introduction, she gave no sign. "Please. I thought we established that you must call me Rachel."

She smiled winsomely at Jason and held out her

hands for him to clasp. He stooped, and she kissed him on both cheeks, before he followed her inside, the rest of us trailing after. She wore green again, a long tunic that fit loosely over her slender form while still showcasing her curves, and her hair flowed silkily down her back to brush her pert rear. I caught Jason checking her out and wondered sourly if it was his "demon antennae" he was *keeping up*, then pushed the thought away. If I clung to the precept that he didn't have a claim on me, then *I* didn't have a claim on *him*.

"My own husband," she said as she closed the doors behind us, "is out at the creek. He will be in shortly."

I'd checked the map app on my phone. The "creek" was the River Moselle, which wound through the region on its way to Luxembourg in the west. If something that big was about to flood their land, I didn't see how Heinrich could have stayed so clean yesterday.

I gave myself a shake. I was over-complicating. Jason caught my eye and lifted a shoulder, telegraphing that he didn't sense any demons nearby, and I let my breath out. This didn't have to be hard. Of course, after last time, which involved both demons of the lower case "d" variety *and* High Demons of the Last Circle of Hell, I had a right to be pessimistic.

Plus, if the Burkes were demons, couldn't they, like Jason, just pop up their shields and hide it from him? It was beyond frustrating, not knowing how any of this worked. And another reason to allow Jason back into our lives, whether I wanted to or not.

But first, I had to get Michael's rock.

I paused in the entryway to try sensing it but still couldn't. Maybe it was locked in Heinrich's safe. Or maybe the house was too large and the shard too small.

Disappointed, I followed Rachel through new corridors to what I assumed was the formal dining room, until she said, "I thought we'd eat in here. It's so much cozier than the Big Hall."

If this wasn't the "big" hall, what was? This room was huge, with cathedral ceilings, ornate gold-paneled walls, and the same green décor, interspersed with splashes of blood red, that defined the rest of the castle.

In the center stood a polished oak table which could easily seat twenty, laid out with tableware bearing symbols which must be the Burke family crest. Each bone-white piece of china sported a gold-leaf zig-zag, bisected by a straight gold line, beside an arrow pointing up, with two "feathers" on the left side of its tail, the whole enclosed in an elaborate gold circle. The flatware was white gold and engraved with the same symbols, plus a few more that I recognized as early versions of the Christian cross, or possibly pagan sun runes.

"Frau Burke," Geordi began, and she bent to his eye level.

"Please. Rachel."

He grinned, and said shyly, "Rachel… Is there more hot cocoa?"

She laughed and straightened. "Did you like it?"

He nodded. "It filled us up. Didn't it, Tata?"

I flinched. I'd coached him on pretending Jason was his father, but I'd forgotten to remind him not to call me "auntie." I'd never heard Rachel speak French, though, so maybe she'd think it was another version of "mama."

Her expression didn't change, and she whispered conspiratorially, "Well, I've got a big lunch for you, if you haven't eaten in a while."

"Oh, we had a big breakfast," Geordi said. "We got

starving at the Black Gate."

An odd expression crossed Rachel's features. A mix of surprise and…displeasure? Maybe she was disappointed because she'd gone all out on our lunch.

I said quickly, "I'm *still* starving. Thank you for inviting us."

The moment passed, and the warm smile was back. "We are happy to have you."

Jason rested a hand on my shoulder. "It's very generous of you." I'm sure to Rachel it looked like a loving gesture between husband and wife, but I felt his warning squeeze.

Surreptitiously, I sought out Eric. He stood near a wall, watching Rachel with narrowed gaze. So he was still suspicious too. He caught my glance and mouthed, *I do not like this*. The fact that he didn't want to speak out loud, despite the fact that the Burkes, in theory, couldn't see or hear him, spooked me even more.

Deliberately I tried to unclench my gut. I agreed the whole thing felt off, but I couldn't figure out *why*. I was almost positive the Burkes weren't demons. No eyes flickering black, no heat when I was near them. If anything, their home was unnaturally cold.

But if not demons, then…what? They seemed like a benevolent rich couple with too much leisure time, or not enough friends, or both. Other than that, I had nothing.

Maybe instead of spending the last two months helping Geordi cope with the loss of his mother and trying to unlock our finances, I should have been at the library, researching which mystical evil creatures were prone to look like friendly German-slash-Americans.

I glanced at Geordi. Nope. He was still more important than anything or anyone. Still, I added *Library* to my list of things to do when this trip was over.

I said to Rachel, "Will Heinrich be back soon?"

"Oh, yes. He should be done any time now. Why don't we start on lunch? We can view his silly rocks much better on a full stomach."

Rachel sat to the left of the head of the table, which must be Heinrich's place, and the rest of us found our own spots. Geordi clamored to be near her, which made me uneasy, but I couldn't stop him without being rude.

Fortunately, Jason sat protectively on his other side, leaving me with the seat at Heinrich's right. Pretending I needed to hang my purse, I tugged the chair next to me out enough for Eric to squeeze in. Rachel might not know he was there, but I felt better with him at my side.

The moment we were situated, the far doors opened and white-coated servants entered bearing lidded silver trays. These were set on the table and uncovered, revealing hot, fragrant food, including everything you'd expect at a fancy sit-down dinner: potatoes and jellied berries, winter vegetables, and the *pièce de résistance*, a roast goose. Then the servants paraded silently back out, closing the doors again with a soft *click*.

Though my mouth watered from the heavenly smells, I said, "This is too much. You shouldn't have."

Even Jason seemed to be softening toward her. I guess he liked a good meal as much as the next demon.

"Don't be silly," Rachel said. "Martinstag is next week. We're just celebrating early." She piled potatoes on Geordi's plate, saying, "Do you know what Thanksgiving is?"

He nodded. That was one ex-pat tradition Lily'd kept alive. I wouldn't have bothered if it was just me, but I drove up to Paris every year to be with her and Geordi.

She really laid it on for him, even after she left Nick. Turkey, stuffing, sweet potatoes, garlic mashed potatoes, plus four kinds of pie. I made a mental note to celebrate it this year when we got home. It was three weeks away, so we had plenty of time.

Rachel explained to Geordi, "Martinstag is the feast of Saint Martin. Very important in Germany. It's kind of like Halloween and Thanksgiving all rolled up together." She raised her eyebrows. "I've just had a brilliant idea. Halloween is tomorrow. Why don't you come back, and I'll take you trick-or-treating around the neighborhood?"

I wasn't sure how to respond. "The neighborhood? Aren't you kind of…isolated out here?"

"The village, then. C'mon, it'll be fun. The Germans don't make as big a deal of it, and it would be such a treat for me to take Geordi around."

"Can we, Tata? Please?" He sounded so hopeful. "I never got to go before. *Please?*"

Even with Michael's references to Samhain, and the eve of All Saint's, I'd forgotten about Halloween. Neither France nor Germany is big on it, but Lily had shown Geordi American TV and movies, exposing him to its appeal. However, I wasn't about to let Rachel take Geordi out alone, no matter how nice the offer.

"We really should leave tonight," I said. "I'm sorry. But thank you. Geordi would have loved it, I'm sure."

"Oh. Of course. I'd forgotten." She sounded genuinely disappointed, but she only went back to serving food and passing platters.

When she got to me, she piled a huge portion of goose on my plate. Jason saw my distaste and shook his head subtly, which I interpreted as, *Careful. If you want something from her, be polite.* I swallowed. It did smell good, even if I had already eaten meat today. I took a nibble. It was tasty, but I couldn't stomach it. I focused on the other goodies and hoped Rachel wouldn't notice.

A few minutes later, Heinrich came in, as neat and dressy as before. Jason rose and shook hands with him while Rachel made the introductions.

"So sorry I'm late," he said as he took his seat. "Very busy this time of year."

"Your wife mentioned a creek?" Jason asked, sitting back down.

He sounded politely curious, but I thought he might be fishing. He was heavily involved in theater at one point, or so he claimed. I tended to believe him on this. He could change from the Jason I knew into whatever character he chose in seconds flat. Today he played Devoted Husband and Sophisticated Guest so well, I half believed we *were* married and Geordi was our son.

Beside me, Eric didn't look happy. "*Mon ange*, he—Heinrich—has been handling the Plutonium rock. I can feel it on him."

I shot him a slight frown, wishing I could respond. At least Geordi hadn't heard and answered without thinking. Eric had reason to be sensitive, but a rock collector handling his rocks seemed pretty normal, particularly as he was sorting them for us. Plus, Heinrich might not even know that rock came from the Plutonium.

Then again, a grown man collecting rocks this rabidly was odd by itself, but what the hey. Even Rachel thought *that* was nuts, and she'd married the guy.

"The creek is actually a river," Heinrich explained, while Rachel heaped his plate with food. "Every year, it overflows. I must supervise its containment, or the boys get it wrong."

"His retainers," I supplied helpfully.

"Ah." Jason's tone was noncommittal. "It must be hard to keep so clean."

Well, bluntness was one approach.

Heinrich laughed. "I have a wood platform from which I observe the workers' progress. It is they who get muddy, not I."

"Come, Heinrich," Rachel cut in. "Don't bore our guests. Let's eat, and then they can see your rocks and be on their way."

She lifted the final platter, which held rolls baked together in groups of six, so that they made fat little brown men. They shone with glaze and sported raisin eyes, noses, and buttons, and Geordi giggled delightedly.

"*Weckmann*," Rachel said. "They are bishops, as Saint Martin was the Bishop of Tours. Don't they look yummy? I made them special for you."

"Can I have a whole one?"

Rachel started to hand him one, but I said, "Let's try an arm or a leg first and save room for our good food."

She looked nonplussed but tore off a round head and dropped it on his plate, then divided the rest of that *Weckmann* between herself, Heinrich and Jason. She tore the head off a new bishop for me, and I tried it warily. It was delicious, sweet, but not overbearing. Maybe the religious overtones of chewing on a priest just creeped me out. Not that gingerbread men bothered me. But those aren't religious. I think.

To counteract any hint that I might be becoming a prude, I took a big bite of bishop, chewing down an eye and the nose with gusto.

The meal finished pleasantly enough. Jason and Heinrich made small talk over Geordi and Rachel, while she chatted across the table with me. Geordi mainly ate, with occasional breaks to allow Rachel to serve him seconds and thirds, and Eric brooded, listening to the rest of us. By the end, he crackled with impatience, but Jason seemed more at ease and gave me a slight *no-idea-what's-wrong* shake of his head.

"Great meal," he said for Rachel's benefit.

I admit I was stumped. Eric thought something was wrong but couldn't say what. Jason was suspicious at first but now appeared reassured. And Geordi had an obvious crush on our hostess, who accepted his shy approaches with aplomb.

Meanwhile, Heinrich was charming to all and self-deprecating about his "childish hobby," as he led us down fresh hallways to what must have been the castle's original kitchen. Big, and open, it held several wood-topped stone worktables, but the built-in shelves were largely bare, except for here and there a wicked carving knife, or an extra-large bacon press.

"In the fifties my grandfather built an addition," Heinrich explained, "adding a modern kitchen for my grandmother and leaving this space as you see it. It's useful for spreading out."

He moved to one wall where eight black cases were lined up, each about a meter tall and fifty centimeters around, with metal trim and padlocks. He unlocked one and swung the door wide, revealing stacked trays which he brought one-by-one to the nearest table.

Most of the rocks were the size of small plums, interspersed with a few larger or smaller ones. Most were also the same rough gray of Michael's sanctuary stones, so it was possible the rock I sought was here. But I hadn't picked up even a frisson of talking-rock energy. This close, I should have felt *something* by now.

Could the metal cases block the rock somehow? Or was it so small I'd have to examine each tray, maybe touch every piece, before I found it?

At roughly fifteen stones per tray, twelve trays per case, that was a lot of work. But I couldn't see another option, as Michael was convinced his rock was here.

Jason lifted Geordi up onto a table, lounging next to him, while Eric paced the stone floor like a caged animal. Rachel smiled at me sympathetically.

"I told you there were tons." She went to a small wooden door in the opposite wall, which led to a pantry. "How about a glass of wine to get the party started?"

I hesitated. Oh, what the hell. This was one instance where drinking on the job might be a good thing. "Thanks. I'd like that."

I pulled a stool up to the table where Heinrich had set up operations, and Rachel disappeared into the pantry, returning moments later with a bottle of something dark red. She retrieved four metal goblets from a dusty shelf, rinsed them in the sink, then brought the wine and a corkscrew to Jason.

"Do the honors?"

He smiled, uncorked, and poured. But not, I noticed, without sniffing it first. And I don't think he was testing its "bouquet."

Three hours later, my back ached from sitting on the stool, my head was fuzzy from the wine, and I'd learned absolutely nothing except that Heinrich took his collection *very* seriously, recalling details of where each piece was found, why he wanted it, and how he'd acquired it.

Geordi, Jason and Rachel had played Go Fish for a while with a deck of cards Rachel found somewhere. When Geordi tired of that, Rachel took him and Jason to the castle library. She returned alone fifteen minutes later, saying we'd retrieve them when we were done.

Eric stayed close by me, frowns deepening as the afternoon wore on, but I couldn't tell him to stop without drawing unwanted attention. When Heinrich move to carry one of the trays back to its case, Eric leaned in and murmured, "*Mon ange*, ask him about that one there."

He pointed to a small, nondescript black stone in the corner of a tray over which I'd already run my hands. A little bigger than Geordi's scarab, it was similarly oval and shiny, with sharp edges.

I said under my breath, "That's not it."

"I know. Just ask him."

Heinrich returned, carrying the next-to-last tray, and Eric stepped quickly away. I said, "I'm curious—where did you find that stone there? It's very pretty."

Heinrich beamed and set down the fresh tray. "Ah, yes. That one is very special indeed. Would your client be interested in it?"

"I'm not sure. It's not what he usually likes, but maybe if you tell me its story…? There's certainly something about it."

Rachel came to peer over her husband's shoulder. "What, that one? It's the same as all the rest."

I cleared my throat. "It's…shinier."

She rolled her eyes and offered me more wine, and when I declined, returned to the style magazine she'd been perusing. Heinrich picked up the stone. It wasn't one of Michael's, and it didn't look like the Plutonium rock from yesterday, but if it was important to Eric, I had to ask.

Heinrich said, "This little beauty came from our honeymoon trip. Remember, my dear?"

Rachel smiled sweetly. "Yes, darling. Wewelsburg Castle. How could I forget?"

At the name of the castle, Eric crackled blistering hot behind me, but even without that, my own non-demon antennae went off. Wewelsburg itself I didn't recognize. But the way they spoke of it, like they shared a *very* important, *very secret* secret, set me on high alert.

Just then Jason and Geordi joined us. My "husband" looked tense, and my gaze immediately went to my "son." He seemed fine, clutching a dusty tome to his chest and grinning broadly. I experienced a moment's relief, then looked at Jason again. His lips were pressed together until they were white, and he gave an unreassuring *not here* shake of his head.

"Tata, look!" Geordi said. "It's fairytales, and it's really old, and the pictures are really cool!" He held it up and I took it, while Rachel grinned at him.

"Ah, the Brothers Grimm. You have good taste. They were German, you know." Geordi's eyes went round, and she added, "That's a very old copy. It's been in Heinrich's family forever."

It certainly smelled old, its leather cover frayed around the edges. "Oh. Sorry." I held it out to her, but she laughed.

"No, no, I didn't mean that. In fact, Geordi's welcome to borrow it if he'd like."

"But…" I didn't know what to say, as I'd repeatedly said we planned to leave tonight. Although now we couldn't, since the rock wasn't in any of the trays Heinrich had shown me.

Echoing my thoughts, Jason said, "We should be going. Did you find what you needed?"

His tone reiterated that something was off. Not *run-for-your-life* time, maybe, but approaching *let's chat now*. I didn't need to see Eric to know he agreed, so I sent an apologetic look Heinrich's way.

"Ah," he said. "But we have two trays to go."

"Of course." I dutifully peered at the one he'd just set down, found nothing, and then waited while he brought the final tray over. None of the rocks gave off any kind of vibe, but for form's sake, I ran my hands above the tray, hesitating here or there and pretending I wanted to pick the rocks up, not that I expected them to talk to me.

"Do you see nothing that interests you?" Heinrich's gaze bored into mine. Then his smile flashed warm and friendly, boyishly excited to find someone who shared his love of questionably interesting mineralia. "Come. Tell me what is missing from my selection—what your client wishes to find."

I straightened. "I already explained he's interested in rocks from Turkey."

"Ah. But clearly that's not the only trait he values." His gesture encompassed all eight cases, filled with rocks from Turkey. "Why that region? What is special about those rocks?"

Now we came to it: the part I'd been avoiding. Demons they might not be, but that didn't make them trustworthy.

Just then Geordi piped up. "Is it because that's where Tonton fought the bad man?"

Heinrich and Rachel both snapped to attention, and Heinrich asked, "Someone was in a fight? At Colossae?"

Geordi nodded vigorously while I put a hand on his

shoulder and pasted on my best *I'm totally innocent* smile. "He means a friend of ours got into an argument with another tourist."

"I see." Heinrich stroked his chin thoughtfully. "You know, I do have a piece that I personally did not find at Colossae, but which may have originated there."

I perked up. Of course he needn't have found the rock himself, or even at Colossae. It was thousands of years since Michael fought Satan; the rocks could and had been passed from place to place, many times over.

"Where is it?"

"I'm afraid it's too late now."

"Too late?" It was barely five o'clock.

Rachel interjected, "My husband is referring to a large stone he keeps outside down by the creek. It is too dark to see it tonight. But if you come back tomorrow…"

Her smile was winsome. Jason and Eric, in yet another twin moment, wore identical expressions of resigned frustration. And Geordi squealed, "Can we, Tata? Can we come back and see the river and go trick-or-treating? Please?"

Hoo-boy. For a "non-demon, easy rock retrieval," this was a helluva lot of work.

Chapter Fourteen

God help those who do not help themselves.

~Wilson Mizner, American Playwright
(1876-1933)

The ride back to town was tense to say the least. Whatever Jason had uncovered in the Burkes' library, he refused to discuss it in front of Geordi. Ditto Eric and the Wewelsburg rock. And Geordi kept reading out bits of the Grimm's Fairy Tales. Naturally, the gorier ones.

I know the House of Mouse glossed over the violence in the stories they cartoonified, but I had no idea how bloodthirsty those German brothers were. Or rather, the peasants from whom they'd done their own co-opting.

"Listen to this one, Tata!" Geordi exclaimed for the umpteenth time. "'Take the child out to the forest. I never want to lay eyes on her again. You are to kill her and bring back her lungs and liver as proof of your deed.'"

"Uh, wow. What fairy tale is that, sweetie?"

"Snow White."

I swallowed a bubble of hysteria. Maybe I should worry less about Geordi's demon blood and more about his reading habits.

Jason sat moodily beside me, as did Eric in the backseat. Neither of them had heard a thing Geordi'd said, which just made me wonder more what they were thinking. I cleared my throat, and Jason frowned at me.

What I had to say didn't need to be kept from Geordi, so I launched into it. "Where are you staying?"

The frown deepened. "It doesn't matter. Go back to your hotel, and I can walk home."

"No, see, that's the problem. There's no room at the inn." He still didn't get it, so I swallowed my discomfort and spelled it out. "We don't have anywhere to stay. The hotel is booked, and we planned on going home today."

"Oh. You can stay with me. Sure, no problem."

"*All* of us?" I nodded toward the back, where Geordi was now reading aloud to Eric, who also wasn't paying attention to him. Or to us. Still, I lowered my voice and said to Jason, "We're kind of a package deal."

"Meaning?"

I shook my head and kept my gaze on the road. I didn't want to spell *that* out, but it seemed he'd make me.

"What exactly is your relationship with Eric now?" His tone was bland, and his expression was so neutral, it was six shades of off-off-off-white.

"It's…complicated."

"Never mind. I get it. A tiny bit of demon blood is a total turn-off. But a dead guy—a *cop*, for Chrissake— makes you hot."

I didn't know whether to laugh or hit him. Sadly, they *both* made me hot. But I couldn't tell him that, and even if I could, it didn't make what he'd said okay.

We were at the outskirts of town, so I pulled off the highway at a side road and parked. I said to Eric and Geordi, "Give us a sec."

Then I got out and waited while Jason unfolded from the passenger seat and came around the car. We stepped a few feet away on the grass, and I faced him.

"You left. You lied, kidnapped my nephew, accused

me of working for Satan, then vanished. Eric stuck around. He's been here for us—for *me*."

"You lied too." Jason's voice was tight, and I wondered if that's how I sounded. "You still won't tell me what's up. You don't trust me, fine, that's my fault. But Geordi's not just your nephew, he's *my* cousin. And I don't care how Eric's acting. He has his own agenda. Everyone does, whether they advertise it or not."

I opened my mouth to deny it when what I wanted to do was pummel his chest. But I couldn't hit him or force the words out, because what he'd said held a grain of truth. Eric did have his own plans, which he didn't always share with me. Plus, like it or not, Geordi and Jason *were* related, and had things in common I could barely comprehend, much less help with.

I consciously unclenched my fists. "Tit-for-tat?"

Jason looked at me, startled. It was a game we'd played in Turkey. One question each, with the promise of a truthful answer no matter what.

Slowly he nodded. "Okay. You first."

"Why did you come back right now?"

"I told you—"

"No. Not the crap about the car. Why *now*, instead of six weeks from now, or three weeks ago? Why track me all the way here? If you knew about this trip, you had to know we'd be coming home again soon."

He glanced uneasily at the car, where Eric watched us through the window as Geordi read aloud to him. For a second, I thought Jason would cry off, then he exhaled.

"I'll tell you, but you won't like it. We've been keeping tabs on you. When you left Switzerland to come here so suddenly, at this season, we…wondered."

My jaw dropped. It was one thing to think he *might*

have been sent to spy on me during Lily's custody battle for Geordi. It was quite another to learn I'd been systematically followed for weeks, maybe months, and I'd had *no* idea. This seemed like a necessary skill for a graverobber turned magic-rock-hunter-slash-demon-avoider, working for the Angel of Death. I gave myself a mental head slap. Then the anger hit.

"We? Who in God's name are we? What *about* this season? And what the *hell* were you—*we*—wondering?"

Tit-for-tat is supposed to be one question, or at least a give and take, not rage-yelling. Jason just looked resigned.

"You may as well know. There's a…sect, I guess you'd call it. Within the Dioguardis. A group of us who dislike what the name now stands for."

"A secret society? Really? But why spy on *me?*"

He shook his head, then raised his hands when I stepped toward him. "I'm not saying I won't ever tell you. But first, my turn. How did you find the Burkes, and why is their rock collection so damn important to you?"

I suppose two questions were fair given he'd answered two of mine. I thought a minute, searching for a response that wouldn't involve Michael or being dead, or any of the things I still didn't want to share, despite Eric's advice to the contrary.

At last I said, "I told you about my client, the rock collector?" He nodded, his expression saying he was prepared for a load of BS, but he'd listen anyway. I sighed. "He's not your average collector. He *needs* these rocks. It…has to do with Satan again."

I flinched, expecting another of his blistering lectures on the dangers of Satan and Hell and blah-blah-blah. Ha. Like I didn't already know.

Instead all he said was, "I know."

I blinked. "You mean you figured it out because of what happened last time?"

"No. Because of what's happening now."

"But you said yourself the Burkes aren't demons."

"No, but…" He frowned. "You don't know?"

"Know what?"

He shook his head, bemused. "You really have no idea who you're dealing with. Christ, Hyacinth. What the hell kind of clients do you have, anyway?"

I got a bad feeling in my gut. "What do you mean?"

"The Burkes!"

He wasn't exactly shouting, but his voice was raised, and Eric moved as though to pass through the car door. I waved him back and forced myself to calm down.

"What about them? You just agreed they're human."

"Yeah, they're human. For now."

"What on *earth* are you talking about? Spell it out for me—pretend I know nothing about demons, or Satan, or anything else. Which I *don't*."

He stared at me for a long moment, then scrubbed a hand across his face. "Sorry. I forget you weren't born into this like I was. And Geordi too," he added pointedly.

"Get on with it. Why are my new besties actually evil and dangerous?"

"Because they're devil worshippers, trying to raise an army of the Dead for Satan."

Eric must have seen my face go white. The next thing I knew, he was at my side, touching my elbow. I hadn't even heard him dematerialize, he was that fast.

"*Mon ange*, do you need to sit down? What has happened? What has *he* said to you?"

Jason scowled. "Nothing she shouldn't have figured

out on her own by now."

I glanced at the car where Geordi pressed his worried face against the window. Eric followed the direction of my gaze, his frustration clear.

"I wish to help, and if you ask it, I will return to him. But I cannot always sit in the car with your nephew. I cannot *help* you if you will not include me."

I squeezed his hand. "Just a few more minutes, until I figure this out. I promise I'll tell you everything later."

"How? When?" Eric shook me off and paced angrily. "We are never alone. Your nephew is there, or people are near us who cannot see me. Unless they are dead, in which case your *friend* must be summoned. *C'est impossible*. You must do your work. But you must also care for your nephew. I am not sure you can do both."

Proving his point, Geordi suddenly pushed the car door open and ran to us, throwing his arms around me. "I missed you, Tata. When are you coming back?"

I hugged him tight, breathing in the sunshine and earth of his silky black hair. The problem was that if I *didn't* do my job, I'd lose him forever. But if I kept working for Michael, at best I'd always be hiding things from Geordi, and at worst, putting him in danger.

Which apparently I'd done now. Though who knew how Jason came to his conclusion about the Burkes, or if I'd believe him when he finally told me. Okay, that was unfair. He would've explained already, except we were all so busy protecting Geordi. Even Eric, surprisingly.

He pursed his lips. "*Mon ange*. I hate to admit it, but it is possible your nephew would be safer with his cousin's family."

Jason straightened in surprise while I tightened my hold on Geordi, making him squirm. "No. Just—no."

Eric lifted a shoulder. "It is something to consider."

Jason's gaze flicked from Eric to me. "We'll figure it out. For now, you need a place to stay. Paolo and I can double up and you can have my room." One corner of his mouth lifted in a combination of irony and regret. "All of you. If you'd like." When I hesitated, he added, "With more adults around, it'll be easier to finish our talk."

Geordi broke free and went to stand by his idol. Jason took his hand, and I tried not to be jealous. They wore identical expressions of hope, their wavy black manes a perfect match, as was the blue of their eyes. No wonder Rachel assumed they were father and son.

I was about to relent when I realized what Jason had said. "Paolo's with you?"

"Yep."

"So he's…what? Your partner in crime? Is he…?" I didn't know how to ask in front of Geordi, but Jason understood.

"One of us? Yep."

"Oh."

It made sense. Paolo was probably in the Super-Secret Sect too. Of course he was. Of *course* he'd been protecting Jason the night Eric died, which also explained why he hadn't intended to kill a cop.

Of course a super-secret sect of Dioguardi Demons were exactly *who I should trust with our lives.*

Suddenly, I was too overwhelmed to care.

"Fine. We'll stay with you, if you can swear to me on—well, whatever it is you people hold sacred, that neither you nor Paolo will try anything funny."

"*Us people* are Catholic, just like you." His glare softened. "But I do swear to you, Hyacinth Finch, that Geordi is in no danger from myself or Paolo. I promise."

Okay, then. The tension left my body and I grabbed Geordi's other hand. "Let's go, sweetie. We got us some new digs."

The hotel Jason and Paolo had chosen was a swanky one in the middle of Roman Trier, not far from Dom Saint Peter. They had a two-bedroom, one-bath suite, with a common area and kitchenette, plus a balcony overlooking the Porta Nigra. Their budget was clearly bigger than mine, and I wondered if being a demon paid that well or if it was standard Dioguardi loot.

Either way, I probably didn't want to know.

Despite my misgivings, the transition to a larger group was a snap. Or maybe it wasn't so amazing. I'd forgotten Geordi knew Paolo, not only from their time together in Turkey, when Jason took Geordi from me, but also due to Paolo visiting Nick and Lily often in Paris.

The first thing he said when I walked in was, "Sorry about your sister." Except he said it in Italian, so it sounded flowery and sympathetic: "*Partecipo al tuo dolore per la tua sorella.*"

He was handsome as ever, with the infamous Dioguardi black hair, short and neat, and blue eyes. He resembled Geordi less than Jason did, as he lacked their long, lean build, instead sporting muscled arms and a broad chest. He wore a faded-green t-shirt, belted jeans, and scuffed sneakers. His boyish face was marred by a nasty scar or two, as was his arm, presumably from when he got shot while shooting Eric. I put him at around twenty-five; he didn't *look* like someone who wanted to die, especially not from the way he was checking me out.

Jason glared at him, but Paolo only grinned and

winked at me. He ruffled Geordi's hair with a "*Ragazzino!* Long time," then peered nearsightedly to where Eric hovered—figuratively—in the background.

Jason had explained that Paolo was sort of a demon "lite." The blood hadn't manifested until he was nineteen, which is almost as rare as Geordi's pre-puberty scenario, but with the opposite effect: very low concentrations instead of high ones.

So Paolo had some demon abilities, but at a lesser strength than his cousin had, even before Jason stole his Rousseau juice. Which amounted to Paolo knowing Eric was present but being unable to see or hear him.

I gestured to the appropriate spot, and he lowered his gaze, peering hard. "If you say so. I thought he was taller." To the air near Eric he said, "Sorry I shot you."

Eric gave one of his Gallic half-shrugs and said, "*De rien*," neither of which Paolo saw or heard. Geordi, watching them, translated before I got the chance.

"He says it's nothing. Why did you shoot him?"

Paolo squatted to Geordi's eye level. "Grown-ups do dumb things sometimes. I didn't want to, and I guess he knows it, so we're good. Speaking of shooting, remember that video game we played in Turkey?"

Geordi's eyes lit up. "The one where you have to kill the aliens?"

"That's the one. It's here. Wanna play it with me?"

Geordi jumped up and down, squealing with excitement, at which point Paolo caught my frown and looked chagrined. "Sorry—your sister let him play some of the non-violent games, so I thought it would be okay. When he, uh, visited me and Jason in Turkey, I wasn't, uh, expecting him."

He was working so hard not to say *when my cousin*

kidnapped your nephew that I relented. "Never mind, I get it. You had to occupy him, and I'm sure you play everything out there."

Jason cut in, "We didn't let him play anything gory or too violent. The game Paolo's talking about has a ten-and-under setting. It's more like the old Space Invaders from the eighties. Little spaceships and asteroids dropping from above, and you shoot them with lasers."

"No blood?"

"None," Paolo said. "And the graphics are cheesy."

"Fine."

Geordi ran to the couch, and I thought, Fun Demon Cousins—*one*, Formerly Fun Aunt Who Is Now His Parent—*zip*.

In truth, I wasn't opposed to video games. I just didn't own a console myself, and like so much else, it was low on my priorities list. Watching Geordi fire up the system and expertly navigate the menus, I thought he must have that natural, next-generation tech-savvy so common in kids his age. I'd have to buy a system when we got back just so he could keep pace with his peers.

Which reminded me: I hadn't figured out what to do about school or anything else for him yet. But I couldn't make those decisions today, so I followed Jason out to the balcony where we sat at the small metal table, while Eric lounged against the railing.

"Okay," I said. "Spill it. Why do you think the Burkes are devil worshippers?"

Eric's head jerked up and his eyes narrowed, and I suppressed a twinge of anxiety at his sudden interest. I was being ridiculous, allowing Jason and his "agenda" speech to get to me. Eric simply wanted to know of this new development. Just because it also made him thoughtful and moody didn't mean anything. Hell, it made *me* thoughtful and moody.

"When Geordi and I were in the library," Jason said, "I happened to check out Heinrich's desk. You know, in case he left any loose rocks on it."

"Did he?"

"Nope. Not a damn one. But he did leave a book out. Maybe you've heard of it." He watched me closely. "The *Apophasis Megale*."

Eric started, his face going white. Another oddity of his ghostliness: he usually still appeared tanned, as he must have been on the day he died. Not now, though. His gaze slid guiltily away, and I looked from him to Jason.

"Say who now?"

Jason leaned forward, templing his fingers. "Okay. All right. You really don't know. But…your dead friend does. Maybe you should ask *him*."

Eric scowled. A tense moment passed, then he sagged in defeat. "Yes, I know of it. It is the *Great Declaration*, the writings of the Gnostic teacher Simon Magus, the Sorcerer. He was accused of founding all things that did not, *comme l'on dit*, suit the church's idea of Christ. Some called him a demon in human form."

Jason's tight lips telegraphed *touché*, so I cut in before the testosterone level rose any higher. "Lots of people are interested in ancient history. It doesn't make them devil worshippers, even if they study the devil."

"Come on, Hyacinth. Think about it. You admitted this whole cockeyed journey has to do with finding rocks for your client, and it involves Satan. You can't possibly believe the Burkes are unaware they own a rock that's *wanted by the Devil*. Especially since you want it too."

Eric blinked. "*Mon ange*, you have told him?"

Jason's eyes narrowed. "Told me what?"

"Nothing," I said quickly, if unoriginally. And unconvincingly, from Jason's expression. Distraction generally worked with Geordi, so I tried it here. "I still don't see your point. Heinrich collects rocks. He's got an old book by a man the Catholic church doesn't like. How do you connect those dots and get devil worshipper?"

Jason hesitated. "I know it sounds circumstantial. It's just an awfully big coincidence."

"*Mon ange*," Eric interjected. "You know how I hate to admit this. But…your live friend may be right."

I don't know who was more surprised, me or Jason. Twice in one day, Eric had backed him up. If I wasn't careful, I'd be a third wheel on my own quest.

Eric continued. "You recall the little black rock I asked about? The one Heinrich said came from Wewelsburg Castle?"

Jason's gaze sharpened, and a look passed between them. It said, *She doesn't know, but we sure as hell do.*

"What? Enough cloak-and-dagger. Get to the damn point."

Eric pushed off the rail and knelt in front of me, taking my hand. I was hyper aware of Jason's gaze and tried not to flinch. I'd made my choice, and so had he.

"*Mon ange*, Wewelsburg was a Nazi stronghold, home to a sect known as the Order of the Black Sun, a racial cult, based on pre-Christian pagan beliefs. There are those who believe the Nazis followed the teachings of the Order far more than those of Christ."

"Well, duh. Everyone knows the Nazis weren't all full of love and tolerance. That doesn't—"

"You recall the first time we met Frau Burke, *ouais?* The belt she wore?"

Reluctantly, I nodded. "The buckle was black with a dozen crooked spokes coming from a central point. Like a sun, I suppose. It's also on their doorknocker."

"*Le Soleil Noir*. As well, it is found on the floor of Wewelsburg Castle, only in green. The spokes incorporate the swastika, among other symbols. I suspected when I first saw it but did not wish to leap to any conclusions. In France, we remember better the horrors of the war. For you Americans, it is more distant. Still, I forebore to blame the Burkes for the sins of their ancestors, even knowing they possessed a rock that came from the Plutonium. But…"

He squeezed my hand for emphasis, though I couldn't possibly have paid closer attention, riveted as I was. "*Mon ange*, I am afraid I have put us—you—in danger."

"How? They didn't even know you were there."

"That is true. But I believe Heinrich displayed that shard on purpose, *comme un test*, and by my asking about it, they now believe you understand its significance."

Eric's expression had gone über grim, and beside me, Jason was so tense, he could've cut diamonds. "What *is* its significance? Why were—are—you so interested in it you'd call attention to it like that?"

"Unless I am mistaken, it is from the crozier of Saint Peter, the staff that raised Maternus from the dead. Some of it was preserved in Trier for a time, then Prague, and then it was broken apart and sold in the eighteenth century. Before the war, Himmler collected as many pieces as he could and sent them to Wewelsburg, to be distributed amongst the highest officials of *l'Ordre*."

"I thought you said the staff was at Saint Matthias'."

"Yes. A piece which was preserved at Cologne until

a few years ago, then presented to Trier upon the inauguration of Bishop Marx. The remainder could be anywhere, including at the Burkes'."

Jason said impatiently, "Get on with it. Why is it important *now*?"

Eric grimaced but continued. "Due to the actions of Saint Eucharius, it is believed the pieces of the staff can restore life to those who have died." He dropped his gaze to my hands, still clasped in his. "It helps if one's body is available, but if not, other arrangements can be made."

At first, I didn't get it. Or rather, I *thought* I did. He wanted to regain his life. He was in an impossible situation, and he wanted to fix it. Hell, that was probably why he was so interested in Eucharius' tomb in the first place. I'd thought it was for me, so I could be permanently alive, but instead, he'd meant it for himself.

Then the last thing he'd said sunk in. "What does 'other arrangements' mean…?"

He didn't raise his eyes, and he didn't answer.

Jason broke in, quiet, serious. Concerned. "It means the Dead can take over someone else's body in certain situations. Your *friend* here was thinking that if he found one of the newly dead and their corpse still together…"

I jerked my hands from Eric's grasp, and he looked up. I wanted him to deny it, to say he would never do something so abhorrent. But the sadness in his eyes told me he'd considered it. And perhaps wanted to try it.

I stumbled to my feet, knocking my chair over, and hurried inside. Geordi and Paolo still sat on the couch, blowing up pixelated aliens. There was nowhere to go—I had to wipe the shock off my face before Geordi saw it.

"Bathroom," I mumbled, keeping my head down.

Then I fled.

Chapter Fifteen

*Body and mind, like man and wife, do not
always agree to die together.*

*~Charles Caleb Colton, English Writer
(1780-1832)*

Next day dawned dreary and dark, like the weather
knew it was Halloween and had planned accordingly.
After I'd had a short but effective cry in the bathroom, I
came out to find Paolo'd gone to get dinner, and Jason
and Geordi were playing some sort of game that involved
throwing rolled up socks at each other.

Fun Demon Cousins—*two*.

I pushed down my jealousy and headed for the
balcony, seeking Eric. It was empty, and when I asked
Jason, he said, "He left after Paolo. Didn't say why."

The implication that Eric had left to pursue his
nefarious purpose hung between us. But with no one to
occupy Geordi, we couldn't chat, so I sat on the sofa and
tried to ignore the socks flying everywhere. At least
Geordi didn't want to play video games *all* the time.

Then Paolo returned, bearing Big Bags O' Meat.
Okay, it was in sandwiches, but they were all hot and
greasy, making me half-orgasmic while also repulsing
me. Jason either forgot to mention I'm a vegetarian or
else he thought I needed the meat. And damn him, I *did*
feel better after snarfing one of the biggest, greasiest

concoctions. My arteries might hate me later, but in the moment, my blood thrummed with life.

But by the time Eric wandered in, my meat-high had crashed. It was Zürich all over again, except where Geordi'd had no idea Eric was there, Paolo did know, but couldn't see him. So he kept jerking to the side as though avoiding Eric when they weren't even close.

I should have appreciated Paolo's consideration, but feelings rarely follow the "rules," so instead it irritated the crap out of me. And when Paolo finally sat down, it was to play another round of shoot-'em-up with Geordi. I had to give up my spot on the sofa or be bombarded with cartoon aliens exploding all over the TV.

All in all, it was a relief when Jason and Paolo holed up for the night. Geordi, of course, stayed with me in the second bedroom, so Eric stretched out on the loveseat nearby, and that was it. Lights out.

Except I tossed and turned and half dozed all night, until giving up at dawn. Leaving Geordi sacked out under the covers, I padded to the window and opened the drapes on the dismal, wet, cold start to the day.

"Perhaps there will be no trick-or-treating, at least," Eric said softly. He watched me from the sofa, looking tired and rumpled and vulnerable.

Who was I to judge? At least I had a body, and a purpose, however impossible it might seem at times.

He moved his legs aside and I sat next to him.

"I am sorry I did not tell you," he said, staring at his hands. "I do not even know if it is possible. I thought perhaps you could accept it more readily if I already…"

He trailed off, and I supplied, "If it was a done deal?"

His lips twisted in self-deprecation. "I suppose I imagined surprising you by showing up in a real body."

"That certainly would have been a surprise." I paused. "Is having a body so important? I can see, hear, touch you, as you are now. Is it worth whatever it might cost, just so the rest of the Living can do the same?"

"I do not know. I think it may be."

"What, exactly, is the process?"

He took my hand, his fingers warm, his grip strong, and I experienced another disconnect. I *knew* he was dead, but he felt so real, so *alive*. Was I crazy? Had I somehow imagined this whole thing? Then he spoke, and the moment passed. I couldn't invent the pain in his voice or the darkness in his eyes.

"I am not sure. What I read is vague, perhaps from fear of retribution, or because *les auteurs* did not know. But *hier soir*, I returned to Saint Matthias'. They have a written history of the legend, including notes culled from many sources. There is a good deal on the so-called research performed by *l'Ordre du Soleil Noir*." He hesitated. "Are you certain you wish to hear this?"

"No. But I think I should. You owe me that, at least."

He nodded reluctantly. "You have heard how *les Nazis* started as, *essentiellement*, a cult dedicated to neo-pagan arts? And that Himmler had a lifelong interest in the occult?"

"I'm no expert, but I know he dabbled in it."

"These writings detail a much deeper purpose. *Mon ange*, many officials are buried at Wewelsburg Castle. Himmler wished to preserve them, so that after the war, he could bring them back to life."

I was speechless. Then I thought of my own situation. Maybe Himmler wasn't so wacko after all.

"But...how?"

"I do not know. According to Himmler's notes, he

thought the pieces of Saint Peter's staff could be used like keys, in combination with…other powerful relics. That the two items, together, could reverse the effects of death and restore life."

He paused, and I exhaled. "Michael's rocks."

"*Ouais.* Among other things."

Odd that I hadn't thought of it before. Michael had restored my life, and his powers were in the rocks, so it made sense. "And the keys? How do they work?"

"Himmler believed they allowed men, saints and mortals alike, to tap into and use the relics' powers for good…or ill. He thought that, by preserving the Nazis' corpses with their spirits, he could later find fresh bodies for them to inhabit. And also that there is a window of opportunity, after *l'esprit* vacates a corpse, when, if another soul is present, a…deal may be worked out."

I stared at him. "Are you saying you can *sublet* a corpse?" I swallowed the hysteria. This wasn't funny— it really wasn't. "I'm sorry. It's just…I'm glad you have to ask permission."

"It is not mandatory. A formality only." That sobered me. He lifted a shoulder. "*Ça ne fait rien.* The point is, *le plus frais le cadavre*, the easier the ritual. If the original soul is absent, but the body has not lain too long, it is still possible. I believe the thinking is up to one day, *pas plus.* After that, the body is…tougher, to inhabit."

I paused. "You mean more difficult—*plus difficile*— right?"

"*Non.* I mean what I have said. The body is tougher—*plus résistante*—the longer it is left out."

I shuddered, and he shifted so that I lay against his side. I put my head on his shoulder, cradled in his arms, his fingers laced with mine, and felt reassured.

"*J'ai pas dit que c'était agréable*. As for what happens with the brain, how long it has gone without oxygen, I do not know. We have all heard stories of the fallen, miraculously revived when no pulse was present for some time. Perhaps they are merely corpses who have been, as you say, sublet."

Creepy. I swallowed. "How would the original soul stop the new one from moving in?"

"Again, I do not know. This is all speculation, for *l'Ordre* never knew if their experiments succeeded." His arm tightened around my shoulder. "I will *not* tell you what they did, attempting to prove their theories. I will spare you that at least."

"Thank you," I said, and meant it.

He nodded, the brush of his jaw gentle on my hair, and entwined as we were, a current of heat shot through me. I moved against him, the slightest of frictions, but he felt it and kissed the top of my head, then sighed.

"*Mon ange*, you say I am as real to you as if I had a body. But perhaps it is that I am not real enough…for myself. If there is a chance I can remedy that, I must try."

He'd thought this through. And really, was it any different from what I'd done? At least I'd landed in my own body. But it was empty for a while. What if I'd come back to find it occupied?

I hadn't considered it before, but…how "fresh" was I when I jumped back in? *I* knew where I was that whole time, so I never considered myself a corpse. But anyone who happened by, alive *or* dead, would have thought of me so. Why not move in? For a soul seeking a body, housing must be scarce.

Put another way, was it any different than an organ transplant? Sure, it was a whole body. But if the owner was willing to donate, or gave tacit permission in absentia, why should it weird me out? I'm sure the Nazis didn't ask the old or the new, spirit or corpse, what they wanted, but Eric wouldn't force anyone.

I said, "But…are you sure you want to stay here? I've offered before. I can call Michael down, and—"

He pulled me close, his mouth demanding as his tongue teased my lips. I opened to him, sliding my tongue into his mouth in a possession of my own. He groaned, angling his hips until he found the right spot, and it felt so good, so *right*. Being in his arms, holding his head in place so his mouth wouldn't leave mine, I knew if he chose to find a body, I wouldn't stop him.

Eric broke the kiss, eyes dark in the weak light from the window. "*Mon ange*, I never want to leave you. Do you understand? If I find someone—I—"

I shook my head. "It doesn't matter. I don't want to know. As long as you—the *real* you—so long as that doesn't change, I'll accept your decision. I'd prefer if you ask the guy first. But I can't tell you what to do. God knows, I can barely figure it out for me and Geordi."

He trailed his thumb lightly along my jaw, then the sensitive skin of my neck. I shivered with pleasure, beyond caring what form he was in, so long as he kept touching me. He groaned, pushing his heat into me. He fisted my t-shirt, twisting it tight, the rough fabric an agonizing friction against my breasts. He took my mouth in another swift, hard kiss, before forcing himself up onto his forearms to gaze tensely down at me.

"*Mon ange*, you must hear the rest. I do not know if this is even possible. I must find a man's body, and it must not be so old or infirm that we cannot be together." I opened my mouth, and he pressed a thumb on my lips.

"*Non. Écoute-moi.* It could be months or years, or never. *Puis*, if I find someone suitable, I still do not know what must be done in order to…move in."

"You're saying it won't be today?"

He nodded, and I didn't know whether to be relieved or, like him, frustrated.

"There is more. That person will most certainly have friends and family. Perhaps a wife, children. Once inside, I do not know if my memories will be my own…or his."

"Jeez." At least he wasn't sugarcoating it. Then a thought struck me, something I should've asked before. "Did you have a wife—or children—before you died?"

He hesitated, a flash of pain in his eyes. But all he said was, "*Non.* I have not lied about the women I have been with. But I did not stay with them. *Ou bien*, not for long. Not as I wish to stay with *you*."

As declarations went it was pretty minimal, and I couldn't help thinking he'd omitted critical details. But with his chest covering my breasts, his arms protecting me, it was enough for now. And then he *pulsed* his desire to me. The solid warm thread of him grew stronger and brighter in my mind, filling me until it was everywhere, but especially *there*, as though he were physically inside me.

I gasped and arched into him, twining our threads, sending my own desperate desire back to him, the possessed in turn possessing. He ground into me, pulsing stronger, bigger, faster, and I couldn't tell what was outside my body and what was in. I wanted him to reach for my undies, to pull them down and slide into me—*all* of him—but then I heard a noise on the bed.

Eric heard it too. He drew back, his thread instantly gone. I ached to pull him back, sink further into the couch, *finally* finish what we kept starting. Luckily, our non-sexual senses returned in time. He shuddered once, then twisted up and off as I scooted away, and we faced the bed as Geordi sat up, stretching blearily.

I drew a relieved breath, not entirely because we'd escaped detection. For in that moment, when Eric was startled, unable to shutter his expression in time, I'd seen a bleakness, a soul-deep desperation that even I hadn't suspected. Exposed, raw, there was a hunger in him for…something. I wasn't sure it was for me.

At that intensity, I hoped not.

###

We pulled up in front of the Burkes' later that day, a silent group, each lost in our thoughts. We'd debated who would come and who would stay at the hotel. I wanted to go by myself and have done with my mission once and for all. Neither Jason nor Eric would agree to that, and Geordi had his heart set on trick-or-treating, so we finally decided we'd all go—safety in numbers—and leave Paolo to man the fort.

I didn't feel great about returning at all. But I had to get Michael's rock, especially after Eric's intel on the key shards. I wasn't sure the Burkes knew about the Wewelsburg shard, or for that matter, if Himmler was right about the keys. I may be biased by historical perspectives, but I tend to think Hitler, Himmler, and that whole bunch weren't exactly sane.

However, I still hadn't sensed the damn rock anywhere on the property, and I had no reason to believe I'd find it at the creek today. So I calmed my nerves, reassured myself that the Burkes weren't demons, and determined to get this over with.

Rachel had said we could come whenever we liked,

but by the time we'd showered, dressed, and eaten, it was lunchtime. Then we had to find a costume for Geordi. As noted, Germany isn't big on trick-or-treating, but he'd already read several of the Grimm's fairytales and promptly chose to be a witch. I couldn't argue with the ease of the costume, which consisted of a black pointy hat and robe, with a bare branch for a wand. But it still meant we didn't get to the Burkes' until after two.

Since my primary purpose was checking out the rock by the river, I glanced at the fading light—no sun poking through the heavy clouds—and herded everyone up on the porch just as Rachel flung the double doors open. Today, she wore her habitual green in the form of a diaphanous skirt topped by a white tunic and darker green vest. The vibe was vaguely Bavarian, but she'd added large gold earrings made from ancient coins, Roman or maybe Greek. In deference to our excursion, she'd completed the ensemble with black rain boots.

"You're here! I was about to give up on you!" She ruffled Geordi's hair. "I have cocoa and pumpkin pie and more *Weckmann*."

Geordi frowned. "And candy?"

She laughed. "Yes. Lots of candy." To me she said, "Heinrich is on an important phone call. If you like, we can go down to the creek to see his rock."

Smoothly, as though we totally didn't have another agenda, Jason said, "Would you mind if Geordi and I go back to the library? We had such fun poking around yesterday."

"That would be fine."

It was Jason's idea to split up. The discovery of the book by Simon Magus worried him, and I must admit, me too. I could stick to my theory that collecting rocks and odd books did not a devil worshipper make, but more than ever, my own antennae were twitching. Sure, the Burkes weren't demons. But Satan coveted Michael's rocks too, or I wouldn't be here. And keeping Geordi far away from anything Satan wanted seemed smart.

Moreover, Rachel taking me to the creek instead of Heinrich was a boon. Call me sexist, but I felt safer with a woman. Besides, Heinrich was the one who brought up the Nazi-castle connection, which seemed to displease Rachel. More points for her, and with Jason watching Geordi, I could hopefully get this all over with by dinner.

Of course, there was still the trick-or-treating, but I could face that with renewed energy if I'd finished my so-called "easy" mission. I still hadn't figured out where Rachel intended to take Geordi. If trick-or-treating wasn't common here, wouldn't the residents of the "village" be confused-slash-unhappy if we banged on their doors, demanding candy?

For his part, Eric opted to go with me. At first, I argued against it. Whatever I'd seen in his eyes still bothered me, though I felt it shouldn't. I'd accepted his plan to find a body, so why should a little desperation worry me? But he insisted and I caved, secretly relieved I wouldn't be alone with whoever took me to the river.

"Go on in," Rachel said to Jason. "If you don't remember the way, find one of the servants."

He nodded and they disappeared into the house.

"C'mon," Rachel said to me and led the way to a path that wound around the side of the house toward the back.

Everything was even more impressive from the outside: all aged stone and manicured shrubs. Though it was autumn, and the deciduous trees were half-covered in colorfully-dying leaves, not a single one marred the landscaping, and I wondered what salary Leaf Collector at the Burkes' earned. Maybe I could do that instead of working for Michael. It seemed much less stressful.

Around the back of the house, the path branched to the right and headed downhill. At first, it was well-defined, with a border of white rocks separating it from the neatly-clipped lawn. But when we began to hear the roaring of water ahead, it narrowed to a dirt track leading to a copse of fir trees bordering the creek itself.

With all the recent rain, we essentially walked in a tiny tributary. I tried the path's edge instead, but the grass made swampy sucking sounds and glommed onto my sneakers, so I gave up, wishing I had an umbrella.

Rachel didn't seem bothered by the weather. She glanced back every now and then to check my progress, always with the same cheery smile. After ten minutes, my own mood soured, and if not for Eric's reassuring presence behind me, I might've given up and gone home.

Eventually, we reached the trees, the "creek" now well and truly thundering nearby, though still not visible.

Rachel shouted over the roaring waters, "Nearly there—just past that bend!" Then she began walking even faster and disappeared around a curve in the path.

Eric sped up until he was next to me on the narrow track. "*Mon ange*, I did not realize we would be so far from the house. Do you not think it odd that Heinrich could not just bring the rock up from the creek?"

"Well, Rachel did say it was a large stone."

I didn't actually know, but I assumed most of Michael's shards were similar to the ones I'd found before, so no larger than an American football. If they were bigger, they wouldn't be "shards."

"I do not like you being here with Rachel by

yourself," Eric said as we rounded the bend into a clearing, with trees at our backs and the swollen Moselle in front of us, many yards wide and brown with mud. The sight that met our eyes surprised us both.

"We're not alone after all," I said under my breath.

This was an understatement. Dozens of Heinrich's "retainers" lined the banks in front of us, hard at work building sandbag barriers against the rising flood. I had no point of reference for how exposed the banks usually were, but I saw no span of dirt between the river's crest and where the grass and trees began. Plus, I was hardly an expert, but I didn't think this was the best spot for the wall. Shouldn't they worry more about flooding in open fields rather than this crowded copse?

Rachel spoke to one of the men, gesturing at a gap in the sandbags through which the Moselle had begun to trickle. The man nodded, then turned to several other men to pass on the message. The whole scene was chaotic and loud, with many men lifting, heaving, and throwing the heavy sandbags, and many more just standing around, awaiting instructions. Maybe they were on a break. But why here? Why not go somewhere dry, with Rachel's hot cocoa? Or better yet, whiskey.

Then all at once, I *felt* it: Michael's rock.

"It's here," I said excitedly to Eric, whose curious gaze had quickly changed to a frown.

"*Mon ange*—" He stepped toward me, but I'd already moved away, following the familiar tuning-fork disturbance in the atmosphere.

By the bank, near the gap Rachel had pointed out, stood a large, flat stone on which were arranged a half-circle of smaller rocks. In the center lay a thin, shiny black stone, resembling the one Eric had asked about yesterday. But it was the rock at the circle's crest which interested me. It was big, as wide as a soccer ball and maybe twice as tall, shaped like an obelisk, with one side sheared straight off, while the others were more jagged. Most importantly, I felt the vibrations coming from it.

I moved toward it, relief at having finally achieved my goal rippling through me. Rachel stood in front of the slab, unaware of my approach as she bent and picked up the small black stone.

"*Mon ange*—wait!" Eric's voice was urgent.

He hurried up behind me, and I sensed his fear, tangible and directed at me, but I was calm with purpose. Here was Michael's rock; I would retrieve it, and then we could go *home*.

"*Mon ange!*" he repeated, more loudly.

One of the men nearby glanced up curiously, and I made a *shushing* motion behind my back at Eric. Not that anyone could hear him, but still.

I reached the slab. Rachel stooped toward Michael's rock, aiming the black stone at a narrow indentation near its center. The rock started to shake. Imperceptible to anyone else, but I felt its shudders, as though it feared what she planned to do.

"Rachel," I said, touching her shoulder.

She whirled, eyes blazing, arm up, stone raised as though to strike me. Instinctively I stumbled back, bumping into Eric.

Except it wasn't Eric. It was the large, burly man who'd glanced up when Eric spoke, and he glared at me.

"I'm so sorry," I said, and Rachel gasped, dropping her arm and the black stone in apparent shock.

"*Hyacinth!*"

Eric's desperation penetrated my all-consuming

purpose, and I looked to where he stood a few yards away, surrounded by several of the idle workers. He regarded them nervously…and they eyed him back.

Shit.

Adrenaline, fear, you name it: they all surged through me at once. I rounded on Rachel. "What the hell is going on?"

"You tell me," she said. But before I could respond she shouted to no one in particular, "Seize her! *Now!*"

I tried to run, but I had nowhere to go. The river blocked me on one side, the trees and Heinrich's men on the other. I struggled, fought, heard Eric shouting my name, but the men—both the Living and the Dead— were too much.

Massive hands captured my arms, an iron grip trapped my legs. I was lifted, carried, the trees moved crazily across my vision. I screamed. There was no way Jason could hear me, but I did it anyway.

Something hard connected with my temple. Blinding white-hot pain exploded in my head, my muscles suddenly wouldn't obey. I shuddered once. Then the blackness came.

Chapter Sixteen

The earth belongs to the living and not to the dead.

~Thomas Jefferson, American President (1743-1826)

"It's an army of the Dead."

Jason's voice, coming from a muffled distance, sounded conversational. That seemed wrong, given what he'd said, but I couldn't pull my muddled wits together to figure out why.

"I know," Eric said.

He sounded closer, and as I came back to myself, I discovered my cheek rested on what must be his thighs, though I couldn't get my eyes open to check. Then I realized they *were* open, it was just too black to see anything. I raised my head, bumping it on Eric's palm, which he'd been using to stroke my hair.

"Ow."

"*Mon ange*, you are awake." He straightened and helped me sit up. "How do you feel?"

"Like I got punched in the head. But I'll live."

"*Merci à dieu. J'avais peur que…* But no matter."

I heard his relief and didn't add that even sitting made me dizzy and sick. He fumbled for my forehead, running his fingers over my skin and hair. I think he'd checked me over before and this was just for reassurance.

"There is not much blood, but you will have quite the bruise, I am sure."

He closed his arms around me, and I allowed myself a moment to hold and be held before extricating myself. I sensed his reluctance to release me, but he recognized my need for action. Or at least, taking stock. The blackness wasn't abating, so I felt around with my hands. We were on a dirt floor, damp and smelling of mold. The air was cold and stale, motionless.

I checked my pockets, but of course my phone was gone. Probably Nazi-loving devil worshippers wouldn't want me flashing a light around, or making calls from…

"Where are we?"

"Underground," Jason said from somewhere to my right. His voice was still muffled, but I thought it must be our enclosure rather than my hearing. His clothes rustled as he stood, his voice coming closer. "In a cellar below the castle. The walls are stone, the floor's earth. I paced it out. It's not big, maybe ten meters on each side."

"How long was I out?"

"Not long. An hour or so, I think."

Eric said, "They gave you some drops. I believe that is why you slept so long."

That explained the sour taste in my mouth. I stood, putting my arms out in front of me, and took a step. Immediately, I bumped into Jason, which I only knew because he was so much taller than Eric. He gripped my arms, steadying me, then let go. I missed the feel of him, which was so not what I should be thinking about that I snapped at him instead.

"Can't you magic up a light or something?"

"Hyacinth."

"I guess that's a no." I tried to sidestep around him

and tripped over his foot. His hand shot out again, and I shied away.

"It's okay, it's just me."

My heart hammered and I tried to relax. It was Jason. Just…Jason.

Only Jason.

Raw panic bolted through me and I jerked upright. "Geordi! Where is he?"

"With Rachel and Heinrich," Jason answered calmly.

Or maybe he wasn't calm; maybe it was suppressed fear and rage that made his voice so steady. Me, I wasn't even trying to stay calm. I pushed away from him, then swayed, dangerously close to passing out. I lowered my head, bringing myself back to consciousness by sheer force of will.

"We have to get him. How do we get out of here?"

"*Mon ange*—"

"No. Don't pacify me! *Tell me how we get out.*"

"Hyacinth." Jason's emotionless voice cut through my panic. "Geordi's safe. They won't hurt him."

"How can you be sure?"

"Why would they? He's just a child."

"What if they know about him?"

"They don't."

"You can't know that."

I couldn't breathe. Geordi, my sweet, innocent part-demon nephew, was in the hands of Satan's wannabe minions. I forced air into my lungs but the panic didn't budge. I was about to pass out—or vomit—or both.

Jason's hands found me, his fingers digging into my arms. I fought but he held on. "Hyacinth, listen to me. I doubt they know *I* have the blood. For Christ's sake, calm down. You think everyone knows, but honestly, most of the world has no idea about any of this."

"*Mon ange*, your friend is right. Truly, most of the Living do not believe in ghosts, let alone demons."

"But they're devil worshippers, raising an army of the Dead! They're—"

Jason squeezed my shoulders, strong and steady against my shaking terror. "All true, as far as I can tell. But I don't think Satan's aware of their adoration."

He sounded so certain. I drew a shaky breath, willing down the fear and nausea. "And you know this how?"

"Because if Satan had heard about the Burkes," he said bluntly, "they'd be demons by now. He'd never pass up anyone with the means and desire to help him, especially not people like Rachel or Heinrich."

Sensing I might not be about to lose it after all, he released me, dragging his fingers over my arms as he dropped his hands. I shivered at his touch, but thankfully, it was after he broke contact. He moved away, pacing, his voice toneless in the muffled dark of our prison.

"I don't know why they're raising an army for Satan, or what they expect in return. But it's obvious they have no clue what they're doing. They didn't even know they'd succeeded until you told them."

"What are you talking about?"

Eric moved closer, filling the void left by Jason's retreat. I don't know if his instincts were *that* good, or if he just saw better in the dark with his ghost eyes. Either way, his presence was reassuring, and I tried to concentrate on his words.

"Do you recall *la riviere?* You stumbled into one of the Dead. Rachel cannot see them and did not know they were there. When you spoke to him, she discovered that the army they have been working for is already here."

I was dumbfounded. "But—you mean they—"

I forced myself to take a breath, then another. Who knew breathing was so much work? I tried again.

"So they've been using Michael's rock, with one of those key rocks we talked about, calling up oodles of dead folk, and they had *no idea* it was working?"

"Who's Michael?" Jason asked, coming to rest a few feet away.

"Erm. Client."

Eric crackled with frustration, and without seeing him, I knew he wanted to lecture me on keeping secrets from Jason. At least as much as Jason wanted me to tell. Sometimes, I wished that in life Eric had been anything but a cop. Truth and justice were a lot to expect from a gal who made her living by lying and bending the rules.

"We don't have time for this," I said. "If the Burkes can't control the Dead Army they don't know they have, then how did you—Eric—get caught?"

At first, I thought he would insist I come clean. Instead, he said, "The Dead heard Rachel order your capture. It was obvious that I was your friend, so they took me too."

"You mean the Burkes don't even know they've caught you?"

I suppressed the urge to laugh at the cosmic irony of it all. At least I *knew* I was hysterical. That counted for something, right?

"Let's see if I've got this straight. They have an army of the Dead at their disposal, but they can't command it. They've caught me, presumably so I can be an intermediary, and without knowing it, they've snagged a ghost and a partial-demon into the bargain." Which brought up another point. I said to Jason, "And how did they get you—Jason—anyway?"

"They put something in the cocoa, but it didn't work like they expected. I could tell by the shock on Heinrich's face when he found me still vertical in the library. Also, he checked my cup and asked more than once if I'd drunk it all."

"Did you?"

"Yep. I also lied and said I'd drunk Geordi's too."

"Why?"

"Think about it. If he thought it would knock me out, and it didn't, he has to wonder why. I didn't want him or Rachel wondering about Geordi. Anyway, he called his thugs in when I had my back turned. They put on a pretty good show for Geordi, pretending you wanted me at the river. But Heinrich made it clear if I didn't cooperate, they'd hurt him."

Which brought us right back to what they did and did not know about Geordi, and how long before they figured out he could also communicate with the Dead.

I moved, arms out, until I found the nearest wall. "Never mind. None of this matters right now. We have to get out and find Geordi." I patted the surface of the rock, scrabbling in the crevices, searching for any indication of a passageway or other means of escape.

"We can't," Jason interjected. "There are no doors, the walls are solid rock, and the ceiling—it's a trapdoor—I heard them push something heavy over it."

Oh, God. I leaned my head against the cool stone. Part of me wanted to work my way around anyway, just to see if Jason and Eric had missed anything.

Eric.

I whirled until I thought I faced him. "Eric—you can dematerialize! Float up to the ceiling, or go through the wall, or something."

There was a pause, and when at last he spoke, his voice was low with disappointment. Or maybe shame. "I cannot. I have tried, but the Dead, they have tied me somehow. I can move about this cellar, but I cannot leave the floor."

I thought back to when he'd been made "full Dead" on a dark hill in Turkey not long ago. The Dead had tied him then too, with visible cords that held tight throughout the ceremony they performed on him.

"There must be a way to cut your bonds."

"*Non.* It is unlike anything I have encountered before. It is as though I am weighted to the floor." I heard the bitter irony in his voice. "As if I am alive, and gravity holds me back."

"Then we'll use our energy to break through the wall or open the trapdoor or something. Like we did in the Rousseaux's villa." I found Jason's hand. It was warm and strong and reassuring, and I fumbled until I had Eric's as well.

Eric's thread, ever present in the back of my mind, grew instantly stronger and brighter the moment I stood between him and Jason, touching them both. I hadn't even noticed how dim it had gotten, until touching Jason reminded me how strong the threads could be. I'd been so caught up in getting the rock from the Burkes, and before that, in adjusting to life in Zürich. Even though Eric and I were now…involved…I hadn't felt *this* connected to him since Turkey.

I couldn't think about it now, though, any more than I could focus on how connected I *did* feel to Jason, despite everything. My utterly bizarre romantic life would have to wait until we'd escaped and Geordi was safe. At this point, I didn't even care if we got the rock back. Satan could have this shard if it meant our freedom. Surely Michael would understand.

"Come on," I said to Jason. "Do what you did in Turkey—let's put our threads together and break free."

Jason squeezed my fingers and let go. "I'm sorry. It doesn't work like that."

"But we broke through a demon barrier! How the *hell* can this be harder?"

"Hyacinth. There has to be someone on the other side. At the Rousseaux's, Eric was outside the bubble of their spell. You found him, and I helped you, and together we attacked their spell from both sides at once. I'm sorry. It won't work this time. Besides, it's not even a spell. It's a plain old prison."

I was getting pissed off. "We can't just give up! What the hell good is being a demon, if you can't blast us out of here or do something useful?" I moved forward and jabbed him in the chest, startling him into an *oof!* and a stumble. "What exactly *can* you do? I thought the Rousseaux's powers made you *more* a demon. Why can't you *use* those powers, for God's sake?"

I raised my arm again and somehow, he knew where it was and caught my wrist in an iron grip. "God damn it, Hyacinth! It's not like that!"

"Then tell me what it *is* like!"

His voice was hard with frustration. "I'm human, okay? I keep telling you, the blood, it's not like being a full-on, Satan-made Demon. We can't use magic. At least, not like what you're asking me to do."

He blew out a breath, its warmth caressing my face, and despite it all—being locked underground, with Geordi God knows where, and Eric six feet away—

despite all that, I remembered the feel of Jason's mouth when he kissed me, the taste of him as we explored each other's depths. His grip tightened and he pulled me subtly closer.

He remembered too.

Abruptly he let go and moved away. "You want to know what it's like, being part demon? It sucks sometimes. Hell, it sucks most of the time. I can sense things—Satan's energy when he's near, or when another demon is. But usually, I can't do a God damn thing about it. Worse, he—they—can feel me too. It's like I've got a big fat target on my head, a fucking Hell tattoo, marking me forever, making people like you think I'm evil or damned or whatever the fuck it is you think about me."

"Jason—"

"You asked," he bit out. "Let me finish. Because that isn't all of it, and I sure as hell don't want your pity. There's good things too. Things I *can* affect, like helping you in Denizli. Or Geordi. Or what I've done for the Dioguardis."

"What do you mean, what you've done?"

"No. Don't ask me to tell my secrets, when you won't fucking trust me with yours."

"You're right, I *don't* trust you." We were right back where we'd been in Denizli, neither of us willing to speak the truth. Now it was my turn to pace, frustration at being trapped boiling up and out, spewing all over one of the few people who could help me. "But it's not because you're a demon. For God's sake, Geordi's one too. I'm not *that* hypocritical. It's because you lied *and* took him from me, and are *still* working with the Dioguardis—the very people I'm keeping him from. Why in the name of anything would I trust you?"

"*Mon ange!*" Eric's excited voice startled me. I was so intent on Jason, I'd forgotten he was with us. "Your nephew—he is on the other side! Could we not use his energy to break through the trapdoor?"

Sudden bright hope wiped out all previous anger, and I said to Jason, "Could we? You keep saying how strong the blood is in him. Could we connect with it and use it through him?"

Jason blew out a breath. Probably, like me, he was shoving our squabbles aside until we could get out of this mess. "It's possible. If we could find his thread and take hold of it, we might be able to direct it from in here. But it's too dangerous."

My heart sank. "Why?"

"Ignoring the fact that he's seven, completely untrained—unaware even that he *needs* training—taking none of that into consideration, and assuming he was able to help us, it could get him killed. Or worse."

"How?" I didn't really want to know, but I had to ask. I needed the facts, and Jason could provide them.

"The Burkes aren't demons, but they *do* want to contact Satan. Based on what I saw in Heinrich's library, they're using some pretty wacko texts—seriously weird shit, that no real demon would touch with a ten-foot pole. If we try to link with Geordi, at the very least, we'll announce our presence—*and his*—to any other demons in the area. Maybe even to Satan. I doubt he'd come himself, but he might send one of his High Demons. And, if the Burkes figure out what Geordi is, you can *bet* they'll use him as a bargaining chip."

Despite my own experience with High Demons and an open pit leading to Hell, Satan was still an abstract concept for me. But Jason spoke of him like a tangible being. I don't know why that surprised me. Wasn't Satan, like Michael, just another angel? If I could see and touch Michael, why should the Devil be any different?

And then I had one of those *well, duh* moments where I wanted to smack my head and punch a wall besides. Instead, I shut my eyes, though I hardly needed to in this godawful blackness, and thought Michael's name.

Nothing happened.

Michael, where are you? I need help, damn it!

I waited a few more seconds. Still nothing.

Eric must have realized what I was doing. He said in a low voice, "Anything?"

"No. It's like something around us keeps the call from getting out."

"What are you talking about?" Jason demanded, but I ignored him, doing a quick mental inventory of my physical state.

My head was better, but the rest of me felt…suppressed. Like after drinking Rachel's cocoa. Not tired, but not awake, either. Not full, but not hungry.

Something tickled my consciousness. I remembered how Geordi and I both suddenly perked up at the Porta Nigra on the morning after the cocoa. I'd wondered then if the iron in the Gate counteracted whatever Rachel had given us. Back then, I hadn't thought the cocoa's effect was on purpose. How times change.

"Jason—you said something was in the cocoa. Any idea what?"

"How should I know? I'm not a chemist."

"I know. I thought maybe there's something people like the Burkes would *think* you need to avoid. Something unusual or, uh, surprising, from one of their wacko demon tutorials."

"You're forgetting, they don't know I'm a demon."

That brought me up short. "Right. Okay, they think you're human. So they gave you something that *should* have affected you. But, maybe because you *are* a demon, it didn't. Any idea what that could be?"

"You mean, what are demons immune to, besides the Eucharist?"

I heard the hurt in his voice. We were running the gamut on emotions. Even Eric, who still twitched and crackled nearby. I wondered if Jason sensed him. I pushed the thought away to ask him later. If he gave me the chance.

"I'm sorry. It could be important. Is there anything you can think of, that Heinrich might think would knock you out, but it doesn't affect demons that way?"

He was silent, then he said, "Not exactly. But the demon blood does give us high iron levels, which can interfere with other mineral absorption in our systems."

Now *that* was unexpected. And odd, given my own sudden needs. "So demons…what? Can't be poisoned by anything that binds to iron?"

"I'm really not sure. I've never been poisoned before, that I know of." He thought a minute. "I still don't get why they tried anything on you and Geordi right away."

Eric said, "*Mon ange*, you came to their door, interested in their rock collection, which contains stones from Hell's Gate, *et puis*, pieces of the staff Saint Peter used to raise the Dead. Perhaps they suspected you might be a demon. Perhaps they have used two different substances, one for you and one for your friend."

He found my hand again, gripping it in excitement. "You did not fall unconscious, but later, your nephew told Frau Burke the cocoa filled you up. She assumed you had not eaten and was disappointed to learn you had—that you had recovered so quickly—*n'est-ce pas?*"

He was right. At the time, I'd thought it was because she'd worked so hard—or the staff had—on preparing our feast. "So maybe they expected it to suppress my appetite for longer, but even though it didn't, the fact it affected me at all proves to them that I *am* a demon?"

"Perhaps. It would explain for them why you are able to commune with the Dead."

Jason said, "Then why drug her at all? Why not announce their intent and invite her to lead their army?"

"I do not know." Eric's tone conveyed his frustration, and I felt him give his standard Gallic half-shrug to accompany his words. "Perhaps they doubted her compliance, or wished to hold her hostage, to lure Satan from Hell."

Jason gave a low whistle. "If they think they can one-up Satan, they're crazier than I thought. Besides, he doesn't even know Hyacinth exists."

He was trying to reassure me, but it didn't help. He might not know the reason for it, but he knew I'd driven the Rousseaux back to Hell, straight to a presumed meet-and-greet with their master. No doubt they'd tattled right away that it was all my fault they'd lost Michael's rock.

"What about Geordi?" I asked. "He admitted the cocoa filled him up too. Won't they think he's a demon?"

"Probably not," Jason said. "It's likely they know nothing about our brand of demon, only Satan-made ones, and he has no reason to turn a child. Adults are much more useful. And anyway, Geordi told her you both 'got starving' in the morning. She probably assumes you fought off whatever she gave you, but for him, it wore off naturally."

"And you lied about drinking his cocoa today. So whatever they laced it with now, they wouldn't know it didn't affect him, and they won't suspect he isn't human."

"He *is* human," Jason ground out. "So am I."

"You know what I mean." I sounded flip, but in all honesty, I was more grateful than ever for his quick thinking and his care for Geordi.

Eric said, "Even so, we must save ourselves and your nephew. If we cannot link to Geordi, so be it. But there must be something we can do."

Jason hesitated. "There is another way. I don't know—it's risky."

"What?" Eric and I asked together.

"From what you've said, these rocks you're collecting—you've got some kind of connection with them right?"

"Yes," I said cautiously.

"If you can locate the rock from in here, I might be able to connect to it through you. The thing is, it would be better if—"

A loud scraping noise came from above us, as of something heavy being dragged across bare boards. With a groan and the creak of dry hinges, the trapdoor lifted, revealing a blindingly bright square of light. A shape moved into view, backlit so that her blonde hair formed a glowing halo around her shadowed face.

"Well, hello in there!" Rachel's sing-song voice floated down to us. "Time to come out and play!"

Chapter Seventeen

*The fear of death is the most unjustified of all
fears, for there's no risk of accident for
someone who's dead.*

*~Albert Einstein, German-American
Theoretical Physicist (1879-1955)*

The light in the cellar above was dim at best, but it still hurt my eyes. Someone lowered a ladder, and a couple of thugs climbed down to guard Jason, while a third grabbed me and pushed me roughly onto the rungs. Two of the Dead followed the thugs' example and floated down in case Eric needed restraining. Smart, given how hard he struggled to get to me.

"*Mon ange*, do not help them!"

One of the Dead punched him in the mouth, then the gut, and he doubled over. Jason took a half-step toward them and I cried out. His gaze snapped to me, and I shook my head subtly, hoping he'd get the message. It was all I could manage before the thug shoved me up the ladder.

"Climb!" he ordered, and I did.

I glanced down once more before I was through the trapdoor. Jason stood rigid, fists clenched, watching me and ignoring Eric. If he could keep the Dead and anyone else from realizing that he, too, saw them, it gave us an edge. Not much, but it was a start.

Then hands pulled me up, yanking me across the

floor to the room's exit. Four beefy guys herded me along, blocking my view. I didn't see Rachel, but behind me the trapdoor slammed, and I heard heavy scraping as the weight covering it was replaced. The men forced me out the door and up a dark stairwell. At the top, they pushed me through another door into a bright hall with green marble floors and wall hangings.

By now my eyes had adjusted, and I tried to get my bearings. This hall was unfamiliar, and the men dragged me along at warp speed, rounding corners and crossing more hallways, until my sense of direction was shot. Every chance I got, I checked for windows, but it was no use as the curtains were all drawn. No bright sun poked through to say, *Hey, this is West*, so I gave it up.

I recognized several of the Dead keeping pace with us, but I couldn't tell if they were the ones who'd just been guarding Eric. I hoped they were, so Eric and Jason were now alone and could formulate a plan.

Eventually, we came to a familiar hall, perhaps one we'd traversed yesterday on our way to the old kitchen. Today, we headed for a door at its end which one of the men flung open, and I was manhandled through, stumbling off the stoop into the yard outside. Someone kicked me in the back, and I faceplanted into the muck and slime, choking on the rotting leaves.

"Ah, you're here."

Rachel's voice was pleasant, friendly even, and I struggled up onto my knees, slipping in the mud. The sky was dark, and floodlights mounted on the castle walls cast the shapes in the yard into sharp relief. Late afternoon or early evening, then. We'd arrived at two, and the trek to the river and my subsequent capture couldn't have taken more than a couple of hours.

Allowing for my time in the cellar and our journey here, it had to be five-thirty or so. Well past sunset this far north.

As at the river, men swarmed the yard, many carrying battery-powered lanterns. They, at least, were probably alive, but who knew about the rest? I twisted until I saw Rachel, wearing the same winsome smile as always, just as if she weren't holding us all hostage.

"Where's Geordi?"

Her grin widened. "Oh, he's having a lovely time, carving a jack-o-lantern with Heinrich. They're eating candy and drinking hot cider."

"Not cocoa?"

She laughed. "Nope. Not this time."

"Where does he think I am?"

"Oh, you and your *friends*—" Her sly smile said she knew or had guessed about Eric. "—got busy down at the creek. I'm not at all sure you'll be done in time for trick-or-treating. Such a shame. I'll have to take your *nephew* around the village all by myself."

I pushed up, ready to launch at her despite the futility of doing so, when her words hit me. *"What did you say?"*

"The internet is a marvelous thing, wouldn't you agree? Last night, I suddenly wondered about Hyacinth Leclerc, living in France with her husband and son, and working as a, shall we say, art collection facilitator? Yet when I searched, I couldn't find you. So I tried you and Geordi together and found a *wealth* of information, about a poor, sad, missing little boy, the son of Nicholas Dioguardi and his wife, your sister, both deceased."

I stood frozen, rooted to the proverbial spot. *Damn, damn,* and *more damn.* Was her plan to ransom Geordi to the Dioguardis? Did she know who—*what*—they were? Or was she only making trouble for me?

And…did she know about Jason?

One of her henchmen stepped forward, a lean, muscled guy with dark brown hair, eyes, and skin. He held a big axe, reminiscent of Snow White's woodsman, who'd been tasked with offing her and bringing her organs back to her Wicked Stepmother. He said something to Rachel in German, and she responded in kind. I took advantage of her distraction to check my surroundings.

We were in a small yard enclosed by a low stone wall, probably the former kitchen gardens, although any vegetables or herbs were long since replaced by weeds. The lanterns bobbed crazily, making it hard to see, but at least the rain had stopped. It was cold, though. I wiped my muddy hands on my jeans, then pulled my sweater sleeves over my fingers and hugged my arms tight.

I considered calling for Michael, but then I wondered what he could do? He'd repeatedly said he had no truck with the living, and sadly, that's all the Burkes were. Besides, what if he saved me but couldn't help Jason or Geordi? And…Eric. I hadn't thought of it earlier, but if Michael did pop down, would he whisk Eric off to wherever he should have gone already?

Finally, the Burkes knew I conversed with the Dead, but they didn't know I kinda-sorta *was* dead. Inviting the Head Archangel to the party would announce that loud and clear, precipitating who knew what results.

In the end, I decided I needed more info first. That's me, and it sucks sometimes: I like knowing what I'm getting into. Except, evidently, when it comes to "hobbyist rock collectors" who are closet devil worshippers intent on…something.

Rachel had finished her convo with Axe Man, so maybe I'd finally discover what. He nodded once before stomping back into the house, and Rachel said to me, "Come, we need to get back to the river."

"Why?" I said without moving.

At her gesture, two men stepped forward and manacled my arms with their meaty fists.

"That's better."

She moved to the garden gate as the men pulled me along, her remaining goons following us. A few of the Dead dematerialized through the stone wall, while others floated over. Probably more came through the gate, but I could only catalogue those who telegraphed their deadness, so that's what I tried to do. Some regarded me curiously, but most ignored me, focusing on Rachel and wherever she was leading us.

Outside the garden, fog seeped from the nearby forest, its thick tendrils brushing against me, and I shivered in my inadequate clothes. Rachel strode purposefully ahead, flanked by two lantern bearers, while everyone else crowded around and behind me.

I couldn't make a break for it, so I asked, "What do you want with me?" The fog muffled my voice, making it eerily hollow in the night.

Rachel stopped, so we all stopped, and she threw a smile over her shoulder at me, her voice as dulled and lifeless as mine. "I think you know, but I'll spell it out." She nodded at my captors, and they shoved me forward so that I stumbled. The men flanking her stepped aside, and I fell in beside her as we began moving again, en masse.

"Run," she said conversationally, "and I kill Geordi."

I swallowed icy fear and nodded. So much for

bravado. I would never again criticize a victim for complying with her captor. I think of myself as strong and independent, but apparently, I'm *dependent*, on Geordi's well-being. I'd do anything Rachel demanded if I thought it kept him safe.

The lanterns' light barely dented the fog shrouding the trail, but while I stubbed my toes too many times to count, Rachel neatly avoided gnarled roots and jutting rocks as though it were daylight. "Heinrich and I are working on a little project. You'll help us finish it."

"What project?"

Was it my imagination or did her smile slip? Certainly, my partly-pretended ignorance must be irritating her by now.

"I know you can talk with the Dead. You will be the *Kommandant* of our army."

"What army? What are you talking about?"

We rounded the final bend into the clearing at the Moselle. Earlier, it had roared by, promising destruction to all in its path. Now, it oozed, its slow, murky depths more threatening, not less, as though it knew it would get us eventually, and not a damn thing we could do to stop it.

Near the bank, two bonfires raged, their grotesque orange glow flickering against the dank fog rolling off the river. Shapes milled about, but I couldn't tell how many or if they were dead. Immediately, I sensed the rock. It still lay on the slab above the half circle of smaller rocks, the "key" shard pointed at it. Except now it crackled with energy, like Eric when agitated.

Rachel and the men crowded me close to the fires, until my skin burned and I wanted to tear my sweater off.

"Don't play dumb. You will command the army that

you showed me is here." Rachel's sweeping gesture encompassed the mass of foggy shapes, her eyes blazing in the hellish light. "You will do it in the name of Satan, or little Geordi will pay."

She had me, and she knew it. But maybe I could stall her while I came up with a plan. "Why are you doing this? What can you possibly hope to gain?"

She lifted a shoulder. "We have wealth and prestige. But Satan can provide things no one else can."

"Such as?"

"His power."

"You mean power in general."

"Not at all. I mean what I say: *his* power. When he sees the army we have raised for him, he will let us feed from him so that we may do his work in this world."

I tried to wipe the astonishment from my face. She was crazy—full on whacked—if she thought Satan would give her his power. Even *I* knew better than that.

"Come," she continued. "You know this already, or else why would you be here?"

"I don't understand."

"Didn't your *boss* send you here to vet us?"

Forget the dumb "act"; now I was genuinely confused. Did she know about Michael? But if so, why would she think he'd want to help them?

She studied me in the popping firelight. "It's not important. *This* is important." She stepped back, raised her arms, and called loudly, "All ye Dead who we have raised, hear me now: I have brought you forth, and it is I whom you will obey. This woman"—she indicated me—"will speak for you. Let your leader use her as a channel. I am waiting—I would hear your words!"

I gasped, staggering back into someone whose heavy

hands clamped on my shoulders. I shook him off, but there was no escape in the crowded clearing. Dead or alive, it made no difference. The very state that made Eric so real to me made all the Dead just as solid.

"You're insane. There is no way I'm letting one of the Dead take over my body."

"I don't believe I gave you a choice." She signaled the man I'd bumped into—guess he was alive after all—a beefy skinhead with dark, beady eyes. He twisted my arms behind my back, and I couldn't break free.

"Shh," he murmured in my ear. "Better do what Mistress says, Princess."

Like Heinrich, he sounded faintly British. He rubbed his unshaven chin against my cheek and I cringed. His breath smelled of alcohol and stale cigarettes, and I fought down the bile that rose with my panic.

Rachel raised her voice again. "Come! Be not afraid! I have brought her here for your use. Make yourself known, that we may begin the work I have planned."

A shape detached from the fog, and this time I knew he was dead. Recently so, from the blood dripping down his face. He turned and I saw his skull was bashed in. I shuddered, but he was beyond physical help now.

"Frau Burke," he began, then continued in German, which I couldn't understand and she couldn't hear.

She demanded avidly, "What's happening? Speak!"

I shook my head, and Smoke Breath dug his fingers into my arms. "Relax," I said. "I'm not going anywhere."

Rachel's face contorted. "Why are the Dead not using you?"

"How the hell should I know?"

She slapped me so hard my head slammed into Smoke Breath's shoulder. He laughed and grabbed my chin, pressing his fingers into my windpipe.

"Let her go." Rachel's tone brooked no argument, and he released me. I coughed, sucking in air and clutching my bruised throat.

"What I wonder is, are the Dead incapable of using you, or do you somehow deny them?"

I managed a rough, wheezing croak. "I…told you. I don't…know…anything…about this."

"And yet you speak to them, can touch and be touched by them. How is that?"

What should I tell her? What would she believe, that would give me an advantage? Or more to the point, endanger us all the least?

"I don't know," I said at last.

"You lie!"

I read the frustration in her zealous eyes and doubted she was stable in the best of times. I still felt the rock's energy; maybe I could connect with it and use it to break Jason and Eric out. It was risky, and anything I did now could get me killed. Again. But what did I have to lose?

Geordi, a voice whispered in my head, but I ignored it. I'd lose him in a far worse way if Rachel succeeded.

So first, I had to appease her. She glared at me, lips thinned, body tense. I held up my hands, palms out. At least my voice was stronger.

"Okay, all right. I can talk with the Dead. I'll ask them to speak to me, and then tell you what they say."

Rachel threw her head back and laughed, the sound sharp in the fog-muffled clearing. "So you can make up anything you like? No. Should I invite little Geordi to join us? Would that keep you from lying to me?"

"I won't!" Desperately I searched for a way to convince her. My gaze landed on the newly dead man.

"You!" He regarded me with suspicion, but he stepped forward. "I'm sorry, I don't speak German. Do you speak English?" He answered in German, which I took as a no. "*Parlez-vous français?*"

"*Un peu.*"

Some was better than none. "*Quel est ton nom?*"

"Hans."

I continued in French, "And how did you die?"

He grinned, showing tobacco-stained teeth. He bent his head, indicating the gash at the back. "My cellmate. He wouldn't give me his peas, so I broke his nose, *und* he bashed my head in with a shiv from a metal chair leg."

"Nice. When?"

"Today. He's here somewhere. After he hit me, I shoved *das* shiv down his throat."

If I did call Michael down, at least I knew where this guy should go. Still, I needed to stay on his good side, so I asked, "Er, why didn't you pass on to the afterlife?"

He shrugged. "Maybe I started to, then I was pulled here. Took me awhile to die. I passed out. Not sure what happened when I was alive and what was after."

Rachel had been listening raptly to my half of the conversation. I told her, "The leader of your Dead Army is Hans. He died in prison, after attacking his cell mate."

Her eyes narrowed. "How do I know that's true?"

I blew out an exasperated breath. "Look, I don't speak German beyond tourist basics. Ask him anything in German, and I'll give you his answer."

"In German. My question *and* his answer."

"Fine. If it makes you happy."

"Very well." She faced the spot where Hans stood. "*Wenn diese Frau tot wäre, möchtest du sie ficken?*"

Hans' eyebrows rose, then he burst into loud

guffaws, as did the men nearby. He gave me an evil leer before speaking his rapid-fire response to Rachel.

"*Attendez!*" I held up a hand. "*Pas assez vite!*" He slowed, speaking a few words at a time, and I tried to mimic him exactly. "*Ja. Aber ich…würde dich…lieber ficken. Sie ist zu…dick…für meinen Geschmack.*"

The men roared again with laughter, and Rachel smiled. "Good. *Very* good. You've done well." To Hans she said, "*Wir fliegen nach das Zentrum der neuen Welt in einem Hubschrauber. Wie werden die Toten reisen?*"

I really don't speak German, but the phrase *Zentrum der neuen Welt* caught my ear. Where had I heard it before? At the Porta Nigra or the Cathedral? Or maybe I'd read it in the guidebook?

Hans spoke and I repeated, "*Busse oder LKW am besten wäre. Wir sind zu langsam auf unsere eigenen.*"

"Very well," Rachel said. She murmured something to one of her henchmen. He nodded and ran off, and she said in Hans' general direction, "*Es wird getan.*"

We went on in this vein for a few more rounds, until finally Hans nodded, snapping his feet together and saluting just as you'd expect a soldier to do in the presence of his commanding officer. I wished Eric were here to translate. Both Hans and Rachel were awfully happy, which seemed like a bad thing for the rest of us.

"He salutes you," I said, and Rachel's grin widened.

"Good. Now I have another job for you."

She led the way to the slab with the rocks on it, Smoke Breath and Hans falling in behind, the remaining crowd parting before us. Watching who moved aside for Hans, I concluded a third of the Burkes' army were dead, or about twenty souls. Either there was a shortage of dead folk, or the Burkes were doing it wrong.

The closer we got, the more agitated the rock became. By the time Rachel stopped, inches away, it hissed and sputtered like water in a kettle. Rachel didn't appear to notice, but Hans eyed it suspiciously, as he did everything and everyone.

"Touch it," Rachel commanded.

I hesitated. Sometimes nothing happened when I touched the shards. At others, they screamed. Given how upset this one was, I anticipated the latter response now.

"Go on!" Rachel grabbed my arm and shoved my hand onto the rock.

The connection was instantaneous. The rock's energy, what I thought of as its "thread," surged to life. Except it was far beyond anything so insignificant as a puny little filament. It *thundered* through my veins, thick with molten heat, and I tried to snatch my hand away.

Rachel forced my fingers down, then grabbed my other hand and closed it over the key rock. Alone, Michael's rock was bad. Touching them both, my blood burned, my insides melted. I *felt* light streaming from my fingertips, for I certainly couldn't see anything.

Someone screamed. I think it was my voice, though it wasn't me—the *real* me—doing the screaming. It came from Michael's shard and the key rock, too much to contain, sound escaping out my eyes and nose and throat. I couldn't move, though Rachel no longer held me. My hands were glued in place, my feet cemented to the ground. My vision refracted, as if I looked through the heart of a diamond, and the screaming went on and on, until I thought my ears would burst.

Then just as fast, it ceased, my sight returned, and I sagged forward, exhausted, needing to throw up. My hands still grasped the rocks, but I couldn't tell if I was holding on for dear life, or if something forced them to stay put. I wanted to cry, but it didn't feel like *me* doing the wanting, and then yet another part of me got angry, but it was muted—again, me, but not me.

"Yes!" Rachel cried, and Hans tipped his head back and roared with victory.

Through the opening in the trees at the riverbank, the Dead poured forth, passing between the bonfires to join their comrades. Countless souls slipped through the fog, a trickle at first, then a stream, until hundreds of spectral forms flooded the clearing, jostling the Living, who reacted as though experiencing a sudden chill, shivering and peering uneasily around.

Once through, the Dead stood silent, waiting, apparently incurious as to how they'd got here or why. I saw a variety of cultures and time periods, mostly men, but some women, all wearing the same vacant and— pardon the word choice—dead expression. Not at all like Eric or the other souls I'd encountered to date. If I met this crowd on the street, I'd *know* they were dead.

"How many?" Rachel demanded.

I tried not to answer—resistance seemed important—but my mouth opened and a voice that wasn't mine spoke in an ancient tongue I somehow understood. *"Five hundred. More should you desire, but later. She will not survive it again so soon."*

Rachel's eyes glittered. "Very well. Enough!"

She clapped once, and my hands were freed and my knees buckled. I collapsed onto the cold ground, shaking, all thought of using the rock's powers for myself gone.

Rachel bent and spoke in my ear, her voice husky. "Now you see what it is to feed off Satan's powers, to drink from his cup. To use and be used by him."

She trailed a hand lightly over my cheek. I shuddered and tried to move away, but my muscles wouldn't cooperate. "Not...Satan," I managed.

"Oh, but it was." She brushed her thumb by the side of my mouth, and it came away red. Was I bleeding? Had...*whatever* that was...made me bite my tongue, or had all the screaming injured my ears? She licked her thumb, eyes closed in ecstasy, then opened them, staring at me dreamily. "Satan poured forth into you and you drank him in, like a dry sponge."

She arched her back, breasts straining against the white of her blouse, and nearly every man in the clearing, dead *or* alive, drooled with desire. Smoke Breath went so far as to lift a hand to touch her cheek. She smiled, leaning in to his caress while saying to me, "I don't know why you bother to deny it. You've done it before."

"No," I croaked, even that one word like a thousand knives inside my throat.

"Yes, you have. All demons do; it's where they get their powers."

No. She was wrong. I shook my head, shrinking from her, and she laughed.

"Hans said you didn't know. It's why the Dead are drawn to you, why when you touched your Master's rock and the key, you opened your veins to him like an addict to a needle." She smiled, her teeth eerily white in the orange firelight. "And now that you have let him in, you must do so again, and again, and again. If you do not, your veins will shrivel and your guts will be ravaged and your brain will want to crawl out of your skull."

She dipped close, her mouth hovering over mine so that her breath filled my nostrils. "You *will* feed off him again, as I will feed off you. It's what demons do."

Chapter Eighteen

*If man were immortal he could be perfectly
sure of seeing the day when everything in
which he had trusted should betray his trust,
and, in short, of coming eventually to hopeless
misery[...] In place of this we have death.*

*~Charles Sanders Peirce, American
Scientist (1839-1914)*

I didn't pass out again, but being dragged back to the cellar is a blur. It was Smoke Breath who dragged me, and he took the opportunity to nuzzle my neck and paw me with his dirty hands. He was too afraid of Rachel, though, to do anything else, which was good because I didn't have the strength to fight him off.

Plus, I was beyond nauseous, utterly revolted by Rachel and her insanity. What had Jason said? *Texts so wacko, no real demon would touch them.* I believed him.

We came to the room above the cellar and Smoke Breath paused, hands fisted in my sweater. "Be back for you, Princess." He bent forward and I cringed, twisting my head so that his tongue landed in my ear instead of my mouth. He laughed and licked my jaw, then gave me a rough shake. "Mistress says I get you when she's done. You'll want me then."

He shoved me to the floor, then removed the chest blocking the trapdoor and opened it, lowering the ladder.

I saw Jason below, shielding his eyes from the searing brightness, and almost cried with relief. Demon he might be, but in that moment, he was a welcome sight. Only finding Geordi safe would have been better.

"Get in," Smoke Breath ordered, and I climbed down, nearly falling onto Jason when the ladder was yanked up before I reached the bottom. Smoke Breath slammed the trapdoor and Jason and I were back in total blackness.

I stretched a hand out and found him, solid and alive, and before I knew it, I was in his arms, holding and being held, shaking and unable to manage coherent speech.

"Shh," Jason murmured into my hair. "It's okay. You're okay. I've got you."

I couldn't help it; I leaned into his warmth, his strength, *him*. In that moment, there was nothing between us except this. He tightened his hold, stroking my back and hair while I nuzzled into his neck, breathing him in, so warm, so *alive*, letting his scent of male sweat and something ineffably him flood my senses, the one thing I couldn't do with Eric.

Eric. I couldn't sense him—hadn't seen him when Smoke Breath opened the trapdoor. Panic reared and I pulled back. "Where's Eric?"

Jason stiffened and stopped caressing me, and the loss was a physical blow. It was too late, though. I'd inserted Eric between us, an invisible wedge guaranteed to drive us apart.

"I don't know. After you left, the Dead took him away. I couldn't see in this dark, but I heard him struggling."

I leaned farther back, wishing desperately that I could see his face. "But that's good! Now we have someone on the outside we can connect with, to escape."

Jason hesitated, which I took as not a good sign. Experimentally, I sent a thread out, searching for Eric's location. Everything was still muffled by whatever was in the prison walls, but I detected a faint spark of something so pale, I almost couldn't sense it. Or maybe it wasn't even him, just my wishful thinking.

Disappointed, I said to Jason, "What? Why can't we do what we did in Turkey?"

"Hyacinth. I felt you when you were up there. Connecting with those rocks. I know what you did with them. I…know what you are."

And there was the *other* wedge that tore us apart. I disentangled myself from his arms. "What's that supposed to mean?"

"Jeez. It's okay. It's not like I didn't suspect. Even after you denied it in Turkey, I had to wonder."

"For the last time, I am *not* a demon!" I sounded petulant, but I didn't care. After what I'd been through, he was *still* accusing me of being on the Dark Side.

"*Hmm*. Let's examine the facts. Sees dead people? Check. Has mysterious job involving Satan? Also check. *Uses one of Satan's own relics to raise an army of the Dead?* Check, check, and checkmate!"

Put that way, it did sound bad.

"You've got it all wrong. I didn't want to raise *any* of the Dead, let alone an army. And the rocks I need, they aren't Satan's. I'm trying to *keep* them from him, for God's sake!"

"If they aren't Satan's, then whose? Jesus Christ, Hyacinth, tell me the goddamn truth for once! Whose rocks are they? *Whose?*"

Even in the blackness, he unerringly gripped my

shoulders and shook me, and I shoved him in the chest.

"They're Saint Michael's! Mr. Big himself, the leader of the archangels, defender of the universe—the *one* dude who *really* knows how to kick Satan's ass!"

Jason was breathing hard. So was I. I couldn't believe I'd just told him, after all this time. Just like that. I found the nearest wall and slid down it, wrapping my arms around my knees, huddling against the cold stone.

"I have some kind of connection to the rocks. Michael needs them back, or Satan will steal his powers and escape from Hell. So you see, I'm not a demon. I work for *Michael*. I have no connection to Satan at all."

"Bullshit." His harsh tone was more startling than the word itself. I heard him walk toward me, then squat down, his voice suddenly level with my face. "*If* any of that is true, why the hell wouldn't you tell me before?"

"At first, I didn't want you to think I was crazy. You know, back when I *thought you were human*." He ignored the barb—so much for delay tactics—so I pushed on. "And now, after you came back, I didn't know what would happen if you knew. It's Michael's *job* to banish demons. I…didn't want to lose you again."

It was as close as I could get to admitting I *might* still have feelings for him, but he seemed not to notice. The silence stretched out, until he finally spoke, still quiet and calm.

"I don't know what you think you're doing. Maybe you really believe everything you just said. But that rock up there—the one you just connected with—that rock is Satan's and no one else's. You just used the devil's own powers to bring forth souls from Hell. If Michael really is your boss, I bet he's pretty pissed right now."

My jaw dropped. "You're as crazy as Rachel! That

rock is *Michael's*. It's a shard off the slab he split at Colossae, after evicting Satan from Heaven. The rocks still contain *his* energy, which Satan wants to *steal*."

"No. I'm a demon. Remember?" He gave a short, harsh laugh. "You certainly *never* let me forget it. But it's true. I can sense other demons, especially when they tap into Satan's powers." He fumbled for my hands, trapping them in an iron grip. "Hyacinth, if Michael and Satan fought at Colossae, and this rock slab got between them, isn't it at least *possible* that some of the shards have *Satan's* powers in them, not Michael's?"

If it wasn't pitch black, I would've stared at him. I finally yanked free and pushed to my feet. "No…"

"*Yes*." He rose also, blocking me. "That rock is Satan's. And it's entirely possible your connection to either set of shards is through him, *not* Michael."

"No! You say that because you *are* a demon. Why should I believe you any more than Rachel?"

I pushed past him with no idea where I'd go. I had to move, to get as far from him as I could in our little prison.

"Hyacinth, stop and *think* a minute. Geordi has demon blood in him—"

"I know, damn you! *You* never let *me* forget that!"

"Okay, but have you thought about this: *Where did it come from?* I told you, it's like genetics. Nick was a carrier. He got the recessive 'gene' only, making him non-infected, in your terms. He passed that gene to his son, but Geordi could not be infected, *only* by him."

He let the words sink in. I had thought about it, but put like this, in a pitch-black devil worshiper's prison, from the lips of the one demon I'd ever remotely trust, I couldn't ignore it.

Jason pressed on. "We suspected all along, as the

second copy of the gene *had* to come from somewhere. And if Lily was a carrier, she got it from one or both of *your* parents, which means *you* have it too. It has to be why you can sense the rocks and see the Dead."

It sounded so logical. Except he didn't know I was half-dead, with the likelihood of that causing at least some of my "symptoms." But the rest of it—*that* couldn't be true.

Could it?

I drew a deep breath, trying to think rationally, to take the emotion out of it. "But you said it manifests in puberty. If I'm infected, why wouldn't it show up until now?" Then something else he said struck me. "You *suspected all along?* What *the hell* does that mean?"

He took a long time to answer. I wished I could see his face; I had enough trouble believing him in broad daylight.

"I'm sorry, Hyacinth. I told you long ago you'd hate me when you learned the truth. I guess you already do, so I might as well tell you the rest now."

He sighed, and I heard him slide down a wall to sit on the ground. In spite of it all, I wanted to tell him how wrong he was about me hating him—*so wrong*—but I couldn't, and the moment passed.

"After Geordi was born, word spread that he might have the blood. It's something the Dioguardis watch for, including our sect." He paused, as though having trouble phrasing the next part. Even so, I wasn't prepared for what he said. "You know Paolo and I are working together. What you don't know is that we flipped a coin for our assignments. He got heads and stayed in Paris, to watch over Geordi. I got tails—and went to Marseille."

And there it was. The admission I'd known was

coming—had suspected ever since I figured out he was a Dioguardi. "Your *job* was to *spy* on me? You set me up—our whole friendship was a *lie*. You *bastard!*"

I moved in the direction of his voice, heard him scramble up just before I pummeled his chest. He grabbed my hands and turned us so my back was to the wall, his body covering mine. Touching him—connected in this way—it was so like when we were in Turkey that I sent another test thread out, searching for Eric. God, I needed him, now more than ever. If I could use Jason just long enough to find Eric and get us out, I'd make sure I never laid eyes on this particular demon, ever again.

There. A faint hint, tentative, a tiny thread of weak, uncertain energy. Not the strong, sure Eric I knew, but a faded, colorless copy. *What did they do to you?*

Jason gave me a shake, and the thread disappeared.

"Damn it, Hyacinth! I told you over and over you wouldn't like it. And yes, that's how I got to Marseille. But for the love of Christ, *it isn't why I stayed.*"

He loomed over me, breathing hard. I tried to twist away, and he tightened his grip.

"You wanted the truth. Paolo and I, our job *was* to protect Geordi, Lily, *and you.* Yes, it was random. But it was good he got Paris, because he was already close with Nick—already knew Geordi *and* your sister. And I'll *never* regret that I got you."

Suddenly, the fight left him. He relaxed his hold but didn't let go.

"Hyacinth—I—it's not what you think. We thought Geordi might have the blood, and Paolo suspected Lily was leaving Nick. We couldn't let Geordi wind up with that branch of the family. I came to Marseille in case Lily ran to you and either of you needed help. But after I knew you…"

His voice trailed off. We stood there, stuck in limbo in the muffled dark of the Burkes' prison. I shook my head, denying him, repudiating his words, and he slid his hands up my arms to cradle my face, brushing his thumbs over my cheeks, my eyes, my jaw. "*Hyacinth…*"

It was a plea, stark, desperate—and then he waited.

I could have pulled away. His touch was gentle, his emotions held rigidly in check as his fingers trailed lightly over my skin. He'd never force me, would take no part of me without my consent. Unlike Eric, who was so overcome with frustration that his passion boiled up and out. Not that *that* was against my will, either.

But this was different. Jason wanted me, and in the dark of our prison, with God knew what happening above us, he could have taken me. I mean, I'm a feminist and all, but he's a foot taller and a helluva lot stronger than me. There wouldn't be much I could do to stop him. But instead, he stood, eternally patient—so goddamn *nice*—giving me time to decide, to choose.

And it was *Jason*. My friend—we'd been so close— he'd done so much for me. Was it his fault he'd met me in the worst circumstances imaginable?

Hesitantly, I lifted my hands and found his face. At the first brush of my fingers he groaned, then leaned in to my touch. I caressed the rough stubble of his chin, the crooked bump of his nose that had been broken at least once, the strength of his jaw, the smooth firmness of his lips. Eric was all passion, emotion, everything on the surface. Ironic, given he didn't *have* a surface. But Jason…his control, the way he held himself back, powerful feelings tightly leashed, something about *that* was sexier than hell.

"Jason…" I whispered, and suddenly the choice was easy. I pulled him closer, standing on tiptoe to reach him.

That was enough consent for him, and the next thing I knew, our lips met, the kiss a surge of feelings we'd both suppressed too long. He slid his hands around my back, under my sweater, stroking my skin, letting his fingers say what words couldn't. Then he pulled me tight, a much less subtle declaration of his desire, as he kissed me harder. His scent filled me, musky and sharp, flooding me with heat, intensifying all my other senses, but especially taste. And oh God did he taste good. I tugged his shirt free, then slid my palms up his chest.

"Jesus—Hyacinth—"

He scooped me up, holding me against the uneven stone wall, as he delicately bit my neck, then licked the spot. I pinched his nipple, making him thrust hard against me. I arched into him, but it wasn't enough, and then his hand was inside my bra. My sweater was up, bra down, his mouth on my other breast, sucking, teasing with teeth and tongue, and in about ten seconds I—

The heavy chest above us scraped across our ceiling.

Jason's head jerked up. "*Shit.*"

We just had time to break apart and fix our clothing before the trapdoor was flung open, bathing us in enough light for me to get one quick glance at Jason's face before he turned away. He looked…shaken.

Good. That's how I felt.

This was a terrible time for *any* of this to happen. In a rush of guilt, I thought, *I'm supposed to be with Eric.* More, I kept forgetting the biggest problem: *I was dead.* Geordi needed me, and I had to figure out how to stay on Earth for him, before I thought about Eric *or* Jason. I needed time to process, to analyze and make informed decisions, and I didn't have it.

Instead, Smoke Breath leered down at us. "Mistress wants you again. And she says bring your friend too."

This time we were herded up from the cellar to find Rachel and Heinrich both waiting in the room above with a selection of Heinrich's "boys." I was pretty sure a few were dead, but no sign of Eric—or Geordi.

"Where is he?"

You'd think it was me asking, but it was Jason, and thank God for it. His quiet fury was far more powerful than my meager rage-screams could ever be.

Rachel's winsome smile didn't slip. She'd changed clothes since our escapade at the creek and now wore all black, from her cap-covered hair and turtleneck sweater to her standard-issue combat pants and boots. The only things missing from the "night ops" stereotype were infrared goggles and black leather gloves. Then I saw Heinrich's ensemble included both those items. So maybe hers were in her Gucci Special Ops bag close by.

She glided across the floor to Jason. "I suppose you mean that charming little boy we have upstairs. Hyacinth's nephew, yes? But...what is he to you, Mister...Jones?"

In that moment, *something* came from Jason. Not like Eric's crackling pops, nor even Jason's own "normal" thread of energy, which I'd connected with in Turkey. This was different, a white-fire flash radiating off every inch of him, so hot it burned my skin and seared my lungs. His eyes went black so fast, I almost missed it.

And then it was gone. His eyes were blue, and he was the cool, collected Jason I knew. I doubt Rachel noticed, and Heinrich was busy conversing with his also-black-clad men.

"Where is he?" Jason repeated, ignoring the fact that she'd discovered his true identity. Rachel laughed and stood on tip-toe to plant a seductive kiss on his mouth.

Though I knew what she was, knew he hadn't wanted the kiss, an unreasonable stab of jealousy shot through me. What was the matter with me? Almost having sex with Jason in the middle of this crisis, then getting *jealous* of another woman kissing him. Just to counteract my lingering guilt, I concentrated very hard, sending out one of my own threads and thinking, *Eric*.

At first, I got nothing back. Then all at once, that same weak thread I'd sensed earlier connected with mine. As soon as I touched it, it grew, but it was still slim, with none of the familiar irony he usually projected. Instead of a silver rope of energy, it was a thin wire, and that buried deep below the Earth's surface. Could the Dead somehow have damaged his energy?

I tried sending a sense of reassurance down the thread—*it will be okay*—but instead of reciprocation, I got back *how?*, followed by a pulse of sheer terror. Eric might be all passion and emotions where I was concerned, but he was pretty stoic about his own pain. Unless his anxiety was for me? I suppressed a shiver of my own panic and tried to secure his thread in my mind, so I wouldn't lose it again.

Rachel caught my eye and arched an eyebrow, like she knew I was up to something. Quickly I shuttered my expression, and she said to Jason, never taking her eyes off me, "Geordi is safe. And he will stay that way, so long as you play your parts."

She surveyed our disheveled appearances, which stemmed in part from our make-out session, but mainly from wandering around our dank prison and, in my case, the muck of the Moselle.

"You'll do," she decided. "We will go upstairs, and you will tell little Geordi you have been down at the creek this whole time. I'm sure he knows the *real* reason for your visit, so you can tell him your precious rock wasn't here after all, and you and Heinrich decided to check somewhere else. We will fly there tonight."

"Fly? Where?" I asked, thankful I sounded calm, since I sure as hell didn't feel that way.

"To the Center of the New World, of course."

Jason gave a visible start; unusual for him, but Rachel's attention was elsewhere. She murmured to Heinrich, who nodded once, and then he and half the men left through a door at the far end of the room.

Rachel turned back to us. "Come. We'll retrieve little Geordi and meet Heinrich at the helipad."

"Why?" Jason asked, not moving.

A small frown creased Rachel's brow. Like many megalomaniacs, I doubt she understood that others might not get her master plan. "Why what?"

"Why are we bringing Geordi *there?*"

The frown vanished, replaced by a slow smile of pure pleasure. "Ah. So you *do* know."

"Know what?" I interjected, but she ignored me.

"Let us just say that Geordi is our insurance. You will both do *exactly* as you are told, without argument or complaint. Make no mistake: If either of you do or say *anything*, I will kill him in front of you."

I shuddered, and managed a nod. Jason stood rigid and tense, the muscle in his jaw twitching as he fought for control before he too, assented.

"Wonderful," Rachel cooed. "Off we go, then!"

Chapter Nineteen

*Hell and Destruction are never full; so the
eyes of man are never satisfied.*

~The Bible, Proverbs 27:20

Geordi seemed physically fine. Glad to see us, but
fine. Rachel brought us to the "small" dining room,
where we found him at the long table, sorting candy.
When he saw me, he jumped up and hurled himself at
my midsection. I admit my first feeling was relief that
he'd run to me first, not Jason. But after that, all I felt
was gratitude that he was safe and in my arms.

I hugged him, and he clung to me, and I thought,
Okay, not totally *fine.* He gave no sign of noticing my
injuries but he might ask questions later. Rachel watched
me carefully, and Heinrich's men were everywhere. I
had to make Geordi understand that he couldn't let on he
suspected anything. But how?

With no better ideas, I closed my eyes and squeezed
him tighter, thinking hard, *Pretend everything is fine—
don't let them see you're scared. I'll keep you safe.*

Geordi squeezed me back, and simultaneously,
Eric's thread pulsed brighter in the back of my mind. I'd
forgotten I still had it, entwined with mine. I'd been
trying to calm Geordi, but I must have reassured Eric too.
He now projected understanding, or…renewed purpose?
Still not up to speed, but better.

Geordi pulled back, frowning. "Tata, where were you? We went trick-or-treating in the village, but I didn't see anybody else. But every house had candy. Rachel made sure they did. See what I got?" He pointed at the table, but before I could look he went on, "My witch costume was nice and warm. Did you see the fog? I thought I'd be cold but my costume was really cozy."

I met Jason's gaze over Geordi's head. He was not a chatty kid.

To cover, Jason said, "Wow, kiddo. That's a lot of sugar. I hope you haven't eaten too much of it already."

Geordi still clung to me, and Rachel frowned, so I gave him a deliberate pat on the back and untangled myself. He let go reluctantly, glancing at Jason for reassurance. "I ate five pieces. That's okay, right?"

"Yep. That's the perfect amount."

"Okay, then!" Rachel said brightly. "We had such fun trick-or-treating, didn't we? And your *parents* had fun down at the creek. Would you like to have more fun? Have you ever ridden in a helicopter?"

Geordi's eyes went round. Either he really didn't know anything was wrong or he'd inherited Jason's acting skills through circuitous routes.

"Tata, can we? Please?"

"Sure. I guess." Rachel narrowed her eyes, and I remembered my cover story. "Actually, yes. Your, uh, father and I didn't find that rock we need at the creek, but Heinrich thinks it might be somewhere else. It's too far to drive, so he offered to take us in his helicopter."

Geordi jumped up and down and clapped his hands, but I saw a hint of uncertainty in his eyes. Acting, then. I gave him a *very* slight nod, and Jason lifted his brows almost imperceptibly. I hoped Geordi would understand us both to mean, *That's it—keep playing along—you'll be okay*. For the hell of it, I sent a similarly reassuring thought down my thread to Eric in case it helped.

And then two things happened: Eric's thread grew a tiny bit stronger; and Geordi winked at me, so fast, I almost missed it. I wanted to cry with relief. He might not be Jason's son, but it seemed they shared more traits than he and scumbag Nick after all.

Rachel stood by the open door with barely concealed impatience. "Time to go!"

Geordi put his hand in mine, asking her, "Where are we going? How long will it take? Is it a big helicopter?"

Rachel smiled her winsome smile, which now seemed creepy, not friendly. "We are going to Wewelsburg Castle." My hand convulsed around Geordi's and Jason stiffened, but Rachel didn't notice. "It will take about an hour, and yes, it's a big helicopter. You, your parents, and me and Heinrich can all fit in it."

"Is Heinrich a pilot?"

She laughed. "No. We have a pilot and a copilot too. Perhaps they'll let you ride up front with them."

"No, thank you," Geordi said politely.

I said quickly, "He hasn't seen me all day. We'd like to sit together."

She looked displeased but let it pass. We trooped out the door and were immediately, if subtly, surrounded by her men. Jason took Geordi's other hand, and we went through the castle and out the back to a gravel helipad.

I'm no expert, but some of my clients have given me rides in their flying machines. The bird warming up on the pad was large and expensive, at least a six-seater, plus the cockpit. Heinrich awaited us at the cabin door with the same genial smile *he* always wore, and I wished briefly that all of them would stop pretending and get on with it. But as that was hopeless, I tried to play along.

And then I noticed something else: a low humming that had nothing to do with the helicopter. *Michael's rock.* The buzz grew as Heinrich stepped aside and Jason, Geordi, and I clamored up, until the rock *shrieked* in agitation from the baggage compartment below us.

The key rock was probably down there too, giving me an inkling of the Burkes' plan. What had Eric said about Wewelsburg, and the dead Nazis buried there? But there couldn't be very many of them, so maybe I was wrong, and we had another reason for our trip. But what?

Axe Man, who'd been one of our entourage, stepped into the helicopter and secured the door. He also was dressed in black and had exchanged his axe for some sort of semi-automatic handgun, which he now tucked inside his very own Special Ops belt. I found myself wondering if Jason still carried a gun. Even if he did, the Burkes would obviously have confiscated it. Still, the thought that he knew how to use one was reassuring.

Axe Man—Gun Man?—sat at Rachel's right, while Heinrich sat on her other side. That left the other three seats for Jason, Geordi, and me, and we arranged ourselves accordingly. Moments later, we were off.

The flight was uneventful. The helicopter was comparatively quiet but too loud for conversation. Besides, at least half of us were too tense to make small talk. Much as I wished I had a plan, I couldn't see what we could do mid-air, with five of them to two-and-a-half of us, and Jason—presumably—unable to fly a helicopter.

About seventy-five minutes after takeoff, so nearing

eleven p.m., we descended to the castle. Though the night was dark, the ramparts were well lit, revealing a triangular shape defined by one large, flat-topped tower to the north and two smaller, pointy-roofed ones to the southeast and southwest, respectively.

We aimed for the floodlit space on the big tower, which served as a helipad. Rachel and Heinrich weren't concerned about being seen, so either they'd obtained permission for this venture or they were so confident in their power, they hadn't bothered to ask.

Probably the latter.

We landed in a whoosh of whipping blades, and Heinrich rose, opened the cabin door, and led us down the extendable ramp. Rachel and Axe Man followed us, and we moved toward a door in the wall surrounding the tower's top.

Jason and I exchanged glances over Geordi's head. We were on the ground again, and now it was two versus three, unless the pilot and copilot joined in. Axe Man still had his gun, but we'd been behaving well, so I thought he might be complacent and slow on the draw.

Before we made a move, though, the door opened, revealing a dozen armed men. Of course they'd sent an advance guard to control us. I squeezed Geordi's hand again, communicating that we would all be okay. I had no idea how, but I wouldn't let him know that.

"Wasn't that fun?" Rachel chirped. "Come on in! We have snacks inside."

She ruffled Geordi's hair, and I saw him try not to flinch. *That's right—you're doing great!*

Then Axe Man took his gun out and chambered a round, and *I* tried not to flinch. But then we were off, marching fast, and I didn't have time for anything beyond keeping up.

Inside, Wewelsburg was a bigger, fancier version of the Burkes' home. The rooms were dark, but fluorescent bulbs in old-fashioned sockets lit the corridors and stairs we traversed. At one point, Heinrich and Axe Man veered off in a different direction, leaving us in Rachel's capable hands. Whatever they were up to, it couldn't be good, but at least now I didn't have Axe Man literally breathing down my neck.

Finally Rachel led us into a small study. Three of the wood-paneled walls were lined with shelves containing books and *objets d'art*, while the fourth sported a medieval-issue walk-in fireplace complete with roaring fire. Two stuffed leather chairs flanked it, and across from these sat a mahogany desk, sporting a selection of breads and cheeses, and a six-pack of juice boxes.

"Help yourself," she told Jason and Geordi, then indicated I should follow her out again.

Reflexively, Geordi's hand tightened in mine, and his anxiety ratcheted up. He'd been doing awesome, but he was only seven. I gave him another squeeze. "It's okay. Remember, I have to get my client's rock, and this is the fastest, best way to do it. Besides, Jas—*Daddy* can't eat all that by himself."

Geordi nodded, looking scared. Luckily, his back was to Rachel. I threw a worried glance at Jason, but what could we do? Half the men were clearly staying here, with the rest following Rachel and me.

Then Rachel ushered me out the door and down more halls and stairs. I tried to memorize our route, but before long, I was hopelessly lost. At last we descended a set of steep stone stairs into a small windowless room. A short, medieval-height door was in the far wall, except it was clear glass with a metal handle. Through it, I saw a dark corridor with iron rings spaced at intervals in the walls.

Here we stopped, and Rachel flipped a switch in the wall, illuminating the room with weak electric light. She gestured at two of the men, who carried black leather doctor-style bags. These were unzipped, and I was surprised to see Michael's rock and the key shard being pulled out. I hadn't picked up any buzzing since we took off in the helicopter, but then, I didn't *always* sense the shards, so maybe it wasn't that unusual.

At Rachel's direction, the men set both rocks on top of a small display case near the stairs, which housed an exhibit of some type of documents. Rachel caught my eye and grinned. Not her winsome, for-show smile, but a baring of teeth that made my skin crawl, and I rescinded my earlier wish that she'd quit pretending. If this was the real her, I'd rather have the fake one.

"The castle is a working museum," she explained. "This is the room they used in the seventeenth century to torture witches until they confessed. That door leads to the dungeon where the women were kept, chained to the walls, between torture sessions."

I shuddered, the bile rising in my throat, and she laughed merrily. "Don't worry, I'm not calling forth any dead witches."

I experienced a moment of relief. So far, most of the dead I'd encountered hadn't suffered much before dying. I wasn't sure I wanted to meet anyone who had died in terrible, awful pain. But then she added, "Just a few dead Nazi prisoners," and the nausea came back.

She went on conversationally, "They weren't generally housed here. Most were at Niederhagen to the east. However, when it was dissolved, a dozen came here to work as slaves before they were killed at the end of the war. You will bring them back." She indicated the shards. "Go on, work your magic."

Hesitantly, I approached the case. I could do this. I'd survived it before, and it seemed I'd be raising far fewer Dead than last time. Still, I was terrified, both of the process, and of who I might raise and what they might do. But surrounded by armed men, with Jason and Geordi upstairs, what choice did I have?

I put one hand on the rock. Immediately it hummed to life, the familiar warmth of its energy pouring through me. Then I touched the key, and the screaming started.

###

I did survive, but I'll never know how. I remember bits and pieces—I think maybe Eric's thread, still twined with mine, grounded me. I'm really not sure. It still didn't feel like him, and when I thought it about it later, it was incredible I could sense him at such a distance. Or maybe it was the rock's thread. One thing was certain: it wasn't Jason. Of the three, he was the only one I had to physically touch to sense his thread.

In any case, I came back to myself sometime later to find, once again, my hands still glued to the rocks, my knees buckling as I leaned on the case. Rachel glanced avidly from me to the dungeon door and back.

"Where are they?" she demanded.

I couldn't speak, so I shook my head weakly. She stepped forward, ready to strike me, when a movement in the corridor caught my eye. Rachel saw my gaze shift and peered excitedly in that direction.

A man approached, wearing a tattered striped uniform that proclaimed him a concentration camp inmate. His face was dirty, his ghostly skin sore-covered, and there was a small, neat bullet hole in his forehead. His fingernails were cracked and dirty, and he was barefoot. The glass door was propped open, presumably in anticipation of his arrival, and he stepped hesitantly through, blinking in the comparatively bright light.

"Are they here?" Rachel demanded. "How many?"

"Just one," I managed around my raw throat.

"One!" She turned blazing eyes on me. "Where are the rest? *Where are they?*"

"I…don't know."

The man stopped in the center of the room and caught my gaze, evidently figuring out I could see him. He said deferentially, "Excuse me…"

"You speak English?"

"Yes. What is happening?"

Rachel looked where I had, then back at me. "What is it? What is he saying?"

"He wants to know why he's here."

She peered in his direction. "What's your name? When did you die?"

"Leopold Hesse," the man said. "I do not know. Early evening, perhaps?"

I repeated what he said to Rachel, who frowned. "What *year?*"

Now it was his turn to frown. He said to me, "Is it not this year? I do not understand any of this. I know that I am dead—I remember dying. But I am a Jehovah's Witness. We believe death is an end to consciousness. It makes no sense that I am dead, and yet I am conscious."

Well, hell. What to do if one's belief system had a glitch like this in it? Or maybe the rock overrode all religious nuances. Either way, it sucked for Leopold, who'd apparently lost consciousness decades ago, only to be awakened now by me and Crazy Rachel.

I said to her, "He doesn't know. But based on his clothes, sometime in the forties."

"*That doesn't help me*," she said through her teeth. "I need someone who was here when the Nazis abandoned the castle in March of nineteen forty-five."

Leopold's face cleared. "Yes, I believe that is the date. They told us they were leaving, then shot us." I flinched, and he said, "It was not a bad way to die, compared to some."

Ew. But…he had a point.

I told Rachel he was at the castle until it was deserted, and she beamed. "Wonderful! He'll do." Then she directed the men to put both rocks back in their bags.

Leopold stared at her curiously, then at me. "Why are your clothes so strange?" Then he noticed the room we were in, the glass case, and the modern door to the dungeon, and his face paled. "What is happening here? This room is so different."

A noise came from the stairs, and Heinrich and Axe Man hurried down, followed by Hans and others who, judging by their outdated clothes, were most likely dead.

"The trucks came—the buses are on their way," Heinrich said to Rachel, then he looked to me. "I know the Dead are with me. Is Hans among them?"

"*Ja!*" Hans said, snapping his heels and saluting, and I translated.

"Good," Heinrich said and spoke in rapid German.

Hans turned to Leopold and questioned him extensively. Leopold responded in the same deferential manner he had with me, except now he spoke in German.

When they finished, Hans gave me his report, which I repeated verbatim for Rachel and Heinrich's benefit.

"Excellent," Heinrich said. "We leave now."

He started for the stairs and without being told, Hans took Leopold's arm and dragged him, unresisting, in that direction. Rachel's men herded me in similar fashion, and we re-climbed all the stairs we'd just descended, until we emerged at the top of the tower we'd landed on.

The helicopter was still there, as were Jason and Geordi, the former white-faced and tense, the latter looking scared, despite obvious efforts not to. Thankfully, Rachel and Heinrich were too absorbed in a low-voiced consultation to notice, so I went to Geordi and took him in my arms.

"It's okay, sweetie. Everything will be okay."

Then I caught Jason's eye and my heart stopped. He looked frightened—*Jason*, who had stolen High Demon powers and survived. It must be to do with Geordi; nothing else could scare him like this. No one paid any attention to us, and the helicopter blades whirred loudly, so I raised my eyebrows at him.

He said in a low voice, "Something happened while you were gone. I've—I never saw anything like it before. *Never*."

"What? What happened?" I dropped to my knees, running my hands all over Geordi. He appeared whole and unbroken but was clearly terrified.

"He—he had some kind of fit. We were at the table, eating. About ten or fifteen minutes after you left, he suddenly started crying and fell on the floor. Like a tantrum, only…I can't explain it. Different somehow."

"Could they have put something in the food again?"

Jason shook his head. Not in negation, but in helplessness. "I don't know."

Geordi stared at me, his gaze pleading.

"What happened, sweetie? Are you okay?" If Rachel had poisoned him, had given him *anything* that made him sick, I'd kill her with my bare hands.

He said, "I'm okay. But I want to go home, Tata. Please, can we go home now?"

Rachel heard him and said in her sing-song voice, "Not quite yet! Your *mama* has more work to do first."

Heinrich was in the helicopter, and Rachel clearly expected us to follow. I pulled Geordi tight and whispered, "Just a little longer. I promise Jason and I will keep you safe."

Then Rachel was tugging at my arm, and Jason hefted Geordi onto his hip, and we climbed aboard.

This time the flight was shorter, about fifteen minutes, most of which was takeoff and landing. We touched down in a small clearing high on a forested mountain. A very cold one. Rachel pulled jackets from the under-seat storage and passed them to us, so at least she didn't plan on freezing us to death.

Hans and Leopold had crowded into the helicopter with us, which made sense since they didn't add any weight. I wanted to ask Hans what they'd done with Eric, but even if I could do it without Heinrich, Rachel or Axe Man noticing, Hans wouldn't understand me. For his part, Leopold still seemed dazed, but Hans must have cleared up some of his confusion as he didn't appear surprised by our destination.

Unlike me. I peered at the dense trees illuminated by the chopper's headlight. "Where are we?"

Heinrich opened the cabin door. "Barnacken. Forty kilometers north of Wewelsburg. Don't you recall? I told you that the rock you are searching for might be here."

"Of course," I said dutifully, marveling at their

oblivion. Geordi's demeanor fairly shouted that he knew something was up, but whatever. I guess megalomania leaves scant room for noticing others' feelings. "I don't remember *how* we're getting it back, though."

Rachel compressed her lips but must have realized I needed *some* information to do what they wanted. She zipped Geordi's jacket, saying, "There is a cave nearby. Leopold will guide us, and then you and the Dead will retrieve what we need from it."

"The Dead?" Jason asked innocently, and she turned her most seductive smile on him.

"Oops. Was I not supposed to say that? Doesn't Geordi know what his *mama* can do?"

"I don't know what you're talking about," Jason said. He sounded so convincing, even *I* half believed him. Rachel's smile slipped, and her gaze flicked from him to me, as though trying to decide if he really didn't know about my skills. Then she narrowed her eyes at Geordi.

Thankfully, he now looked mainly exhausted, as any seven-year-old would in the middle of the night, on a cold mountaintop, after a long day of trick-or-treating and kidnapping.

Just then we heard the loud rumble of several buses, and I saw headlights through the trees off to our right. They illuminated a narrow dirt track, barely wide enough to accommodate the army-style vehicles. There were twelve in all, seemingly carrying half a dozen men each, unless you could see the Dead, in which case, they were jammed full of the army I'd raised.

Leopold's eyes widened. "*Was ist das?*"

It suddenly occurred to me that he spoke English *and* German—and nobody was paying any attention to us. Rachel and Heinrich were at the first bus, having another confab while it unloaded, while Hans waited at attention close by, though they of course couldn't see him.

I drew Leopold away from Geordi and Jason and said under my breath, "That man and that woman are raising an army of the Dead for Satan."

He gasped and stepped back, and I grabbed his arm, which shocked him even more. "You can touch me? Are you dead too?"

"It's a long story. We don't have time. Quick, can you tell me what we're doing here?"

He glanced from me to Rachel and Heinrich, and then at Hans. "He—the dead man—he has some kind of control over me. Or perhaps they do. I have no will to disobey. I am sorry."

"Never mind. It's okay. But please, telling me what we're doing isn't disobeying. Anything might help."

He struggled visibly, then nodded. "You say they are raising an army of the Dead, and these are their troops so far—a mere five hundred men. But do you know of the *Totenkopfring*—Death's Head rings?" I shook my head, and he threw another glance at Hans' back, then said hurriedly, "They are the *SS-Ehrenring*—honor rings— silver skulls carved with runes, commissioned by Reichsführer Himmler as gifts to leaders in the Schutzstaffel. What you would call the Nazis."

The buses were almost unloaded, the Dead filling the clearing, and I had no idea who might tattle on us. Plus, the rest of the Burkes' retainers, including Smoke Breath, were also now here. I made a *hurry up* motion to Leopold.

"When the leaders died, their rings were returned to Herr Himmler and stored at Wewelsburg. Before it was abandoned, we—the remaining prisoners—were ordered to hide them deep in this mountain."

"Why?"

"Herr Himmler was interested in the occult. Some say he planned to resurrect the dead officers after the war, using their rings to draw them back from the grave."

Okay. Not entirely new information, but at least now I knew the MO.

"So…Rachel and Heinrich want you to find the cave, so they can dig up the box of rings. Then they'll force me to use the rock and the key, and poof! Instant Nazi leadership? Which will what, double their army? Making it one thousand strong?"

Rachel spoke in Hans' general direction—she must have guessed he'd stick close by—and he saluted and came toward us.

Leopold said in a frightened rush, "You don't understand. Herr Himmler collected nearly *all* the rings. There are a dozen chests, each weighing fifty pounds. If we are successful tonight, the Burkes will have *twelve thousand* dead Nazi war criminals at their disposal."

Chapter Twenty

I am become death, the destroyer of worlds.

~J. Robert Oppenheimer, American Theoretical Physicist (1904-1967)

Hans reached us and spoke in clipped German to Leopold, who translated unnecessarily, "It is time to go."

I still reverberated with the shock of his words, but I managed a nod. A small army of the Dead was bad enough. But twelve thousand dead *Nazis?* Not just foot soldiers who maybe participated for their own survival. No, these were the leaders, the worst of the worst, men who'd engineered unspeakable horrors against millions of innocent people and been *rewarded* for it, with Himmler's literal undying gratitude.

I allowed myself a single shudder of nausea, then followed Leopold and Hans to where Rachel and Heinrich waited. At least now I had a translator and possible ally, if I could break the Burkes' hold on him. I scanned the arriving Dead for Eric but didn't see him, and his thread waned, growing thinner and dimmer by the minute. Jason and Geordi were similarly wan: pale, anxious shadows of their usually vibrant selves.

I forced down my anxiety. Jason had been my pillar of strength for so long, even when we fought or were miles apart. If *he* was frightened, what right had *I* to be brave? And for the past months, Eric had been constantly by my side, so much so that I now relied on his calm cynicism as a buffer between me and the series of crises my life-after-death had become.

I tried sending a pulse out to him—*Where are you? What did they do to you?*—but got nothing back. I've been a loner most of my life, but for the first time, amidst hundreds of the Dead and the Living, I felt wholly *alone.*

I won't bore you with the details of our hike, which was long, uphill, and arduous, nor with the unending game of intermediary-to-the-intermediary we played— also arduous—whereby Heinrich or Rachel said something in Hans' direction; he queried Leopold, then responded to me, both times in German; and I repeated his words verbatim to the Burkes.

Rinse, repeat, and do it all again.

As we were the necessary cogs in this freakish wheel, Leopold and I walked in front with the Burkes. Rachel put Leopold at my left and Hans on my right, so she'd know where to direct her questions, while Axe Man and Smoke Breath flanked us. Jason and Geordi were forced to walk behind us, surrounded by more of the Burkes' living army. The rest of the Dead followed obediently, if uninterestedly, bolstering my suspicion that the Burkes controlled them as well.

In all, we were about two dozen Living and the five hundred Dead. So to me, it sounded like a great racket of branches breaking or snapping in or out of place, or the crackle of spirits dematerializing through the trees, but in fact, we moved pretty stealthily up the mountain.

Axe Man and Smoke Breath had headlamps, while Rachel and Heinrich carried flashlights, but it was still too dark to see beyond a few feet of forest floor and the endless trees surrounding us. At Rachel's instruction, Smoke Breath held a compass up for Leopold to examine, but he didn't need it. To him, the last time he'd made this trek was mere hours before, and he remembered the way. Like Eric, he could see well in the dark, and I wished I'd acquired that skill when I died.

But even were it broad daylight, I couldn't escape. If I managed to break away—*if* I could bring myself to abandon Jason and Geordi—I had no idea where I was or in what direction civilization lay.

After an hour we came to an embankment, an outcropping of rock too steep to climb. Leopold turned unwaveringly to its left, and I followed, and everyone else followed me. A short time later we found the embankment's edge, where it met the trees.

"Here," Leopold said to me, and I said to Rachel, "He says it's here."

She and Heinrich shone their lights, illuminating a narrow fissure in the hillside. Due to the color and composition of the rock, it was almost invisible. Probably the prisoners who buried the chests were so emaciated that they easily slipped through. Now, even Ghost Leopold would barely fit, much less Heinrich's beefy "boys."

Rachel came to the same conclusion and frowned. "Are you sure? This is too tight. How did you get the chests inside?"

Leopold also frowned at the fissure. "It was wider before. No man will pass through now."

I repeated his words, and Rachel's expression changed, lightning fast, to fury. I raised my hands. "It's been seventy years. Maybe there was a rock slide or an earthquake."

"Yes, my sweet," Heinrich said soothingly. "Remember our research? The terrain may change, but we know what to do."

She nodded, appeased, and spoke in German at Hans, who immediately said "*Ja!*", which I repeated. Then he faced the Dead and spoke rapidly.

I looked at Leopold, who explained, "She asks if any of the Dead can move through rock and carry solid objects. He asks for volunteers."

A dozen dead men stepped forward, and Hans queried Leopold, who nodded and spoke in the same deferential tone he always used, probably saying they would be sufficient.

There followed a lengthy back-and-forth between Rachel, Hans, Leopold, the dead volunteers, and myself, in which I assumed Rachel told the Dead what to do, while Leopold gave pertinent details about the chests' precise location, and Hans strategized. Though I wasn't doing much, my brain was too occupied to think my own thoughts or formulate a plan.

I did get one short break while Rachel and Heinrich consulted with Axe Man and Smoke Breath. They no longer seemed to care what I did on my own time, so I turned again to Leopold for an explanation.

"I will lead the Dead into the cave," he said, "and we will dig up the chests and carry them out."

"I got that. But…how?"

As noted, Eric could push small objects around or briefly levitate larger ones, but only when deeply agitated. I'd never seen him lift a solid object, other than Geordi's very small and possibly "magic" scarab.

"Herr Muller"—it took me a moment to realize he meant Hans—"says it is a skill learned over time. I have been dead many years, but I am newly awakened, and Herr Muller died today. The men who have volunteered have been dead longer, and believe they can dig through the earth and carry the chests."

"Have they said what I'll be doing during all this?"

"Nothing, until it is time to reunite the men with their rings."

Hans, who'd been eavesdropping on Rachel and Heinrich, beckoned us over. He and Leopold spoke in German, and then Hans said something through me to his leaders. Heinrich smiled, nodded, and gave his official seal of approval, and then Leopold and the twelve Dead disappeared into the fissure, and we were off.

In the movies, when the main character has to wait for their Next Big Scene, there's usually some emotional conflict or a crisis in a subplot to keep the audience interested. In reality, this part was pretty tedious. I hadn't asked Leopold how far in the chests were, so I had no idea how long it would take a dozen ghosts to find them, dig them up, and lug them out. After a few minutes of standing around in the cold, most of us found somewhere to sit while we waited in silence for something to happen.

Jason wormed his way free—probably his guards figured we couldn't escape anyway—and brought Geordi to where I sat, backed against a thick tree trunk. Geordi stretched his arms out before Jason even lowered him to the ground, then climbed onto my lap. I tried to talk to him, but he burrowed deeper into me, so I just held him tight.

Jason sat next to us, wrapping his arm around my shoulder, and I let myself be comforted. Until I thought about what I had to do when the chests appeared, and then I shook.

"Shh," he murmured. "It will be okay."

"I can't," I said. I didn't want to scare Geordi more, but I *had* to talk with someone, and this might be my only chance. "I can't do what they want—it's too much. I can't do *any* of this. Not for them—not even for Michael. I do other stuff for him, besides just the rocks. But I can't anymore. It's too much responsibility. I—I'm not qualified."

Jason was silent a moment. Then he pulled me closer and said, "You're stronger than you think."

"No, I'm not. You don't know what I've been doing—what they want me to do now."

"Hyacinth. I'm not an idiot. I can guess what else you do for Michael. And I understood enough of what I've overheard to know what the Burkes want."

I'd forgotten his gift for languages. "You speak German?"

"Enough to get by."

"And they still don't know you can see the Dead?"

"I think they suspect, but I've been careful. Mostly, they're so focused on you, they haven't thought much about me."

"Gee, thanks."

"Seriously, you're selling yourself short. Obviously, I don't know the…process…for what you're about to do, but I *know* you can handle it. Your strength is one of the things I—" He paused. Seconds ticked by. Then he said simply, "You should have more faith in yourself."

He said nothing more, and I wondered how far he would have gone if he hadn't stopped himself. How far did I want him to go? His heart beat strong and sure under my cheek, his chin rested on my head, and after a moment, he wrapped his other arm around me, so that

Geordi and I both were cradled in his embrace.

For now, it was enough.

I must have dozed off. From his deadweight in my lap, so had Geordi. A flurry of activity near the cave woke me, both the Living and the Dead shouting and crowding the entrance. Blinking, I realized it was no longer dark out, but rather a soft gray, lightening to a damp, misty pre-dawn. Either several hours had passed, or it was later than I thought when we got here.

Jason said in a low voice, "The Dead got the chests to the cave's entrance, and the Living are widening the fissure to pull them through. I think it's time."

Sure enough, Rachel detached herself from the crowd and walked to us. "Up."

I shifted Geordi toward Jason and he woke, immediately clinging to me. "Tata, no! Don't go! I want to go home!"

Rachel frowned at him. "Your aunt has something to do for me, and you can sit quietly while she does it."

Guess Make-Believe Time was over.

"It will be all right," I said and gave him a quick kiss, because anything more would break my heart.

Worse, I didn't know if it *would* be all right. I was more frightened than I'd ever been in my life *or* death, and the one thing that kept me from losing it completely was Jason. He took Geordi gently from me, his gaze boring into mine, as though to say, *I've got him. You don't have to worry about him. You can do this.*

To Geordi he said, "It's okay, kiddo. Your Tata will be fine."

Geordi glared at him. "I know that! But she shouldn't have to help Rachel. Make them let her go!"

If I'd thought Rachel was angry before, my heart stopped now. "It's okay, sweetie," I said, standing quickly and blocking him from Rachel. "I just have to do this one thing. I promise. Easy-peasy, lemon squeezy!"

It was a total lie, and I doubt Geordi believed me. But I had to do *something* to appease her. If I didn't survive this, or even if I did, and the Burkes succeeded in raising their Nazi army, I needed him to be safe. I clung to the hope that Jason would get him away, or that once we were done, Rachel would turn them both loose. What use were they to her, except as a hold over me?

"Come," she said imperiously, and I followed her to the cave's entrance.

The boys had been busy. Arranged in a semicircle in front of the fissure were the twelve iron-banded wooden chests. They were smaller than I expected, maybe twenty-five centimeters long by twenty wide, and fifteen-ish tall. Even so, they must hold a thousand Death's Head rings each, and that much silver weighed a *lot*. They had been treated with something before burial, so most had only mild discolorations here and there, and just one was slightly warped.

Right by the fissure at the semicircle's heart lay the rock and the key. "Go," Rachel commanded, and I went.

The rock's hum filled me with its anxiety and dread, mingling with my own, as Axe Man and Smoke Breath opened the chests. I half expected a movie-land whirlwind-of-evil to fly out, but instead, there were just piles of silver rings, some glowing like new, others tarnished from years of wear. They looked pretty ordinary, but then, I knew who commissioned them and why, and what their purpose now was.

When she deemed all was in order, Rachel nodded at

me. Heinrich stood at her side, wearing an expression of avid expectation equal to her own. I glanced at the tree to find Jason and Geordi standing several paces in front of it, facing me. Panic roiled through me—bad enough I had to do this. I couldn't do it while Geordi watched.

I shook my head at Jason, who mouthed, *He insisted.*

I shook my head more violently, ignoring Rachel's furious impatience. *No.*

Jason gripped Geordi's hand and lifted his shoulder, communicating, *Whatever happens, it's better he knows.*

Maybe he was right. Or maybe it was the worst thing ever. It didn't matter. Heinrich, who I'd noticed mostly let Rachel handle the details, frowned at me, then motioned to Axe Man and Smoke Breath, who drew their weapons and moved toward Jason and Geordi.

"Okay!" I gasped. "Okay, I'm doing it!"

And then I did.

I touched the rock and grabbed the key and the screaming began, except this time it echoed inside my mind *and* out. Eric's thread, which had been glowing palely in the back of my mind, shrank until it was almost gone. I cried out, but there was nothing I could do. It was better he wasn't part of this, anyway.

My own thread latched onto the rock's, whipping it into a frenzy, while I stood in the half-circle of chests, the fissure at my back. Mist seeped from the forest, and the Living and the Dead swarmed, and chaos crescendoed, and light came from my hands and eyes and ears and mouth. My vision refracted, kaleidoscoping the clearing and trees, the men and spirits, into tiny facets of color that swirled, coalesced, and refragmented.

The rock's thread snaked through me and out my fingers, connecting with the rings in the chests, their molten energy like red-black lava burning my veins. They vibrated in time with the rock, the chests shaking, and then the earth shook too. Rocks tumbled from the embankment, hurling down around me, but I couldn't move, could do nothing but stand and channel the volcanic energy of the rock and the rings.

The rings pulled hard, calling to their owners, thousands of souls stirring, awakening, rising from graves and oceans, valleys and hills. They came, rushing forth from all directions, gathering swiftly in the trees. I shuddered with their evil but couldn't stop it, powerless in the twin grips of the rock and key, so strong they'd overwhelm me, obliterate me, there'd be nothing left.

And still it went on and on and on, until the forest teemed with dead soldiers, jostling to be near the rings. And then…it wasn't just the rings and the dead Nazis.

A…*presence*…began crawling up from deep in the fissure at my back. A presence I'd sensed once before, inside a burial mound in Turkey, when the Rousseaux tried to send the first rock to Hell. The fissure's slab cracked, the earth fracturing behind and below me.

I felt a *rage* beyond anything I'd ever known. It called to the Nazis—*YOU ARE MINE! WHO DARES TAKE YOU FROM ME?*—and it drew closer.

I had to do something—he *couldn't* escape. I would have called Michael down and damn the consequences, but I couldn't form the thought. I knew what I did, and what I wanted to do, but my mind wasn't my own.

Then—I don't know why, let alone how—I found myself twisting the rock's thread and sending it toward the fissure. It passed through the opening, dipping deeper, and then abruptly it arced into white-hot light, like a downed powerline landing in water. The *presence* jerked back, but the electric energy bounced off the rock walls, rending the fissure apart, a spider web of cracks snaking through its sides. I reached for the thread, wresting it back from the deep, forcing it away from the fissure and back toward the clearing.

And suddenly, my vision silvered, then cleared. I saw Rachel and Heinrich, glowing with anticipation. I saw the Living, rapt or terrified in equal measure, the Dead in similar states. And I saw Jason, struggling to restrain Geordi, who fought madly to get to me.

And then from deep within the mountain came a hiss, like air from a balloon, which increased to the sound of wind in a tunnel, until finally it became a hurricane's roar. The *presence* surged, heat blasting from the fissure, dozens of molten-lava shapes spewing into the clearing, cooling, growing, stretching into man-shapes.

"Yes!" Rachel cried out. "He has sent forth his demons!"

"NO!"

The sound ripped through me, but it wasn't me who said it. Suddenly my thread and the rock's were joined by Eric's, strong and sure, but not familiar. It had to be him, but it was not *him*. Before I registered his intent, he wrenched the rock's thread from me and twisted it away, not into the fissure, but *back onto the rock itself.*

What in God's name was he doing? I couldn't stop him—he'd almost got it—*there*—it touched the rock dead center.

And with a sonic *boom*! the rock exploded and the screaming stopped, and the only thread was my own, and I collapsed on my knees in the clearing, surrounded by thousands of dead souls, and the demons and the Living, while hundreds of tiny rock shards rained down.

Chapter Twenty-One

Put on the whole armor of God, that ye may be able to stand against the wiles of the devil.

~The Bible, Ephesians 6:11

When the last piece fell there was a frozen moment of shocked silence. Rachel and Heinrich stared at the wreckage of the rock. The Living and the Dead stared.

The demons stared.

And then they ran for the shards. Dozens of demons, a crazy collection of expensive suits and tattooed goths and everyday men and women, tearing through the clearing and the nearby trees, collecting pieces of Michael's rock.

Rachel whirled on Heinrich's men. "Seize them! *Get the shards*, before the demons take them! *Now!*"

The clearing erupted in chaos again. The Living could see the demons, running for the shards. Some tried to stop them, others collected their own shards, while the Dead aided and abetted according to their abilities.

And suddenly, I realized why Rachel was panicking. If the demons got the shards, they'd send them down to their master in Hell, and the Burkes would have no way to raise more Dead and nothing to bargain with. It was the death of all their plans, the ruination of their evil dreams.

As though reading my mind, Geordi lurched free

from Jason's grasp and screamed, "*NO. You can't have them—they aren't yours! They are Tonton's or no one's!*"

He faced the clearing, his blue eyes flashing black as his gaze darted from one person to the next. Then, just as Jason reached him, he suddenly stood stock still and shut his eyes. And…

One by one, the shards exploded.

Boom! One gone.

Boom! Another. Obliterated—even its dust.

BOOM! Right from the hands of a nasty-looking demon in a navy silk suit.

With every explosion, Eric's thread grew stronger in my mind.

And then I knew. Oh, dear God, I *knew*.

Not Eric.

Ohgodohgodohgod—it was *Geordi's* thread in my mind. All this time, I'd thought it was Eric—had wondered why he felt so small and scared. But it wasn't him—it never had been—not since he was taken from our prison at the Burkes'.

No, it was Geordi's voice that screamed with me when I first touched the rock and the key together; Geordi who'd had a "fit" with Jason at Wewelsburg while I brought Leopold forth in the dungeon below; and it was *Geordi* who'd now taken the rock's thread from me and aimed it *right at Satan*.

He was using his *own* thread to destroy not just the Burkes' bargaining chips, but the one thing Satan needed above all else to escape from Hell and wreak his vengeance against Michael: the pieces of Michael's power, trapped in the rocks.

Boom! Boom! BOOM!

Geordi wasn't just stopping the demons or anyone else from picking up the rocks. Somehow, he was obliterating every last bit of them, *including* Michael's powers.

The fissure crack glowed a vicious angry red: Satan had reached the same conclusion. He rose, pulsing at the walls of his prison—he *would* break through. I felt his utter and complete wrath and outrage—and oh God, he'd use it to destroy Geordi.

I had to protect him. But how?

With every piece that blew up, the demons were comical in their dismay. They ran around, seeking the source of the destruction—they knew it was someone in the clearing, but hadn't noticed Geordi.

Yet.

I tried to go to him, but a wave of heat at my back knocked me flat. I gasped, choking, as Satan sent out tendrils of his power. Geordi's thread glowed bright and strong in my mind—Satan would sense it—would see him—

Boomboomboom!

Only a few shards remained.

Satan raged, seeking his enemy—

—and then an ice-cold wall rose up before me, slicing off Geordi's thread, and I wanted to scream in terror—until I realized it was *Jason shielding him.*

It was like the bubble I'd unwittingly helped him with on Malta. I sensed Jason's powers surrounding Geordi, blockading him in even as Jason threw him to the ground, physically covering him with his own body.

But if I could sense Jason's powers, Satan could sense them too. Why wasn't Jason shielding himself?

Oh God—he couldn't shield them both—he was

sacrificing himself to save Geordi.

A scream of my own pure rage tore through me as I scrambled up and whirled around, seeking an ally—*any* ally—and then I saw Leopold.

"*Help him!*" I shrieked, pointing at Jason. I didn't know what Leopold could do, but I couldn't let Jason die, or worse, be sucked down to Hell, for saving Geordi.

Leopold instantly saw what was happening and began shouting at the Dead nearby. They looked to him and then at me, and I suddenly found I could see their threads in my mind. I sent my own thread out, twining it first with Leopold's and then with the others.

More souls saw us and came to help, and I worked furiously, pulling in dozens of threads, until I had a rope, thick, strong, and pulsing with light. Then we—Leopold, the Dead, and I—hurled it toward Jason, and he caught it, holding on for dear life. We couldn't shield him; I had no idea how I'd helped him before, and the problem didn't seem to be the strength of the shield, but rather, that the entire thing covered Geordi. I'd have to create a shield from scratch to cover Jason, and I didn't even know if non-demons could do that.

Once, in Turkey, I'd made something similar to protect Eric from the vacuum of Hell, by pulling elements from the soil and rocks around him. But that was a thin bubble, protecting one soul from the distant threat of Hell far below. This would have to be big enough to protect Jason and Geordi from the very immediate, very close threat of Satan himself. So the best I could hope for was that Jason would cling to the lifeline the Dead and I had created—and that it would hold.

As soon as Jason grabbed the rope, I felt Satan's power, as though he pulled me too, and his voice roared through my head at Jason.

YOU—YOU ARE TAKING MY SOULS. YOU HAVE DESTROYED WHAT IS MINE—HAVE STOLEN POWERS FROM ME. DEMON, YOU ARE MINE, AND I WILL END YOU.

Jason's grip on the rope slipped, and the shield around Geordi flickered, like a bulb burning out. I shouted to Leopold, "Send everything you have to him! Tell the others!"

The rope pulsed with renewed energy, and suddenly a piece of Jason's thread broke free and twined with it, tying him to us. Satan yanked harder, but we'd anchored Jason, and he wouldn't be sucked away.

There was a moment of frustrated fury from the fissure.

And then Satan noticed me. *I* was the one preventing him from getting Jason, who he thought the cause of all his other troubles.

SEIZE HER!

Every demon in the clearing stopped what they were doing and turned on me.

I didn't know what to do—they were advancing, a few of them clutching the last tiny shards of Michael's rock, his powers pulsing into and through them, making them stronger, while they also shared that power with the others.

Of course! They were stealing the power from the rocks.

Leopold and the Dead had a solid hold on Jason, so I pulled my thread back, and instead sought the thread that came from the shard in the first demon's hands. It was different somehow, and all at once I realized the demon's own powers were intertwined with it.

Too late—I couldn't stop—I twisted the thread with my own, and the demon's power surged through me, stronger, so much stronger than when I'd taken a teensy-tiny sip of the Rousseaux's powers back in Turkey. The white heat of it burned through me, and I shuddered and used everything I had to master it. Then I hurled it back at the demon, straight into the shard itself.

It didn't boom.

It imploded with a violent *CRACK!*, nothing but a black hole remaining—the absolute absence of matter— between the demon's hands.

She wailed an ear-splitting screech, and then her thread arced into her and she screamed, her own power attacking her, *through* me. She lit up from the inside, her veins glowing orange-hot, and then they turned black and shrank into her core. Her scream was cut off and she crumpled to the ground, curling in on herself, before all at once, she, too, imploded, leaving nothing but a smoky black stench behind.

I faced the next demon, echoes of the first's powers reverberating through me, but the rest had seen her demise and dropped the shards, releasing their threads and backing away. In seconds I'd retrieved my thread and began sending it to the remaining rocks. Not being commingled with demon powers, these were easier to destroy. Or maybe I retained the first demon's powers and that helped. Either way, they vanished as soon as I "touched" them.

Then Satan realized what I was doing and released Jason, turning instead to me, but...

He was too late. The last rock vanished with a soft pop, taking Michael's powers with it. There was nothing left—nothing Satan could steal or latch onto to aid him.

His demons scattered into the woods. His power surged and pulsed around me, a tangible, angry mass of heat and impotent fury, but he was helpless to break free.

His awareness was a physical thing, taking in me, Jason, the escaping demons, and the Dead and the Living, frozen in place, awaiting the outcome of our battle. I felt his energy, prodding, testing me, determining my very essence. He withdrew a little, as though pulling back to strike, and then suddenly, his focus shifted. He saw the Burkes, two commanders avidly watching their soldiers execute their campaign, and comprehension dawned.

And he was *pissed*.

YOU ARE THE CAUSE OF ALL THIS. YOU HAVE STOLEN FROM ME—FIRST THE ROCK, AND NOW MY DEAD AND MY DEMONS.

For the first time, Rachel looked frightened, but Heinrich remained calm.

"Please," he said with false subservience. "We have done all this for you, O Great Master. Our only wish is to do your work on Earth. See—we have raised an army for you, that we will send forth to do your will."

WHO WILL LEAD THIS ARMY?

"We will, your Greatness. It is our pleasure to serve you."

FOOLS! MY DEMONS DO MY WORK IN THE WORLD. THE DEAD SERVE ME IN MY PRISON. A PRISON FROM WHICH I WOULD BREAK FREE, HAD I THE POWER.

Heinrich's pleasant demeanor cracked. Perhaps it had finally dawned on him that Satan *might* not like to share his power, or to have it stolen from under his nose.

"Your—your Greatness," Rachel broke in, white-faced and shaking. "W-we thought t-to please you."

BY DESTROYING THE ONE THING THAT COULD SET ME FREE?

She shrank from his words but managed to continue. "We are most humbly sorry. We thought to aid you." Abruptly her spine stiffened, and she whirled and pointed at me. "Besides, it was *her*—*she* destroyed the rock. I will kill her for you!"

NO. SHE IS NOT TO BLAME.

No one was more shocked than I at Satan's refusing an offer to see me dead. But apparently, he had other plans.

YOU SAY YOU WISH TO SERVE ME. IT IS MY PLEASURE TO ALLOW IT.

A noise like a cosmic vacuum came from the fissure. The air moved, a hot suction that bypassed me, snaking out on either side, aiming for the Burkes. They panicked and tried to run, but it was too late. It pulled them—not their bodies, but the blackness of their souls, sucking it out like dirt from a gutter. They screamed—they were turning *inside out* in front of us. Their eyes burst, blood streamed from their ears, their fingernails ripped off. Their bodies convulsed, and then their evil essence was free, a black cloud that hovered briefly before vanishing with a wailing screech, sucked into the fissure.

Rachel and Heinrich's shattered corpses toppled over, and for the second time that morning, the rest of us in the clearing were enveloped in a stunned silence.

Then I realized it really *was* morning. A pale pink light glowed over the mountain's peak to the east—we were very close to the top—and the mist in the clearing receded, giving form to the souls milling around. Heinrich's men stood slack-jawed, staring at the bloody mess that was their former employers. I don't think they'd realized until now exactly what the Burkes intended. Then the Dead suddenly awoke from their stupor, moving agitatedly, bumping into the Living who couldn't see them, but who could feel their presence as shimmers in the atmosphere.

Heinrich's men darted uneasy glances around the clearing and closed ranks, forming a semicircle in front of me. They weren't protecting me; rather, they wanted the embankment at their backs. Released from the Burkes' control, the Dead shouted excitedly, hailing comrades and asking questions. As they moved, they naturally sorted themselves, probably based on their assignments in life. But some groups seemed displeased with others, and fights broke out as the tensions spread.

A rumble came from the fissure: *CHILDREN, RETURN TO ME*.

A ripple moved through the Dead. Jason curled more tightly over Geordi, but Satan had ceased pulling at him. Still, he kept his shield up, thank God, though I doubted Satan cared about one small child, even a part-demon one, now that Geordi wasn't directly opposing him. Besides, Satan was focused on the Nazi souls, urging them back. Unfortunately, they'd tasted freedom and had other ideas.

So did Hans. His masters might be in Hell, but he was ambitious. He began shouting in energetic German, and I didn't need a translator to get the gist: "Come to me! To me! You don't have to go back!"

A few Nazis heard him, realized what he was doing, and joined in, beckoning their compatriots over, calling "*Wir dienen Deutschland!*" or "*Man drup, man to!*"

NO! YOU ARE MINE!

Satan's fury was as strong as ever, but he couldn't force the souls to him. The groups solidified and became orderly, looking for all the world like battalions, with certain souls as their leaders, and Hans directing the whole. It was like a barrier existed between them and Satan, like he was a shark in a tank, and all his thumping against the glass didn't faze them.

The battalion leaders barked orders, and suddenly thousands of souls advanced toward the semicircle of chests at the fissure. But instead of breaking into the circle, they stopped at its edge, stooping toward the chests. One by one they bent, then straightened, each now displaying a Death's Head Ring proudly on the third finger of their left hands, until the chests were emptied.

Heinrich's men gasped and shrank from the thousands of souls they could suddenly see. Plus, the rings seemed to further weaken Satan's hold on the Nazis, as though they no longer belonged to him.

He must have decided to cut his losses—his demons had run off, and twelve thousand Nazis had escaped the prison *he* couldn't leave—because suddenly he receded like a video on rewind. One moment he was there, his power pulsing in the back of my mind; the next, he was gone, and I staggered with relief.

Jason cautiously rolled over, still holding Geordi in a death grip. Geordi struggled, and a moment later the shield disappeared. My nephew calmly freed himself and came to stand at the center of the semicircle in front of me. He didn't look at the bloodied Burkes or the Nazis or anyone but me, just stood straight and tall and proud, my little black-haired, blue-eyed, part-demon angel.

"I blew them up, Tata. Just like in the video game— I blew them all up."

I swallowed. "Yes, sweetie, you did. Good job."

Jason was ash-white. "I didn't know he could do that. I swear—*I didn't know.*"

A bustle of activity came from the forest. Hans was shouting orders, and Leopold hurried to me, followed by several of the Dead who had helped save Jason.

"What shall we do?"

I stared at him blankly. "About what?"

"This!" His gesture encompassed the amassing Nazi troops, Heinrich's men, and the fissure.

"I don't know!"

Most of the Dead I'd called forth at the Moselle had reached the trees near the southern end of the semicircle and hovered—figuratively—waiting for whatever I would do next.

Should I call Michael? But no, these were souls who'd already passed on to wherever they were supposed to be. Michael or whoever had his job in their belief system had already dealt with them. Maybe I should ask if they wanted to go back? How would that even work?

Then beyond our small group, I saw an odd thing. Not *all* the Nazis were marshalling to Hans' call. Some glanced uneasily at each other, then at him. And then…they began quietly moving away from those groups…toward me.

Chapter Twenty-Two

*Regard your soldiers as your children, and
they will follow you into the deepest valleys;
look on them as your own beloved sons, and
they will stand by you even unto death.*

~Sun Tzu, Chinese General (544-496 BCE)

At least they started out quietly. But then the other
Nazis spied them, understood what they were doing, and
raised the alarm, crying, "*Verräters!*"

Heated arguments broke out, and in some cases,
fistfights. The defectors clearly thought they were in the
right, their tones declaring, "We don't *have* to follow
Hans if we don't want to," while the loyalists expressed
the opinion that, "Yes, you *do*. We're Nazis, dammitall!"

Leopold repeated, "What shall we do?"

Jason rose, also looking at me. So did Heinrich's
men. In happier times, I'm sure they would've killed me
in a heartbeat. But now I was the one person who might
be able to make sense of all this Magic-Ring-Nazi-
Demon insanity.

And suddenly, I knew what to do. I said to Jason,
"How are you at bonfires?"

His eyebrows rose. The shock of Geordi's abilities
had worn off, and he seemed mostly recovered from his
extended period of shielding-slash-fighting Hell's pull.
"I can do a decent one, with enough wood."

"Good. Find some. And can you get a sense of how big the army is, space-wise? Like, how far we spread?"

"Sure," he said, and I turned to Geordi.

"Can you help Jason find some nice, dry wood in the forest?"

Though he'd been awake nearly a day, he also seemed recovered. Part of me wanted him to never leave my sight again. But I had work to do, and at least he'd be with the one person that I knew would, beyond *any* doubt, lay down their own life to protect him.

Geordi grinned and nodded and they went off together, skirting the edges of the woods where most of the souls milled. A few of these had thrown down figurative gauntlets and moved to "our" side, despite opposition from their former comrades, and many more looked like they wanted to, but weren't sure how.

I said to Leopold, "Tell them to take off their rings and throw them on the ground in front of the fissure. Any who want to join us—tell them!"

He nodded and hurried to the trees, speaking with a few souls before disappearing into the crowd. The defectors not actively engaged in infighting came immediately and tore off their rings, then went to help their friends spread the word. Soon, hundreds of rings were piled up, and more souls were coming, but it was difficult to determine numbers through the trees.

A woman standing nearby watched me carefully. She looked to be in her mid-forties, very capable, with blonde hair loosely knotted at the nape of her neck. It was an old-fashioned style, as were the brown wool skirt-suit and World War II-era sensible shoes she wore. I guessed she was from the Moselle group, as Himmler probably never gave a Death's Head Ring to a woman.

"Do you speak English?" I asked, and she shook her head regretfully. "*Français?*"

Her expression cleared. "*Oui.* How may I help?" She had an accent I couldn't place, less "polished" than the French I was used to, but at least we could communicate.

"I need to know how many souls have switched to our side and how many are left with Hans. Can you…levitate?" Eric could on occasion, but if I'd learned anything about the Dead, it was to never assume.

She nodded. "*Oui.* I will take some scouts and report back to you."

"Er, good. Thank you."

I turned next to Heinrich's men. They were still armed and could have shot me by now, but either they were too stunned by recent events, or they weren't as loyal as Rachel thought.

"Listen up," I said, hoping enough were fluent in English to translate for the rest. "If any of you want to leave, now's the time. You saw the demons loosed from Hell and Satan trying to escape, and you can see the Dead. Mostly."

I'd just remembered that only the souls wearing rings were visible to the Living, and I'd told our guys to take them off. But I felt certain I was right about this, so I pushed on.

"In any case, you saw the Dead Army your bosses raised. I can't say *they* won't harm you, but *we* won't. If you want to leave, go now, before they remember you. But if anyone wants to stay with us, you can."

There was some translating back and forth, followed by an awkward silence and some foot shuffling. Then a dark-haired, light-eyed guy in his twenties stepped forward and asked, "Vhat, exactly, are you doink?"

Uh…good question.

"Trying to stop them, I guess. I don't know how, but I have, er, connections, who may be able to help."

He nodded once. "I'll stay. I am Yvo."

About half of the others also stayed, while the rest vanished into the woods, including Smoke Breath, who leered at me one last time over his shoulder. Axe Man also left, but as usual, didn't make a big deal about it. Definitely the strong, silent type. He'd spoken with the Burkes once or twice, but never to me. Our one personal interaction was when he menaced me with his gun.

Which reminded me: I probably should've made the men who left relinquish their weapons. Oh well. Maybe it was better I hadn't reminded them they *had* weapons, or they might've used them on us.

At least our guys were also armed.

Okay, then. I had a dozen living men to my name and no idea what to do with them, long-term. Short-term was another matter. "Uh, how about half of you go collect dry wood with Jason and Geordi—the two I already sent out—and the rest can keep watch here."

Ordering them around felt surreal, and I'm sure I sounded ridiculous, but no one noticed. Yvo translated, the men decided who got which job, and that was that.

The "keep watch" part also felt silly, mainly because Hans had seemingly given up on the deserters. There were too many on our side now to reasonably control, and we must not be worth the effort. Instead, he'd moved his troops a short way into the forest and appeared to be focusing on strategy. For what, I had no clue.

But the souls on the edges did keep glancing at us, so I told Yvo to tell our guys to keep an eye on *them*, which they did, albeit nervously. I could sympathize. It wasn't that long ago that I first saw the Dead, and it still freaked me out if I thought about it too much.

Then the scouts returned, and the first woman gave me her report in French. "Most of Herr Burke's *armée originale* has joined with us, though I believe some have joined *la nouvelle*. Of the souls raised here, not many— *deux mille, pas plus*—appear to be on our side."

Twenty-five hundred total with the Moselle group. We were outnumbered at least four to one, and whatever Hans intended, it couldn't be good. He was marshalling an army of dead Nazi war criminals; I doubted it was to do community service.

I said to the woman, "What's your name?"

"Sabine Vezinet. *À votre service.*"

"Er, yes, likewise. Hyacinth Finch."

"I know."

My face heated. Obviously, this group knew me, as I was the one who'd interrupted their eternal sleep.

To cover, I asked, "You're French?"

"Belgian."

That explained the accent. "So…do we know why the Moselle faction is joining us? Or the Nazis, for that matter?"

"The Moselles, it is because they did not volunteer. Herr Burke controlled us with the rock. When you destroyed it, his hold was broken. *Et puis*, you killed the demon. We—the Dead—do not like demons. They are not nice to us. We join with you that we may fight *them*."

I wondered how she'd feel if she knew Jason—and Geordi—were part demon? But now wasn't the time to find out. "And the Nazis?"

"They swore loyalty to the Schutzstaffel during the war, but not all agreed with Hitler's regime. At the time, they were too afraid, for themselves and their families, to stand up to him. But now, what have they to lose?"

She lifted her shoulder in a Gallic half-shrug, and a new thought struck me. "There was a man—a dead man named Eric Guilliot. Some of the Moselle Dead took him. Do you know what happened to him?"

"*Oui.* We helped him to escape."

"You did? How? Where is he now?"

"I do not know. Is he not with you?" I shook my head, and she frowned. "*Je ne comprends pas.* But let me explain. A few of the Moselles, perhaps one in ten, we resisted the rock's control. It just did not affect us. But we pretended, and Herr Muller was fooled. When we boarded the buses to come here, your friend Monsieur Guilliot was there. Herr Muller's men had taken him, perhaps to torture him as leverage against you."

She saw my face, and added hastily, "But they did *not* torture him. They ran out of time and sent him with us instead. They thought he was shackled, but when we disembarked here, we set him free. In all the commotion, no one noticed. I believe he planned to find a different group, who were unaware he was your friend, then pretend he was another soldier and help you escape."

Hope soared—he was *here*—I hadn't lost him. But then…where was he? I cast my thread out, seeking him, but got nothing back.

Sabine obviously knew more about this than I did, so I asked, "Why can't I sense him, if he's nearby?"

"Ah, that I can explain. We showed him how to block himself, to avoid detection."

"The Dead can do that?"

"*Mais oui, bien sûr.*"

Of course. It made perfect sense. And yet…

"But why hasn't come to me now? He must know the Burkes are gone and the Dead are free again."

"I do not know. But the two men who helped to release him are here. Would you like me to find them?"

"Yes, definitely. Please do."

She didn't click her heels and salute, but she did give a small bow before disappearing into the crowd.

Maybe he *was* here somewhere. We were in a state of mass confusion, with Hans' army and ours at an uneasy standstill. It was a lot to sort through. Maybe Eric came back but didn't know where to look for me.

On the other hand, if everyone knew me, how hard could it be to find me?

It was frustrating, but somehow, I didn't think he was permanently gone. Or maybe that was wishful thinking. What did I know? I couldn't even tell his thread from that of a seven-year-old demon.

Speaking of whom, Geordi and Jason reentered the clearing, followed by the six men who'd gone to help—I really needed to learn their names—all bearing armfuls of wood.

"Great, tell them to stuff it all in there," I said to Yvo, pointing at the fissure.

They obliged and set to work, building the bonfire, while Jason and Geordi joined me. I scanned our troops, congregating on this side of the trees. I hadn't noticed any new defectors in a while, but I asked Jason to be sure.

"I think this is it," he said. "Whatever Hans is promising, the rest prefer it."

"What about capacity? How big are we, including both factions?"

"Counting those under the trees, I'd say we take up the area of a large city block."

"That can't be right. Twelve *thousand* of us in a single block?"

"Think about it. An American football stadium holds sixty thousand fans just around the edges. Even spread out, one person per square meter is a good estimate."

"O-kay. Huh. So our twenty-five hundred should be pretty easy to, uh, store."

"And move. Also, there's a river in that direction."

He pointed south, based on where the sun was. This was also where most of Hans' troops had spread, whereas ours were on the north side of the clearing.

"How far away?"

"Maybe five, six hundred meters."

"Perfect! That's exactly what we need."

He narrowed his eyes. "What are you planning, anyway?"

Before I could answer, Leopold appeared at the edge of the clearing with Hans in tow.

They crossed to us, and Leopold said, "We walked throughout Herr Muller's men. I believe all who want to have thrown in their rings. As I passed through, Herr Muller asked to speak with you, with me as translator."

I'm sure Hans wasn't so polite about it, but I nodded graciously, and he spoke in German to Leopold, who said, "He asks that you vacate this mountain immediately. He also warns you to expect an attack from his soldiers in ten minutes' time."

"Ten minutes?" I said, hoping I sounded appropriately outraged. At my back, the heat of the bonfire grew, but with luck, Hans had even less idea of what I planned than Jason did. Or better yet, thought I had no plan at all.

Hans smirked and spoke to Leopold in a derogatory

tone. Leopold translated this as, "Perhaps the lady should appoint a male *Kommandant* to help her with strategy."

Maybe I would. I never wanted to lead an army of the Dead, on top of everything *else* I was doing. But for now, I was it. I smiled sweetly. "Tell him thank you for the advice, and now he can go *fuck off.*"

Jason choked on a laugh and covered Geordi's ears, while Leopold looked horrified. I don't know if he translated literally—I did hear a *ficken* in there—but Hans reddened. He said something final-sounding, flattened his lips, and went back to the woods.

"He says now we have nine minutes."

"Good. That should be about right." To Jason I said, "Can you keep Geordi away from the clearing? On that side?" I pointed to the north.

"Hyacinth—"

"No. I know you want to help. But I can do this. Really. What I can't do is keep Geordi safe *and* do this. You and Eric were both right about that. Luckily, today I don't have to multitask, because I've got you."

Geordi looked up at him, then at me. "It's okay, Tata. Jason and I will wait over there like you said."

Jason stayed tense a moment longer, then caved. "Okay, fine. I told you to have more faith in yourself. Big mistake, right?" He hesitated, then stepped toward me. "Don't go getting yourself killed…again."

He leaned in for a swift kiss, then grabbed Geordi's hand and headed for the trees, disappearing into the woods before his words sank in. *Merde. Did he know?*

I couldn't deal with it now anyway, so I turned to Yvo. "Tell the men, including the ones on watch, to grab the rings. As many as they can hold at once."

He nodded and translated, and Leopold asked, "Shall

I tell the Dead to do the same?"

"No! Exactly the opposite: tell the Dead to move as far from the fissure as they can in that direction." I pointed north again. "Tell them to stay two hundred meters back, maybe more. And if any from Hans' army run that way, they should force them south instead."

He left to follow my orders. Another surreal moment. I faced Yvo's group, now holding handfuls of rings, awaiting further instruction. In the woods, Hans' army had formed into ranks and was marching toward us, chanting, "*Wir dienen Deutschland! Man drup, man to!*"

To Yvo I said, "When they enter the clearing, throw the rings onto the fire, then grab more and keep going until there's none left."

Yvo nodded and translated just as Hans' front line stepped from the trees.

"Now!" I said, and the first fistfuls of silver hit the flames, then the next, and then even more. The souls poured into the clearing, and I saw Hans was not among them. Probably he was a "lead from the rear" type. But it hardly mattered. Yvo and his men kept throwing rings into the fire until all two thousand were gone.

Silver has a melting point of just under a thousand degrees Celsius. I know this from my, er, former job. I also know bonfires burn at around eleven hundred degrees. Add to that, we'd built the fire in a crevice— plenty of oxygen on either side to feed the flames, but no room to spread out—and we had a pretty hot little forge going.

By the time the Nazis were lined up, awaiting orders, the first rings had melted, causing a chain reaction whereby the next batch melted more quickly, and so on, until with a sudden surge, the final rings were consumed by the flames.

Except consumed is the wrong word: they melted, but didn't disappear. Instead, their energy—each ring's thread—was released into the fissure, and with a *ROAR*, the fire vomited that energy back out. Freed from the rings, it was formless, whipping around the clearing, seeking an inlet into anything in which it could re-form.

And Hans' troops still wore *their* Death's Head rings, created in the same original forge as ours, imbued with the same evil that Himmler had imparted to all of them. The Nazis' rings suddenly glowed white, tiny beacons calling to the silver light, like to like, Death to Death.

The soul who was clearly Hans' general, a thin, older man with the grim, pinched face typical of Nazi Upper Management, saw the light's frenetic energy but mistook its meaning. He raised an arm, shouting, "*Attakieren!*"

The souls swarmed forward just as the silver light surged into a ball of white heat that exploded in a giant mushroom cloud. But instead of flattening the souls, the released energy shot out in thousands of tiny threads that sought and connected with the Nazis' rings.

There was a moment of frozen shock among the souls as the energy from the melted rings connected with that of the not-melted ones, two thousand of ours to two thousand of theirs. And then with a thunderous *CRACK* of lightning, all two thousand souls vaporized, including the general, disintegrating into a shimmer of silver-gray.

Yvo and the men and I threw ourselves against the embankment, but the light was gone, vanished with the souls. The troops who were now Hans' front line erupted in chaos, screaming and fleeing south, away from us, telling their comrades behind them to run.

I saw Leopold under the trees at the specified

distance and yelled, "Follow them—push them toward the river!" as he was already giving the command. I didn't see Jason, but I assumed he knew to stay put with Geordi while I joined the pursuit.

Hans' army had been pretty orderly in the clearing, but now the survivors ran helter-skelter, hampered by the trees and our herding. Before long, the souls who'd initially formed the rear guard reached the riverbank and stopped, realizing their mistake. Here, the river curved in on itself, and they were now surrounded by water on three sides, with us blockading them in from behind.

Of course, it might have occurred to them that any destruction of souls had happened because of the melted rings, which we no longer had. Ergo, we were out of ammo. Luckily, at the moment, they were incapable of that level of logic and milled around in as much confusion as before, if not as much chaos.

This was as far as I'd got with my plan. Two thousand obliterated wasn't much, but we'd made a dent. And in many cultures, water is a transition between the lands of the Living and the Dead. I doubted it would permanently deter the Nazis, but it might give them pause if they hoped to stay out of Hell. Maybe we could pick some off before they rallied. I had no idea how the Dead could, er, kill the Dead, but it was all I had.

I pushed to the front of our line, at the apex of the river's loop, prepared to shout...something. I didn't know what, but I seemed to be good at improvising, and maybe I'd put them further off their game. Then, when I got to the river, something strange happened.

I mean, stranger than the rest of this.

The morning was well advanced, the day sunny and bright, but suddenly, a black mist rolled downriver from the northeast. It thickened into a heavy fog tinged green around the edges, and as it approached, it made a *whirring* sound which grew to a deafening *BUZZ*.

Then I realized it wasn't a fog: it was a cloud of grasshoppers. *Millions* of them. The Nazis shrank back, though I don't know why. I mean, the bugs creeped me out, but I assumed they'd just fly through the Dead.

Their hordes parted, revealing a gigantic, rust-colored barge. At its helm stood a large hairy man, clothed in earth-toned Greco-Roman garb. He was bearded, his hair knotted above his forehead, with heavy brows over light-green eyes. He used a pole to steer the boat to the river's loop in which the Nazis stood.

He frowned at them, and then his gaze landed on me. "Ah," he said in a rough growl that I recognized deep in my core. "It is you. I gave you souls before. Now, I will take some back with me."

It was *he* who spoke through me at the Moselle. I'd told Rachel he wasn't Satan, mostly from defiance. But this *wasn't* Satan. "Who are you?"

His face split into the ugliest grin I've ever seen, his teeth green with decay. "You do not remember me? Pity. You were so helpful to the Burkes."

"Not on purpose," I said, beyond caring if it was smart to argue with him.

"Me, neither. But they paid me well, so I cannot complain."

I repeated, "Who are you? What do you want?"

"Why, some of these souls. I find myself rather short. It makes no difference who comes with me. I will take these men as an even exchange, since you have paid their fare with two thousand silver coin."

And suddenly I figured it out. "You're Charon! The

Ferryman!"

His grin widened. "I heard you were quick. It seems he did not lie." He faced the souls cowering on the bank, "Come. It is time to return from whence you came."

"Are you taking all of them?"

He laughed, a booming sound reminiscent of Michael. "*All* will not fit on my boat. But I can take two thousand, since that is what you paid for."

Worth a shot. Then his earlier words registered. "*Who* said I was quick?"

Before he could respond, an angry-looking man pushed his way forward and pulled off his Death's Head ring. He threw it in the river, saying, "*Ich werde gehen! Ich bin müde vom Kämpfen.*"

He hurried onto the boat without waiting for a reply, so I took this to mean, "Take me, I'm yours." A few others came forward, and soon souls were lined up, waiting to fill the boat. Apparently, they didn't *all* want to stay, and trading an eternity in Hell with Satan for the Underworld with Hades seemed like a bargain.

When the boat was full, Charon pushed off the bank, heading upstream, the cloud of grasshoppers swarming around him. Just before it covered him, he called out, "I will tell your partner you have done well for yourself."

"What…?"

Did he mean Michael? He must. Jason was alive—or he'd *better* be—and Eric wouldn't "pass on" with Charon, he'd go with Michael. Wouldn't he?

And then the "partner" bit hit me. Did he mean *Vadim?* Holy shit.

"Wait!" I ran to the riverbank. "Stop! Come back!"

But he was gone, the grasshoppers and his boatload of Nazis vanishing around a bend.

Chapter Twenty-Three

*Make sure to send a lazy man for the Angel of
Death.*

~Jewish Proverb

The rest of Hans' army didn't wait for anything *else*
to happen, but instead, beat a hasty retreat, leaving
Leopold, Yvo, and the rest of our side alone at the river.
A great cheer went up, and they all beamed at me. It was
a small victory; Hans still had over six thousand men to
our two. But it *was* a victory, and I gave myself a
moment to enjoy it before the next crisis hit.

Which turned out to be Sabine hurrying up, followed
by two of the Moselle Dead.

"Mademoiselle Finch! I have found the men who
aided your friend. They are here to make their report."

"Thank you. Can you do something else for me? Can
you take some scouts—ones who can, uh, fly—and find
out where Hans' army is retreating to?"

"*Mais bien sûr,*" she said and was off again. I
suspected her plain, sensible garb hid a more energetic
personality than advertised.

I faced the men she'd brought, but unfortunately,
they had no new information. They'd freed Eric after the
buses arrived on the mountain, just as Sabine described,
going with him a short distance into the woods, before
returning to their comrades. They'd even posted rebels

to watch for him, so he could be quickly integrated into a new group, but he never showed up.

Not since he was taken from me to be made full Dead had I been so worried about him. If he was here, he would've found me by now. My face must have shown my anxiety because both men were abjectly apologetic.

"It's not your fault," I said, but they clearly didn't believe me, so on inspiration, I gave them a new job, to boost their morale. At least, Lily used to say that worked for Geordi.

"Can you find Jason and Geordi—my living friend and the little boy—at the cave? Tell them it's safe to join us now. They can see the Dead, so it's not an issue."

The men seemed puzzled by that but merely saluted and left me there, half hysterical at the absurdity of being their "commander," and half shaking with fear. Eric *couldn't* leave me. Not now, when we'd gotten so close.

Unless... Was our connection so strong that he sensed me with Jason and took himself out of the picture? That didn't seem like him. He understood my feelings for Jason and had essentially said he was happy to wait it out until I came to my senses. Why leave now?

Then a new thought struck: *Geordi* now sensed my emotions. Could he "eavesdrop" on my most intimate moments? I put my face in my hands. On top of shielding, I'd have to ask Jason about this too. Or maybe Sabine could teach me how to "block" others, as the Dead had apparently taught Eric.

As though my thoughts conjured her, she and her scouts returned then. They were really very speedy.

She said, "There is a military training ground west of here, *a peu pré un kilomètre*, occupied by British soldiers. It covers a large area. Hans' army is there."

"Thanks." She didn't leave, so I added, "Er, dismissed." That did the trick, and she pivoted, no doubt off on some critical mission I should have thought of myself.

Sudden tiredness overtook me. I'd been up for over twenty-four highly eventful hours. Most of the Dead sat, quietly talking, and I thought I should take a break too. I found a fallen tree near the river—I'd learned it was the Strothe—and sat against it, waiting for Jason and Geordi.

I also had many unanswered questions, the first and biggest of which was: What about Michael?

Last night, I didn't call him down because the Burkes were live humans and therefore out of his purview. Then today, I'd thought there was no point, because Satan had obliterated the Burkes, I'd handled the demons, and the remaining Dead had all been previously "processed."

But now I remembered that the demons were all loose in the world somewhere, not back in Hell where they belonged. I'd have to tell Michael, which would lead to uncomfortable questions. Such as, how were they freed in the first place? What was my role in that? Or in sending them away?

Which in turn led to, what happened to Michael's rock? He loved each shard like it was a living piece of him, and since they contain his powers, I suppose that's true. Either way, he'd be pissed this one was destroyed, or at least demand to know how it happened and who did it.

Which led to the biggest issue of all: Geordi and his demon powers. No getting around it.

So... Did I call Michael down and lie like hell? Or hope he'd forget all about me and this one rock? Okay, even in my current brain fog, I knew that was a stretch.

He was probably up there now, plotting his next surprise inspection. Maybe I should tell him the truth about my part, but let him think it was *only* me who blew up the rock. In which case I first needed to send Jason and Geordi far, far away, maybe even to Paolo in Trier.

Speaking of which, what was taking them so long? We weren't that far from the fissure. Even accounting for Jason not being able to fly—as far as I knew—his long legs should have brought him and Geordi here by now.

Sudden shouts and scuffling came from the western edge of our ranks. I rose and headed that way, intersecting with Sabine a few yards into the trees.

"Someone is here," she said. "After I left you, I sent your living men to guard the edges of our troops."

I stopped. "How? If you're dead, and not wearing one of the Nazi rings?"

She seemed puzzled. "It is not so hard. But perhaps you do not know. It is only the newly dead who cannot be seen. With time, it can be learned, like flying or lifting objects. We can allow the living to see us if we choose."

All sorts of new possibilities whirled through my mind. "Can you touch them? Can they feel you? Like this—" I grabbed her hand, startling her.

"I do not know," she said regretfully. "In general, I think not."

I hid my disappointment. For a moment, I'd thought Eric could learn to be visible and perhaps even touch the Living. But of course he couldn't. If ghosts could solidify at will, the world would be a very different place.

"And the rings?"

"They made it so the men were seen whether they wanted to be or not."

That made sense. "Go on," I said, and we moved

toward the noises, which had grown louder and angrier.

"The guard I set were to signal if anyone approached. I would say, they are signaling now."

We came out of the trees to the site of the conflict. Yvo and another of "my" men argued heatedly with one of the Burkes' retainers who I thought had left earlier. I circled around, and sure enough, it was Smoke Breath. He waved his gun angrily and shouted, while Yvo and his friend brandished wickedly sharp hunting knives.

"What are they saying?" I asked Sabine.

She listened. "The newcomer accuses Yvo's men of being traitors. He says they must return with him or die."

"Not on my watch," I said and stepped forward.

Wrong move. Smoke Breath turned from the men and saw me. His face lit with an evil grin. He leveled the gun at my chest, finger poised on the trigger. "Mistress said you'd be mine today. Think I'll take you now."

Before I could react, Yvo snarled "*Nein!*" and leapt forward, bringing his knife around and across Smoke Breath's throat so fast, none of us could stop him.

If you're wondering, in this situation, blood really does spurt everywhere, so most of us jumped back. Also, Smoke Breath looked very surprised at this turn of events. The gun fell from his hands, and in a slow-motion daze, he touched his throat, even more surprised to discover the blood leaking out.

I opened my mouth to shout, *Help him!*, but it was obviously too late. I know he brought it on himself and maybe deserved to die, for stuff he did long before I met him. But I guess I thought he'd just go on his merry way, leaving us to our business. Instead, he sank to his knees, mouthing fish gasps, and sometime later, maybe a minute or less, fell over dead.

At least, that's what the Living saw. The Dead and I saw his corpse topple while his soul still knelt before us, looking the most surprised of all at *this* turn of events.

"What the fuck?" he said, then noticed his body and jerked back like it was a de-pinned grenade. "What the *fuck?*"

"You're dead," I said, then faced Sabine. "I have a job to do. I need to call down Michael the Archangel to send this guy on his way."

She nodded calmly. "Ah, *oui*, you are a sorter."

For the second time in ten minutes, I stared at her open-mouthed. "There's more of me?"

"*Oui*. I do not know how many, but I have seen it before." Her face suddenly cleared. "Ah, yes. To answer your earlier question, I believe some, but not all, can touch and be touched by us."

"They can?" I felt like a parrot, almost adding an *awk!* on principle.

"*Oui*," she said, then switched gears as if it was so common, she needn't dwell on it. "We should move our Dead some distance away. It is not Michael's job to take souls who were already taken. But you may wish for privacy. I will find Herr Hesse and we will move them."

I assumed she meant Leopold, so at least our side was in capable hands. Which was good, because I hadn't regained my powers of thought, let alone speech, before she was off again.

I gave myself a shake and said to Yvo. "You should leave too." I assumed Sabine was still in "visible" mode, and he had heard-slash-seen our exchange.

"I am sorry," he said bluntly. "He vould haf killed you, maybe all of us. He had a gun. If I hadn't—"

"It's okay. You did what you had to do. But for now,

go wait somewhere else."

He nodded, and he and his friend disappeared into the trees, followed by the other onlookers, which left me alone with Smoke Breath. He'd recovered enough to assimilate the situation and took one menacing step toward me. So much for conferring with Jason first.

"Michael," I said, and there he was.

It's probably obvious by now that Michael likes to dress for the occasion, whether it's tourist garb in Turkey or a conductor's uniform on a train. I hadn't known what to expect in the Great Outdoors of Germany, which is just as well, because I could never have imagined *this*.

He was dressed like a nineteenth century British explorer, from his multi-pocketed khaki jacket and pants to his thigh-high leather boots. He'd topped it all off with a double-billed pith helmet tied with a white *puggaree*. The thin muslin would have been great as a sun-shade in the tropics; high in the mountains of Bavaria, in November, it seemed out of place. So did his beard, which, for mysterious reasons, he'd braided into a rope that hung down to his wide leather belt.

At the sight of him, Smoke Breath was too stunned to run. Michael said "Child," then looked from Smoke Breath's soul to his bloody corpse, and back at me.

"It's a long story," I said. "Very long." I opened my mouth to spout the first fib that came to mind, and instead said, "Why didn't you tell me I'm not the only sorter?"

"You never asked." I glared at him, and he sighed. "Very well. I could have announced the fact. But we have not worked together long. It did not come up."

"How many are like me?"

"No one is like you, Hyacinth," he said with a roguish twinkle in his eye.

Smoke Breath—I *really* should have gotten his name by now—said, "What about me? What the fuck is happening?"

"Be quiet," I said to him. Then to Michael, "You know what I mean."

"Yes. But I am serious. There are other sorters, but not in your situation. And they do not sense the rocks."

By "not in my situation," I assumed he meant *not dead and brought back to life*. "So they're fully alive?"

He lifted a shoulder, which I interpreted as, *Employee records are private*. But he hadn't denied it, so that was something anyway.

"Sab—er, someone told me some sorters can touch the Dead, but not all."

Michael just looked at me. I stared back. At last, he said, "Child, I am not keeping anything from you. I honestly do not know the ins and outs, the whys and wherefores, of your abilities versus anyone else's. In most cases, sorters are born that way. You were not. Therefore, it is likely other aspects of your situation are to blame."

Smoke Breath said to Michael, "What the fu—?"

"Be still, my son. Your turn will come. Hyacinth, your report?"

"First, how many sorters are there? Besides me?"

"Not many. A handful, no more." He clearly wouldn't elaborate, so I pushed ahead.

"Okay, one last question that's been bugging me. The norm seems to be for souls to hang around here until you or I, or whoever, gets to them. But when Lily and I died, we went straight to the landing pad. Why?"

He appeared amused by my name for the square, white room. "Generally, you are correct. Souls wait here until I can take them away. But in your case, I suspected there might be…complications."

"What the hell does that mean?"

"Child. Now is not the time. What happened here?"

I blew out a breath. He was probably right, and it wasn't like this was the last time I'd ever see him.

"Erm, yes. Okay." Now that the moment was here, I drew a blank. I really was better at this before I died. "Okay, fine. Here goes. I tried to get your rock from the *harmless* collector, but he was a devil worshipper whose wife made me raise an army of the Dead using the rock. But then I destroyed it—sorry—and now there's a bunch of dead Nazis on the loose. And some demons. Not sure how many. But some of the Nazis went with Charon, so really, only about six thousand are left."

Michael stared, probably amazed I'd told the truth. Mostly. As far as *he* knew, anyway.

"What the f—?" Smoke Breath began again, and I cut him off.

"Right. His turn. He worked for the Burkes. He was going to shoot me, so another of the Burkes' men— Yvo—he switched sides—he killed this guy to save us all. Self-defense really. Sorry, I still don't know this guy's name. But I'm sure he did lots of bad stuff before now, so he should go down. Definitely down."

Suddenly, I couldn't take it anymore. I needed to sit, so I did, collapsing inelegantly with my back at the base of a tree.

"So that's it. The whole story. I'm sorry about your rock, but I've been thinking. If the problem is Satan stealing your powers, and I can destroy the rocks, wouldn't that be better? He can't steal your powers if there's no powers to steal. And instead of sending me all over the place to retrieve the rocks, I think I can destroy them from a short distance. Meaning maybe I don't have to be in possession of them to do it."

Michael still stared at me. The one other time he'd been this speechless was when he first learned I sensed the rocks and had stolen one from two High Demons.

The spurt of adrenaline that had carried me through until now waned fast, and I felt sick. "What? Why are you looking at me like that?"

Michael closed his mouth. Then he found a bigger tree and sat under it himself. Now I was really scared. Would he fire me? Blast me down to Hell? I'm pretty upfront about my lack of a moral compass. But did blowing up his precious rock really merit an eternity with the likes of Smoke Breath? That it wasn't really me who blew it up scared me even more, and I prayed that Jason and Geordi would *not* show up after all

"Hyacinth. You did not destroy my rock."

My heart stopped, and the nausea roiled. "Yes. I did."

"Child, my rocks can only be destroyed by me."

"But that's what I did. I, er, took the rock's energy, twisted it back, and blasted that sucker into oblivion."

"Impossible. I would know if you used my powers."

Now it was my turn to stare. My heart started beating again, wildly. Of course he'd notice something like that.

Smoke Breath took this moment to interject, "Are you two done? I want to know *what the fuck* is happening."

"*Shut up!*" Michael and I said in unison.

I'd never seen Michael aggravated with anyone. He was the most patient angel I knew.

He said to me, "There is more. My rocks cannot be used to raise the Dead. Only Satan's can. You did not use my rock or its powers—you used Satan's."

It was too much. I shot to my feet. "For the last goddamn time, I am *not* a demon!"

"No one fucking thinks you are," Smoke Breath snapped, startling us both. "Look, Princess, your friend here is right. That big rock you blew up? It belonged to Satan. That's why the Burkes fucking *had* it. So whatever the fuck you stole, powers or magic or whatever, it was *Satan's*."

"But…" I was at a loss. I faced Michael. "You *told* me the Burkes had a shard of *your* rock."

"They did. It is still here somewhere. I can sense it."

"Crap. The key rock. *That* one's yours." I frowned. "But we, er, *I* thought that rock came from Saint Peter's staff. Plus, it's black and shiny, not gray like yours are."

"The slab was not uniform, or Saint Peter may have polished it. And yes, he could have used it in his staff."

He rose, leather boots creaking as he hefted his bulk.

"Child, we will discuss this further. This is not the first time you have borrowed Satan's or his demon's powers. I know what you did in Turkey." My face heated, but he only continued, "This is a gift. If you can destroy Satan's rocks, then the balance between our powers may be maintained after all. However, I will need to consider the implications before we formulate a plan."

"No."

He stared at me again, mouth open.

"No. Not unless you give me something in return."

"Ah."

Now or never. I took a breath. "I'm not leaving Geordi. Ever. You want me to blow up rocks from Hell, fine. Sort souls for you, fine. But I stay here on Earth until Geordi is grown up, dead, *and* buried himself."

"Very well," he said, and I exhaled. And then he chuckled. "I would have allowed you to stay in any case. You are really very transparent, child."

With that, he turned his full attention to Smoke Breath, who suddenly looked all calm and trusting, the way everyone did when Michael took them away. Even, evidently, those destined for the down escalator.

"Come, my son. It is time for you to meet your master in person."

Then they were gone, and I sank back down by the tree and put my head between my knees.

Literally seconds later, the two souls I'd sent after Jason and Geordi reentered the clearing. Some leader *I* was. I didn't even know the names of my own aides. I looked behind them, expecting to see Jason loping in, carrying Geordi.

Then it dawned on me: I hadn't *heard* anyone coming, because the only ones here were the souls. I scrambled to my feet. "Where are they?"

The men were even more ashen than before. The older of the two stepped forward. He was a man who'd known hard work in life, dressed in the gray garb of a factory worker from just about any period after the start of the twentieth century.

"*Nous sommes désolés*—we could not find them. We checked all around the hillside, even the mouth of the fissure itself. We searched the woods in all directions. There is no trace of them." He paused. "Except…"

"What?"

"You had better come see."

I followed them back to the clearing. Smoke still spewed from the fissure, but the fire was mostly out. In the center of the clearing was the key rock. Someone had pushed it into the earth so it stood point up. Definitely not where it fell after Geordi blew up the big rock.

Also in the dirt was a message, scratched in with a stick: *I told you that was Satan's rock.*

I wasn't even stressed. I mean, I was so angry, I wanted to rip up a tree and bash something with it. But somehow, I was pretty sure Jason had just taken Geordi back to Paolo. That's where I was at now: My nephew had been ripped from me by a *demon* and taken to *another* demon, and that didn't seem so bad when compared to the alternatives. Hell, I'd even thought of sending them to Paolo myself.

Just to be thorough, I pocketed the key rock. Now that it wasn't masked by Satan's rock, I sensed its energy. But it was weird how similar Michael's and Satan's powers felt to me. I'd have to consider that sometime when I wasn't distracted by my visceral need to get Geordi back and kill Jason.

I turned to find the two men cowering in despair. I blew out a breath. "What are your names?"

"François," said the older man. "And this is Henri."

"Okay. You aren't to blame for not finding them. They've done this before, and I have a good idea where they went. You did excellent work, and I appreciate you showing me this." I indicated the message. "Now, you deserve a break. Go find your comrades."

"If you are certain there is nothing else…"

"Positive. Thank you for your, er, service."

They did salute this time, and I tried to appear serious and appropriate, and not giggle hysterically. When they'd gone, I took another slow breath in and out, prepared to finally take some time to process. But it was not to be. Several men entered the clearing, led by Yvo and all talking excitedly.

He saw me and shouted, "*Da ist sie*—there she is!"

"Here I am," I said, the wearied irony lost on him.

Two of the men brought a third forward and pushed him to his knees in front of me. It was Axe Man. His dark hair was matted with blood, and more blood stained the left side of his black t-shirt near what looked like a bullet hole. It must have grazed him because he didn't seem too concerned. The men forced his arms behind his back, but he shoved them away. He was big and obviously into bodybuilding, but he was also unarmed and outnumbered, so I made a cutting motion with my arm.

"Enough. What's going on here?"

"Vee found him," Yvo said, "*und* ozers spyink on our troops. Some vere armed, *und* vee chased zem off."

I suppressed more hysteria. My exchanges with Yvo so far had consisted of me telling him to do stuff and him doing it. Now I flashed back to the hotel concierge. Forget a drama: Yvo's even thicker accent, plus all the crazy-ass Nazis wandering around, made it feel like we were in a World War II spoof on a comedy channel.

Oblivious to my struggles with hilarity, Yvo said, "Vee found him, bleedink under a tree. He claims he vaz defecting ven his *Kameraden* shot him. I belief he *ist ein* spy, and ze vound vas intentionally small, to gain our trust. He vas *very* close viz Herr Burke."

He had a point. At Wewelsburg, Axe Man and Heinrich were pretty chummy, slipping away for some alone time and looking pretty pleased with themselves when they came back. "So why did you bring him here?"

"He insists he vill speak only to you. *Allein.* Vee felt vee should gif you ze opportunity to question him. But say ze vord, *und* vee vill remoof him."

Why did everyone want to talk with *me* all the time?

Okay, I knew why. Because somehow, I'd been elected leader of this ragtag, half-dead army. And at least Axe Man didn't creep me out the way Smoke Breath had.

He watched me, silent as ever. Besides the blood, he had bruises around his throat, as though he'd been choked. Probably by his own Fancy Special Ops belt, as it was now missing from his waist. So was his gun.

He certainly *looked* like he'd been attacked. But if it were one of him against five or six armed men, surely his very survival meant he was left alive on purpose. Presumably to infiltrate us and steal our plans.

Not that I *had* any plans. But he didn't know that.

The whole thing felt off. But "my" troops surrounded us, and he was by himself. What's the worst he could do?

"Fine," I said. "I'll hear you out. But not alone."

"*Bitte*—please." His voice rasped, as though speaking took great effort, but I couldn't tell if it was from emotion, or his injury, or just his natural tone. "Vill you not…reconsider?" His English was good but with German overtones. Which made sense, as he was one of Heinrich's original "boys."

Speaking of the Burkes, his gaze suddenly bored into me, the brown depths burning with a heat reminiscent of Rachel's fervor. I shivered, which he noticed. With his erect, alert stance, I was sure he'd had military or law enforcement training. He flicked a gaze at the clearing, assessing, taking in my "retainers," considering his options. Which weren't many, and he knew it.

When he met my gaze again, he was visibly fighting for control. Of what, I had no clue. It wasn't reassuring, although when he spoke, he kept his voice low. Non-threatening. Soothing, like I was a horse that needed gentling. Which pissed me off more.

"*Please*—you really do *not* v—w—" He struggled to force the "v" sound into a "w," downplaying his accent. "—*want* to hear zis—*this*—in front of oz—others."

I frowned. "Actually, I do."

With every word, he seemed to be mastering both his voice and his body, and I wondered how many men he could take down before my guys took *him* down. And…what if he got to me first?

What was the big deal, anyway? He wanted to beg for his life? *I* wouldn't take it from him. Yvo, I couldn't make promises for.

Proving my point, Yvo and another man sidled closer to me. "Should vee remoof him now?"

Something in Axe Man's expression changed. From excitement and fervor, it softened, and a note of desperation crept in. Or maybe it was panic. For some reason, he believed I was his last chance. But at what?

I chewed my lip. "No. I'll hear him out."

"*Danke*," he breathed, his relief palpable. "*Merci*—thank you."

I waited, and he twisted, taking in the fissure and the remnants of the fire. Then he peered into the woods, where most of my army had joined us.

"Come *on*," I said, my brief spurt of compassion ebbing as exhaustion spiked my temper. "Get on with it. What have you got to say that's so damn important? I've got stuff to do—people to find. *Three* of them, in fact. Talk, right here, right now, or shut up and go away."

He shook his head slowly, looking bemused.

Then he raised a shoulder in a Gallic half-shrug.

"*Eh bien*, if you insist. But do not say I did not warn you…*mon ange*…"

A Quick Favor Please?

Before you go, would you please leave this book an honest review online? Reviews are so important for authors, as they help us reach more readers. Please take a minute to visit one or two retailer/review sites, such as Amazon, BookBub, or Goodreads, and leave this book a review. I promise it doesn't take long, but it would mean the world to me! This Book Riot article breaks it down into six easy steps, if you need tips: http://bit.ly/BookReviewTips.

Thank you for reading, and thank you so much for being part of this amazing journey!

~ Kerry

Psst! Read on for a sneak peek at Damning the Dead (Book Three of The Dead Series)...

Damning the Dead
(Book Three of The Dead Series)
©2022 by Kerry Blaisdell

Used by permission from The Wild Rose Press.

Chapter One

In the world to come, I shall not be asked,
'Why were you not Moses?' I shall be asked,
'Why were you not Zusya?'

~Rabbi Meshulam Zusya of Hanipol
(1718-1800)

The alarm on my phone went off at noon, and I rolled over to hit snooze, thinking I'd cuddle in bed a little longer before facing the world. But when I snaked my arm out from under the covers, the biting cold alerted me to the fact that my "bed" was two down jackets laid out on rocky ground, with two more spread over me for warmth. And it wasn't even my phone blaring loudly, which I discovered when I fumbled it closer. Then, when I finally silenced it, the rumble of male voices nearby told me "the world" needed me now, not later.

I considered hibernating anyway. But head-burying never solves anything, so I sat up, hugging one of the jackets close, and the low conversation stopped. I didn't turn around, because I already knew who'd been speaking, and I had even less desire to face them now than I'd had earlier. Unfortunately, they had other ideas.

"Frau Finch—" Yvo began, while Axe Man said, "*Mon ange*—" and they moved into my line of sight.

Two of my best minions, and I didn't want to see

either of them, but especially not Axe Man—er, Eric. For one thing, I didn't even know his new name.

If you're wondering, that's because the beefy Black Ops specialist I knew as Axe Man died a few hours ago, and his corpse was appropriated by the ghost I've been "dating," Eric Guilliot, a former French police detective.

Also in case you're wondering: I'm Hyacinth Finch, former graverobber turned antiques dealer—okay, I fenced stolen collectibles for the über-rich backstabbing Marseille elite—and former dead person myself. But not for long before I reinhabited my own corpse, became a magnet for the newly Dead, and launched my third career, sorting souls for Archangel Michael to whisk up to Heaven or down to Hell, as needed.

Which brings us to today. When I realized what had happened with Axe-Man-now-Eric, I dismissed all my other minions—long story—then decided to take a nap. This isn't as weird as it sounds, since I'd been up for more than a day, so I lay down where I was, in a clearing on Mount Barnacken in Germany, telling Axe-Eric and Yvo we'd talk when I woke up.

Yvo's a twenty-something hired gun who worked for Heinrich and Rachel Burke, devil-worshippers who held me and mine hostage for a time. He and a few comrades defected after learning the Burkes were raising an Army of the Dead for Satan. Many of the dead also defected, and now Yvo's my top living guy. He found the coats and loaned me his phone, and though unhappy about it, moved a respectable distance away while I slept, keeping one eye on Axe-Eric, the other on me.

"Frau Finch," he said now, cutting Axe-Eric off. "*He* says he vants to join our side, *und* because he is trusted by ze ozer side, he can spy on zem for us. *If* vee set him free, of course, vich I do not zink is a goot idea."

Did I mention his heavy German accent? It makes me feel like I'm in a high school production of *Springtime for Hitler*, minus all the singing and dancing.

I stood, dusting off my jeans to buy a few more seconds. Ostrich head, meet sand. Okay, I know that's a myth, and in any case, it didn't work.

"*Mon ange—*" Axe-Eric began, but Yvo rounded on him, firing off a string of German, which I don't speak, but which clearly translated to, "How *dare* you call her that, you so-and-so!"

"*Mon ange*" is Eric's pet name for me—French for "my angel." It's how I'm sure he's Eric, as Axe Man *couldn't* know to call me that. He was another Burke employee up until Satan turned them, literally, inside-out, at which time he went off with his buddies, later showing up dead with Eric's spirit in residence.

Yvo worked with Axe Man, but never met Ghost Eric, and knew nothing of the *mon ange* significance. He continued shouting in German, getting in Axe-Eric's face, until Axe-Eric got a calculating glint in his eyes that I'd never seen in *Eric's* before, and I blew out a breath.

"Enough! Yvo, I appreciate your concern, but I really do need to talk with…"

I paused expectantly, and Axe-Eric suddenly looked panicked. Oh God—he didn't know his own name.

In times like these, I tend to get bubbles of hysteria that are both inappropriate and annoying. But the absurdity of the situation the Burkes set in motion—dozens of Hell Demons and thousands of resurrected Nazi war criminals on the loose, plus my upstanding cop *petit ami* now in the body of an unscrupulous private mercenary—it was all too much, and I covered my mouth while my shoulders shook.

Yvo unwittingly came to the rescue. "*Sein Name ist* Sieg. Siegfried Sauer. Or so he *says*."

I still wheezed with suppressed laughter. "Wh-what's that supposed to m-mean?"

Axe-Eric-Siegfried blinked, then said drily, "SIG Sauer. It is a Swiss-German gun brand. *Ses parents*—that is, *my* parents had a sense of humor."

I shook harder, belly clenched, and an ironic smile crept onto Eric-Sieg's face.

Yvo regarded us both with suspicion. "I do not trust him. He vas *very* close viz Herr Burke. If you must speak viz him, I vill vait over zere in ze trees. I vill even turn my back. But I vill stay close, in case you yell for help."

"Erm, yes, that works." I sobered, because really, none of this was funny. "Thank you. For everything. I'll be okay, but I'm glad you're nearby, just in case."

Yvo cast a final glare at Eric-Sieg, then moved into the trees. The rest of "my" troops must also be close by, a dozen living men plus twenty-five hundred of the Dead, so I felt reasonably safe. Not that they could help with *this*, but still.

On the other hand, the Burkes' men who hadn't joined us, roughly half their so-called "retainers," were also nearby, along with six thousand of the opposing Dead Army and their fearless leader, Hans. Though dead himself, he'd barely waited for his former bosses' last bloodied chunks to hit the ground before assuming command and launching his own campaign against us. We'd defeated his first attack and were now at an uneasy standoff while he plotted, and I dealt with this.

I faced…Eric. He might look wildly different, but it *was* him on the inside, so I might as well get used to it. I opened my mouth, then closed it again.

His expression was a little sad. "Surprise!"

"Yeah. You could say that." I gestured at his left side, where a bullet hole and dried, caked blood showed in his black t-shirt. "Do you need medical attention?"

"*Non*. It is not serious." His dark eyes clouded. "*Mon ange*, I understand this is much to take in. When we discussed *la possibilité*, it was theoretical. The reality must be *très différent*."

Hysteria threatened again, and I shook my head. "It's just…weird. I'm sorry. Probably not the reaction you hoped for."

He gave one of his Gallic half-shrugs, the gesture so familiar, I relaxed a little. "*Eh bien*, I did not know what to expect myself. I can hardly fault your reaction." He lifted a hand. "May I…touch you?"

"I'm not sure that's a good idea. We need to talk, about, well, *this*. And…other stuff."

Like that while the Burkes' dead soldiers were manacling him, I'd made out with our mutual "friend" Jason Jones in an underground prison. He's another of my minions. Sort of. He was my neighbor in France, but it turns out he's related to my seven-year-old nephew, who I'm raising since my sister Lily and her scumbag ex, Nick Dioguardi, were killed by the demons who killed me. Only unlike me, they—Lily and Nick—stayed dead.

And *then* I found out that Jason and my nephew, Geordi, are both infected with demon blood, which was introduced into *la familigia* eons ago by a corrupt priest. But despite that, supposedly some Dioguardis are "good" demons, fighting against Satan and *his* minions.

Anyway, Eric knew most of this, including that I had feelings for Jason. But not about the recent making out, or that Jason had absconded with Geordi again—it's a bad habit he has—and we needed to find them. Or that earlier, while Eric was busy corpse-hopping, Geordi and I accidentally unleashed the aforementioned chaos on the world, and now I had to contain-slash-eliminate it.

In other words, lots to discuss.

He dropped his hand. "Of course. You must have questions. Ask."

I took a breath. "Does it feel weird? Like, are you *you*, or do you feel like *him*, but also yourself?"

He watched me for a beat. Jason always said Eric had his own agenda, and even at our best, he'd only shared what he deemed absolutely necessary.

"*C'est moi.* Truly. And yet, this is not my body. I move—" He stepped forward, demonstrating. "—and I am awkward, as if I must relearn the use of my limbs."

During the short time I'd been body-less, I'd barely learned to control what Michael called my "non-corporeal limbs." How would it feel, after months spent mastering an ephemeral existence, to have a body's limitations again? A broader, heavier one than before?

"I lift an arm, *comme ça*—" Again, he demonstrated. "—and it is more difficult than expected. But I have greater reach." He shook his head. "*Bah.* I cannot complain, for the choice was mine."

"Speaking of which… You said you wouldn't take over a corpse without permission. I get that, absent the owner, you might assume squatter's rights. But…"

"You wish to know how Sieg Sauer felt regarding my use of his corpse, is that it? For that, I cannot say. I did not see where he went. Down, I presume. *Moi*, I saw only a body—fresh, young, whole—and empty. The decision must be made *tout de suite*. And so, I chose."

He'd been inching toward me as he spoke. I saw the bruising on his neck where Sieg must have been choked before being shot. Or after. Who could say for sure?

He was near enough to touch if I wanted. And part of me *did* want to. When we'd attempted intimacy before, my brain had flipped out, *knowing* he lacked a body, despite how he felt under my hands.

Talk about a disconnect. But now…

True to his word, Yvo had his back to us, so before I second-guessed myself, I stepped toward Eric and took his hand, lacing my fingers through his.

Instantly, I felt his thread, his energy-light source, except it became *more*. His eyes lit and he pulled me to him, holding me tight and burying his head in my neck.

"*Mon ange…*" He murmured it over and over, stroking my back, arms, everywhere, as though to memorize me. "I—to touch you—hold you, solid and real, not as a ghost. *This* is what I dreamed of—why I made the choice. Can you understand? *Please?*"

His heart beat beneath my cheek, not in Eric's trimly muscled chest but in the bodybuilder one Siegfried had honed, both familiar and different. And the smell of him—not bad, just that I *could* smell him—previously, my single constant reminder that he lacked a body. His scent was manly and clean, despite his recent activity, and getting shot, and whatever else had happened to him.

And yet… That smell was *not* Eric; could never be him. Like riding in a car that's the same model as yours: the interior is the same, but it feels different. Except in this case, Eric *looked* different, but *felt* the same. Mostly.

I stepped away. "Yes. But I need time to adjust. It's just so…." I gestured helplessly, but he understood.

"*Bon.* I am not going anywhere."

I glanced again at Yvo. He hadn't moved, but I *felt* someone's eyes on me. A check of our surroundings showed no one else in sight, but the forest brooded, dense and menacing, and I lowered my voice.

"We'll have to be careful. This isn't something we can announce, even to the Burkes' men. They know about the Dead now—" That surprised him, but I added it to the *explain later* column and hurried on. "—but they may not appreciate you hijacking their former comrade."

There was a sudden flurry of activity in the woods. Yvo raised an arm in greeting toward someone, and I said quickly, "I'll have to call you Sieg in front of the others. And…" I hesitated. I'd only just gotten him back, but his situation presented a unique opportunity. "Were you serious about that whole double-agent thing?"

He drew himself up, alert and purposeful. "*Ouais*. Sieg's plan—I overheard him and his comrades before he died—was precisely as your man suspects. He told his friends to shoot him in a non-fatal place, so that he could pretend to defect to your side. *Alors*, I will continue the pretense, while spying on them instead."

"What if they figure it out and kill you for real?"

"*Mon ange*." Though the rough voice was Sieg's, Eric's natural cynicism bled through. "I can hardly die again. I am already dead."

"But what if they kill you in *this* body and Michael shows up? He'll notice your spirit is from a French cop, not a German militant." I paused, suddenly struck. "Did he guide *Siegfried?* If you were there, how did he miss you? Or did someone else do it?"

I now knew I wasn't Michael's only sorter, a person able to sense whether dead Christians or other believers should go up to Heaven or down to the Bad Place. Yet no one came to guide Eric, a devout Catholic.

I mean, *I* was there. Yet I never got the sense he should go up or down, that I got with other souls. But maybe in this case, Siegfried was an atheist, so not Michael's business. My head spun with all the ins and outs, and it was a relief when Yvo and the two dead men who'd joined him headed our way.

Another thing I'd learned: the Dead can make themselves visible to the Living, which simplifies things. Of course, the rest of the Living *know* who's dead, whereas I can't distinguish the two to, er, save my soul. Plus, I still didn't know why Eric never learned the skill. Or maybe he'd tried, but it didn't work? If so, why not?

The newcomers were François and Henri, who'd helped Ghost Eric escape the Burkes, and who I'd later sent on the fruitless errand of retrieving Jason and Geordi. Was that really mere hours ago? Time flies.

Speaking of which, was I worried about Geordi? Yes…and no. Jason would *never* hurt him, and in fact, would risk death to save him. That's not hyperbole; it's literal truth, as evidenced by previous actions.

So, while it irritated the snot out of me that I had to chase after them again, I knew deep down Geordi was safe. Possibly even safe-*er* than here with me.

I hate it when Jason's right.

François was the older of the two men, somewhere near sixty if his close-cropped gray hair was any indication. He wore a timeless ensemble of gray factory-issue coveralls and heavy black boots. The younger man, Henri, resembled an anxious puppy: early twenties, with pale hair and eyes. He wore loose-fitting jeans, a faded flannel work shirt, and a nondescript baseball cap.

True to form, François did the talking.

"Mademoiselle Finch, we have information about your two living friends. They stole one of the Burkes' buses and, we believe, drove to Horn-Bad Meinberg."

"Where's that?"

"About one and a half *kilomètres* to the northeast."

I blinked. "There's a *town* a *mile* from here?"

"*Oui*. Mademoiselle Vezinet's scouts say it has perhaps fifteen thousand inhabitants. We crossed the road to it when chasing Hans's army to *la rivière*, but in the commotion, it is understandable if you missed it."

I blinked again. "There's a road, and we *crossed* it?"

Duh. The Burkes' cavalcade had to drive up on something. But I'd pictured a gravel road leading to the dirt track I'd seen the buses on. That impression, plus the heavy forest surrounding the clearing where the helicopter landed, led me to conclude we were isolated, with rejoining civilization high on my list. But apparently, if we just walked for twenty minutes, we'd find food, showers, even beds. Which sounded heavenly.

Except, I had no plan. It seemed important to do something with the twenty-five hundred souls in my Dead Army, and get a bead on what Hans intended, before I found a nice Airbnb. But at least I could rent a room. Horn-Bad Meinberg probably didn't have enough Dead Hostels to support an influx of our size.

Still, if Geordi was there, that's where I'd go. Gah. Priorities. *Everything* was top priority, which paralyzed me as I agonized over what to tackle first.

Eric sensed my distress. He'd shown no surprise that my "living friends" were gone, or that we weren't lost in the woods after all, so maybe he already knew both.

"*Mon*—that is, Frau Finch. Please, I can help you figure out what Hans is up to if you let me. Then you can make a decision regarding him, at least."

His voice hitched as he tried not to pepper his speech with French. Who knew if Siegfried spoke either English or French, as he was the Strong Silent Type, but from Yvo's frown, I guessed not. He took a step toward Eric-Sieg, while François and Henri eyed them both warily.

Just then, another of my living minions came from the trees, a tall, muscled guy, late thirties-ish, with pale, freckled skin, medium red-brown hair, and green eyes.

"Ms. Finch," he said in a clipped British accent. "We'd best move. Someone's here."

Oh God, were the demons back? Or Hans? I glanced at the trees. Where were my troops? Should I marshal them? What did that even mean? What if we were attacked and everyone died? Or whatever decimation happened to those already dead. They were my responsibility, but I couldn't protect them. My heart pounded and sweat slicked my palms.

The man saw my panic and said quickly, "No, it's only a family. Man, woman, two young children. On a picnic. Only, I thought…"

He trailed off, unable to voice his concerns for a family picnicking at the very site where thousands of dead Nazi war criminals were recently loosed on the world, along with dozens of demons, plus however many living men who wished to continue the Burkes' evil deeds post mortem.

Well, hell. So much for my downtime.

Ready for more? Find all Kerry's books at
https://books2read.com/kerryblaisdell!

<h1 style="text-align:center">A word about the author…</h1>

Kerry Blaisdell is the bestselling and award-winning author of the acclaimed Dead Series, including DEBRIEFING THE DEAD and its sequels, which InD'tale Magazine recommends for "fans of shows like 'Constantine' or 'Supernatural.'" She also writes award-winning Romantic Suspense (PUBLISH OR PERISH, a Publishers Weekly BookLife Prize Quarterfinalist) and Historical Mystery.

She has a B.A. from U.C. Berkeley in Comparative Literature (French/Medieval English), and a Master's in Teaching English and Advanced Mathematics from University of Portland. Kerry lives in the gorgeous Pacific Northwest with her family, assorted animals, and more hot pepper plants than anyone could reasonably consume.

To connect with Kerry online, visit https://bit.ly/kerryslinks or scan the QR code below to join her Facebook Reader Group, follow her on social media, or subscribe to her Very Occasional Mailing List for freebies, news, and more!